Critical Failures

ROBERT BEVAN

SPECIAL THANKS TO:

No Young Sook, who has believed in me from the beginning.

Joan Reginaldo, without whom this would have been a much shittier
book.

Tom DeHaven, who made the difference between me wanting to be a
writer and me *really* wanting to be a writer.

CONTENTS

Chapter 1

Tim stared out through the grimy front window of the Chicken Hut. The red neon sign cast a pink glow on the parking lot, and Tim kept one hand in the pocket of his jeans to restrain against its natural impulse to flip off the switch. His watch said nine o'clock, Time to close. They hadn't had a customer in over forty-five minutes, and he didn't want one coming in now. He'd already had three beers and was well into a fourth. Thoughts of chicken and customers would have been well drowned out had it not been for the continued flickering and buzzing of that damned sign. It was a beacon in the darkness, inviting just one more fat asshole to come in for some chicken after all of the equipment had been shut down. But he couldn't turn it off. The new Cavern Master would need the sign to find this place.

He hadn't noticed the dull banging until it stopped suddenly. His gaze turned from the parking lot to the interior of the restaurant. Everything was as it should be. Cooper was drinking a beer. Julian, Cooper's coworker who he'd brought along for the game tonight, was engrossed in the Caverns and Creatures Third Edition Player's Handbook. The banging started up again.

"You guys hear that?" Tim asked.

Julian didn't look up from the book.

Cooper got up and grabbed another can of beer from the refrigerator. "You mean that banging noise? Yeah. It's fucking annoying as shit. This place wasn't built on top of an Indian burial ground, was it?"

Tim turned back to the window. "No, Cooper. I don't believe it was."

Cooper made a sound that was something between a snort and a burp. "From the state of this shithole, I think it's a safe bet that it predates any Indian tribes." He put his feet up on the table and cracked open the can.

"Nobody's begging you to stay," said Tim, turning around to glare at him. "Come on, man. Get your feet off the table. People eat here." He looked back out the window. "Where is this Mordred character anyway? He was supposed to be here like fifteen minutes ago."

"He'll show," said Cooper. "Anybody willing to drive all the way from Biloxi just to play C&C with a bunch of strangers has obviously got a hard-on for the game."

"That's another thing," said Tim. "What kind of weirdo did you invite to my restaurant?"

"I don't know," said Cooper. "I just put an ad in the paper. Really, though. What was the alternative? I'm not going back to taking turns being the Cavern Master. It's too much like being a designated driver."

"You mean in the sense that neither one of those responsibilities actually stops you from drinking?"

Julian glanced up from the book. "What's the difference between a halfling and a gnome?"

"An inch or two," said Cooper. "Your vagina will be the same size no matter which one you choose."

"I think I'm going to be an elf."

"Great."

"What is that noise?" asked Tim again. "It's driving me nuts!"

"Calm down, dude," said Cooper. "It's probably just some hobo fucking your mom against the side of the building."

"I can't stand it anymore," said Tim. He walked into the kitchen area. "Katherine!"

"Yeah?" said his sister without looking up at him. She was in the office, looking at herself in the cracked mirror and applying a coating of red lipstick.

"Do you hear that noise?"

Katherine puckered her lips. "Yeah," she said. "I think one of your friends got stuck in the freezer."

"Fuck! And you didn't... Dave!" Tim ran to the freezer door and opened it.

Dave stared at him through narrowed eyes. He pulled the Popsicle out of his mouth. "Do you have any idea how long I've been banging on that door?"

"Sorry man, the safety latch is broken," said Tim. "You're supposed to wedge this block of wood between the door and the frame when you go in there."

"Do you know how dangerous that is? I could've frozen to death."

"No you couldn't have," said Tim, grabbing a beer. "Look, this beer has been in there longer than you have, and it's barely cold enough to drink."

"Whatever," said Dave. "Listen, just don't tell Cooper about this. I can only take but so much of his shit tonight."

"You got it."

"Hey Tim," Cooper shouted from up front. "Time to stop jerking off back there. I think he's here."

"Come on," said Tim. He and Dave ran up to the dining area.

Tim, Cooper, and Dave peered out of the window, squinting at the headlights shining at them. Julian remained where he was, his face buried in the book.

"God, I hope it's not a customer," said Tim.

"Oh, hey Dave," said Cooper. "Where the fuck have you been?"

"Glad to know I was missed," said Dave.

"Did you bring me a Popsicle?"

"Here," said Dave, handing a second Popsicle to Cooper.

"Fuck," said Cooper. "Orange?"

"You're welcome," said Dave.

A car door slammed shut.

"Oh my fucking God," said Cooper.

A fat guy in a purple velvety cape stood next to the car, looking back at them. He had a good ten years on everyone in the Chicken Hut, and a lot more hair on his face than he had on top of his head. He drew up one corner of the cape, revealing a faded gray T-shirt underneath, and made an elaborate bow.

"Katherine!" Tim gasped. He started to run back toward the kitchen and intercepted her just as she was walking into the dining

9

area.

"Fuck, Tim!" she said. "Watch where you're going."

"Hey there, Kat," said Cooper. "You up for a little fantasy role-playing later on?"

"Go fuck an orc, loser," she said with a fake smile and a middle finger.

"Maybe you'd better go out the back," suggested Tim, trying to keep the panic out of his voice. "There's a cop out front."

"Oh right, thanks," said Katherine. She hadn't taken more than a few steps when she turned back around. "Wait a second. I haven't even done anything wrong yet. Why do I need to worry about-"

The bell on the front door jingled as the door swung open. Tim lowered his head.

Katherine's silence behind him suggested that she was too shocked to actually laugh.

"Is this where tonight's tale of wonder shall unfold?" asked the new Cavern Master with alarmingly wide eyes and a broad smile.

"On second thought," said Katherine, "maybe I will just go out the back." She slapped Tim on the back. "Have fun, bro," she said, retreating into the kitchen. If she had left out of courtesy, she shouldn't have bothered. The guys all exchanged uncomfortable glances as laughter rang from the kitchen.

"You must be Mordred," said Tim. "I'm Tim." He put out his hand.

Mordred accepted his hand disinterestedly and craned his neck to look past him. "I take it the lady will not be joining us tonight?"

"No," said Tim. "The lady will most certainly not be joining us."

The side of Mordred's mouth twitched, and his nostrils flared. He refocused his attention on Tim. "Were you the one who summoned me here this eve?"

"That would be me," said Cooper, standing up. "I put the ad in the paper, if that's what you mean. I'm Cooper, this is Julian. You've met Tim."

"I'm Dave," said Dave after waiting a second to confirm that Cooper wasn't going to introduce him.

"You may address me as Mordred," said Mordred. "Or Cavern Master if you like."

"Yeah," said Cooper. "We'll see about that."

Mordred inspected the dining area of the Chicken Hut. "Is this where you intend to play?"

"Yeah," said Tim. "This is where we always play."

"I suppose it will be adequate. However, I will require my own table."

"Right away, your majesty," said Tim, sliding one of the tables from the cluster the guys had already prepared.

"Thank you." Mordred sat down and put a large duffel bag on the chair next to his. "Have you all prepared characters using the guidelines I emailed to Cooper?"

"Yeah," said Tim, pulling a piece of paper from a folder on the table. Dave and Cooper did likewise.

"May I inspect them?" Mordred snatched the papers out of their hands. His piggy eyes ran back and forth across them as he made approving and disapproving hums and grunts. "A dwarf, a half-orc, and a halfling," he mused. "Quite an unlikely group of comrades. You do realize, of course, that dwarves and half-orcs don't get along, don't you?"

"That shouldn't be too hard to role play. Dave and Cooper don't get along anyway."

"Very well," said Mordred. "If that's what you want. Wait, why are there only three characters here?"

"I didn't make one," said Julian. "I've never played before, and I don't know-"

"A virgin player!" Mordred exclaimed. "How wonderful!"

Cooper choked on a swallow of beer. If Mordred had spoken a second earlier, he might have been rewarded with a coating of beer and Cooper spit. "Dude, if anyone in this room is a virgin player,-"

Dave cut him off with an elbow to the ribs, for which he received a much harder punch in the arm in return.

Mordred walked Julian through the steps of rolling the dice to determine his character's ability scores. "What race do you think you might want to be?"

"Jew isn't an option," said Cooper.

"I don't know," said Julian. "I guess I'm cool sticking with white. That should be easier to role play since I'm new at this." Cooper, Dave and Tim snickered, but Mordred merely offered a friendly smile.

"In this game, races include human, elf, dwarf-"

"Oh, that." Julian's face flushed. "I want to be an elf."

"Excellent," said Mordred. "And what class?"

"Choose upper-middle," suggested Cooper.

Mordred cut off any potential for further disruptions with an explanation. "Classes include fighter, wizard, cleric-"

"I want to be a wizard," said Julian

"Really?" asked Mordred doubtfully.

"What the fuck do you want to be a wizard for?" asked Cooper. "You only have an intelligence score of eleven."

"I want to use magic."

"Then be a fucking sorcerer. You've got a really high charisma score."

"I read in the book that an elf's favored class is wizard," said Julian, looking to Mordred for confirmation.

"An excellent point!" said Mordred. "I award you three hundred experience points.""What the fuck for?" asked Cooper.

"For role-playing, of course," said Mordred. "He has demonstrated to me that he put more thought into his actual character than he put into tweaking the numbers to get the highest bonuses." He took another glance at Julian's character sheet. "Besides," he muttered, "with this character, he'll need all the help he can get."

Julian shrugged and wrote down his three hundred points.

"Can we get started now?" asked Tim.

"But he isn't finished yet," said Mordred. "He still has to choose skills and feats, and buy equipment."

"Just let him take the starting package," suggested Dave. "He's never played before. If he has to sort through all that, we're going to be here all night."

Mordred considered it. "Do you want to take the starting package?" He opened the Player's Handbook to the appropriate page and showed Julian.

Julian looked it over. "I don't know what most of this means, but sure. Oh... except that I'd rather fight with a sword than with a quarterstaff."

"Wizards fight with sticks," said Cooper. "If you wanted to use a sword, then you shouldn't have been a pussy wizard."

"Ah," said Mordred. "But swordplay is a part of elven culture.

All elves are proficient in the art of the sword."

"Great," said Julian, looking smugly at Cooper. "So can I get a sword?"

"I'm afraid not."

"Why not?"

"A quarterstaff is free. It's pretty much just a stick, after all. A sword costs money that you don't have."

"Oh," said Julian. "Okay."

"I'll tell you what," said Mordred. "Since you're new to the game, I'll throw in the magical materials you will need to summon your familiar. That's a one hundred gold piece value."

"Can I sell it and buy a sword?"

"You can pick up a sword anywhere," said Tim. "We're bound to fight someone with a sword sooner or later. Trust me, Mordred's offering you a good deal. Take it."

"What's a familiar?" asked Julian.

"It's like a little animal friend that wizards and sorcerers can get," said Dave.

"Like a pet?"

"No,... well yeah, sort of. But you share an empathic link, and it can run little errands for you and stuff."

"Like fetching the newspaper."

"For fuck's sake," said Cooper. "Just take the bag of magical shit and let's get on with it."

"Fine," said Julian. "Bag... of... magical... shit," he muttered to himself while writing it in his inventory.

"Okay," said Mordred. "So we have a halfling rogue," He passed Tim his character sheet. "A dwarven cleric," he handed the sheet to Dave. "A half-orc barbarian," he passed the paper to Cooper. "And an elven wizard," he said, passing the last sheet to Julian. "This is your last chance to change your minds. I'll warn you that a group like that isn't likely to be accepted by certain areas of society."

"I'm a barbarian," said Cooper. "I shun society!"

"And society thanks you," said Tim. "Now shut up."

"Fine," said Cooper. "Let's get this shit started. Do you want a beer, Mordred?"

"I don't drink alcohol."

"Seriously? The decision to wear that cape was a sober one?"

Everyone laughed. Mordred frowned at Julian. "It's a cloak," he said.

Dave held his eyes and his lips shut tight. Tim's eyes started to tear up.

"We haven't even started yet," said Mordred. "And you're already acting like a bunch of drunken imbeciles. This is precisely why I have never partaken in the drink."

Tim reined in his laughter. Mordred wasn't responding well to Cooper's brand of humor.

Mordred reached into his duffel bag and pulled out a black silk bag. Its surface shone like liquid metal, held shut by a silver braided cord. He placed the bag in front of him and ran a finger along its side, smiling an unnerving smile to himself.

"How about a Coke?" asked Cooper.

"Huh?" said Mordred suddenly as if waking from a dream. Cooper stood over Mordred, holding a Coke. Mordred let go of the bag.

"What's in there?" Cooper started to reach for the bag. "Your nuts?"

"Back off!" Mordred screamed, snatching away his bag with one hand and swatting away Cooper with the other.

"Jesus fuck, dude. I'm sorry."

Mordred regained his composure. "I'm sorry," he said. "This is a special set of dice. They are rare and very valuable. I don't let just anyone use them."

He pulled a second pouch out of his duffel bag. This one was dull brown and leather. He poured a matching set of marbled blue plastic dice onto his table. They must have been brand spanking new.

Tim poured his own dice from a Crown Royal bag. They were dirty, dull, and scuffed. No more than three were from any matching set. Among them was a Lego man's head with the face worn off, a cockroach wing, and a pubic hair.

Cooper grabbed another beer and sat down.

Mordred closed his eyes and inhaled deeply. "Shall we begin?"

Chapter 2

"For months the four of you have wandered, a life of adventure having called you to leave your homes and families and seek your fortunes. Along the way, you have crossed paths and decided to travel together, putting aside your racial and philosophical differences. You come to the outskirts of a town."

"What's the name of the town?" asked Cooper.

"You don't know," said Mordred. "You can't read the sign."

"Is it a magical sign?" asked Julian. "I can read magic."

"No," said Mordred. "It's an ordinary sign. He can't read it because he's a barbarian, and barbarians can't read."

"So what does it say?" asked Tim.

"In the common tongue, it reads 'Welcome to Algor.'"

"Al Gore?" asked Dave.

"Is this a green city?" asked Cooper.

"Algor!" snapped Mordred. "One word. No 'E'." His hand crept toward the silk bag beside him.

Tim gave Cooper a pleading glance, and Cooper shut up.

Mordred put both hands firmly on the table and continued. "A tall wooden palisade surrounds the town. The main gate is guarded by a single soldier, and traffic moves in and out freely, so far as you can tell. Outside the gate, on either side of the road, stand two big black menhir, relics of a people long since-"

"Do they have to stand outside because they're black?" asked Julian.

"What?"

"I want to talk to one of them."

"Who?"

"One of the big black men."

"Menhir?"

"Yeah, sure. Here, there, wherever they are."

"Um... okay."

"Good day to you, sir!" said Julian. "I am Melvin the White, no offense, son of Zorbin the Great! My friends and I have traveled far and-"

Mordred interrupted him. "The guard at the gate asks you why you're talking to an inanimate object."

"What a racist prick!" said Julian. "I'll shoot an arrow at him."

"You don't have a bow."

"Can I hit him with my quarterstaff?"

"No," said Mordred. "He's fifty feet away."

"You're a wizard, dipshit," said Cooper. "Why don't you use some magic?"

"Oh right," said Julian. "I'll use magic on him."

"What spell would you like to cast?"

"I don't know. Lightning bolts or some shit."

"Lightning Bolt is a third level spell. Right now, the best you can do is Magic Missile."

"Awesome. I'll use that."

"Did you memorize it?"

"I have to memorize shit?"

"Julian," said Tim. "You have to memorize what spells you want each morning. Well played Mordred. Can we move on?"

"Move on?" asked Julian. "Are you guys really cool with the way they treat big black men in this town?"

"Menhir," corrected Mordred.

"Okay fine," said Julian. "The way they treat big black men, here in this town. Are you happy?"

"Oh for fuck's sake," Cooper shouted. "M-E-N-H-I-R. It's a fucking pillar of stone or something."

"Oh," said Julian. "Well excuse me. I guess I haven't run into as many menhir as you guys have."

"Your mom has run into a lot of men here," said Cooper. "The big black ones were always her favorite."

"Julian, mark down another hundred experience points."

"What the fuck for?" asked Cooper.

"For attempting to stay in character and role-playing. He put some thought into his back story."

Julian marked down another hundred points on his character sheet and grinned at Cooper.

"The guard approaches and shouts 'Halt!'."

"Good day, sir," said Tim in response.

"Where do you think you're bringing that beast?" Mordred pointed to Cooper.

"Who are you calling a beast, motherfu-"

"This is our friend," Dave jumped in. "He means you or this town no harm. We have traveled far, and we seek-"

"Why you should choose to associate with the likes of him, I care not. No orc shall set foot in Algor. 'Tis the law of the land."

"I told you this guy was racist," said Julian.

"He's only half-orc," said Tim. "His mother was human."

"So I should grant him passage because his mother was an orc-fucking whore? Perhaps I should bow down at his feet as well. All hail he whose mother spreads her legs for-"

"Fuck this," said Cooper. "I kill him."

"Really?" asked Mordred.

"Hells yeah," said Cooper, picking up a twenty-sided die. "I chop the fucker's head off." He rolled the die. "19."

Mordred shrugged. "Okay, you swing your great axe around your head and its blade meets his neck just above the shoulder. It's a clean slice and the head tumbles to the ground."

"Sweet. I put it in my bag."

"If you like."

"Do I get any experience points?"

"No."

"Why not?"

"This guard offered no challenge. He was just a piece of scenery. He only had two hit points."

"What about role-playing and staying in character?"

"You call that role-playing?"

"I'm a fucking barbarian, and he called my mother an orc-fucking whore. Would it have been more in character for me to challenge his views through rational discourse?"

"Fine. Take fifty points."

"Your mom took fifty points," he muttered, but wrote down the fifty points without arguing for any more.

Mordred spoke suddenly, calling all attention his way. "People are screaming. It's not long before you hear a bell ringing and guards shouting from within the gates."

"Shit, Cooper," said Dave. "We're going to get our asses kicked."

"Fuck you, Dave. My mother's honor was at stake."

Tim addressed Mordred directly. "You said there's a lot of traffic heading in and out of the city, right?"

"A fair amount, yes."

He turned to the group. "Let's hijack a cart or something and get the fuck out of here."

"Sounds good to me," said Dave.

"A good plan right about now," said Mordred. "Give yourself a hundred experience points."

"I'll find a cart headed away from the city," said Cooper. "If I have time to be picky, I'll choose one with a couple of healthy horses attached to it."

"You find an appropriate vehicle. A covered wagon with two horses you judge to be in good condition."

"I'll brandish my axe at the driver and order him to get out."

Mordred rolled some dice from behind the cover of his screen. "He does as you say."

"Quick. Everybody in the wagon."

"Okay," said Tim. "We're all in the wagon. Let's go!"

Mordred smiled. "Does anyone have any ranks in the Handle Animal skill?"

Everyone looked at their character sheets, and then at each other.

"I have diplomacy," said Julian.

"You can make an untrained check with your high charisma score."

"Um... Go horses!"

"Roll a die."

"Is six enough?"

"No. The horses don't move. You can see a cloud of dust rising above the palisade as the sound of hoof-beats thunders increasingly toward you."

"I'll grab Julian's quarterstaff," said Cooper, "and poke one of the horses in the ass with it."

"The horses bolt forward, out of control. Make a Dexterity check."

Tim, Dave, and Cooper grabbed a twenty-sided die, and Julian quickly followed suit.

"Four," said Cooper.

"Twelve," said Dave.

"Six," said Tim.

"Ha!" shouted Julian. "Twenty!" His look of triumph was met with looks of concern from the rest of the players. "What?"

"You want to roll low for ability checks," Tim explained.

"Shit," said Julian.

Mordred spoke. "You lose your balance and start to fall off the wagon."

"I made my check by a lot," said Cooper. "Can I try to catch him?"

Mordred considered it. "Okay. Make another check and you can catch him."

Cooper rolled the die again. "Fourteen! I made it."

"Fair enough. Mark down a hundred experience points. That's fifty for getting the horses moving, and fifty for saving your comrade."

"So are we heading back the way we came from?" asked Dave. "What's back that way?"

"You head down the road for another five hundred yards or so, but the road curves and the horses continue to go straight. You can see a group of five horses following you. Unlike your horses, they are unencumbered by anything but their riders, and they are gaining on you quickly."

"What are the riders wearing?" asked Tim.

"They are dressed in chainmail armor and armed with crossbows and longswords."

"What's ahead of us?" asked Dave.

"The edge of the forest. The horses won't be able to maneuver through the trees with the cart. You estimate that your cart will reach the trees at roughly the same time as the town guards catch up to you."

"Fuck," offered Cooper. "Who wants a cigarette?"

"What?" asked Mordred.

"Yeah," said Dave. "That sounds about right."

"I'm in," said Julian.

"I'll run to the shop and get some more beer," said Tim.

"But we're about to have an encounter," objected Mordred. "You're interrupting the flow of gameplay!"

Cooper lit a cigarette as he stepped out the front door. "Why don't you interrupt the flow of blood from your vagina for a minute and relax?"

Tim started walking to the corner shop near the Chicken Hut. It was run by an elderly couple, and Tim suspected that their Friday night gaming sessions might be responsible for keeping them in business.

Cooper shouted after him. "Pick up some tampons for Mordred while you're out! Velvety purple ones!"

Tim returned a couple of minutes later, a case of beer in each hand, to find Dave and Julian laughing. He peeked in through the door at Mordred. He sat alone with his elbows on the table, the little tufts of hair on either side of his head sticking out between his chubby fingers. "You guys mind taking these inside?"

Dave and Julian each grabbed a case and walked inside. Cooper started to follow, but Tim stopped him.

"You got a cigarette?"

"Sure." Cooper lit Tim's cigarette, along with a second one for himself.

Tim exhaled a long column of smoke. It hung in the humid air. "What did I miss?"

"Not much."

"He looks pissed."

"Who?"

"Mordred, dickface. Who do you think?"

"Oh yeah," Cooper said, smiling. "He'll get over it."

"Get over what? What did you assholes do to him?"

"We were just fucking with him. He's a big boy. He can take it."

"Dude, I don't know if he's ever had..." he paused, trying to find a better word, because the one that he wanted to say was too depressing. He failed to come up with anything better. "...friends before. He might not realize you're just fucking with him."

"Oh come on, man. You know-"

"Yeah, I know," said Tim. "Just take it down a notch, okay?"

"All right."

When everyone had gotten a fresh beer, they all sat back down at their table.

"Are you all ready to play now?" asked Mordred. His nostrils were flared and contempt resonated in his voice. He gripped his black dice bag tightly in one hand.

"Yeah, go ahead," said Cooper. He and Tim sat solemnly. Julian and Dave sat still, holding in giggles. They looked like two first-graders who had to go to the bathroom.

Mordred waited a few more seconds, and then continued when he was sure he had everyone's attention. "The soldiers surround your wagon on all sides. One shouts 'We have you surrounded! Surrender your weapons and exit the vehicle!'"

"Okay," said Tim to the other players. "What should we do?"

"They're just guards," said Cooper. "I've already taken down one's head off with one swipe."

"You got lucky with that roll. Anyway, these guys might be tougher."

"I don't see a bright future if we surrender," said Julian.

"Your time is running out!" shouted Mordred in the voice he had used for the soldier.

"Keep your pants on!" said Cooper. It was unclear as to whether he was saying this to Mordred or the soldier.

Mordred made that distinction for him. "My pantaloons are none of your concern! I insist that you lay down your arms, and-"

"Why don't I lay down your mom?"

Mordred began rolling dice behind the cover of his screen.

Dave spoke up. "If we can all stay alive for the first round, I should be able to get an attack in before I have to start healing-"

Mordred interrupted, speaking in his own voice. "Cooper, you are hit with a crossbow bolt in the shoulder. The canvas roof of the wagon absorbed some of the impact, but you still lose two hit points."

"Hey," said Cooper. "What the fuck was that for?"

"That was a warning shot!" Mordred was speaking in the voice of the soldier again.

"Your warning shot hit me in the fucking shoulder, shithead!"

"You have ten seconds to comply!"

"Your mom has ten seconds to-"

"Ten!"

"Dude, come on," said Cooper, clearly to Mordred, trying to sound reasonable. "We're trying to work out a-"

"Nine!"

"Shit," said Julian. "Cooper and I will jump out first and take care of the guard behind the-"

"Eight!"

"Would it be possible," Tim addressed Mordred, "for me to see one of them out the front of the wagon without being seen myself? I'd like to use my Sneak Attack."

"Do you want to do that right now?" Mordred asked in his normal voice.

"No," said Tim. "I just want to get into position."

"Roll for it."

Tim rolled a die. "Sixteen."

"You see one soldier, and you don't think he can see you. You can get your Sneak Attack in, but you'll take a penalty because you don't have a lot of room to maneuver inside the wagon."

"Fair enough."

"Seven!"

"Mordred," said Cooper. "Dude. Relax. We need some time to get ready."

"Six!" shouted Mordred, and then spoke in his own voice. "You have six seconds to get ready. It's unlikely that the soldiers outside would give you time to formulate a plan to murder them."

"It's a fucking game, dude. That's not how we play."

"It's how you play when I'm the Cavern Master."

"Really?" said Cooper. "This is your big show of power? We tease you about your cape a little, and now you're going to pepper our characters with crossbows?"

Mordred gave a hollow, snorting laugh. "I assure you, I don't let my personal opinions of players interfere with gameplay. If that were the case, you would have all been eaten by dragons in the beginning."

"See," said Cooper. "That's what I'm talking about. What the fuck have you got against us? We invited you over here, and you waltz in with your faggy little cape and tell us where to move tables and shit, and you-"

"You have insulted me and berated me since I walked through the door. You're a bunch of drunken hooligans."

Julian laughed, and everyone turned to face him. "I'm sorry," he said. "I just think the word hooligans is funny."

"Tim," said Mordred. "I think I would like another Coke, please."

Tim stared back at him in disbelief. "Sure." He got up and walked to the refrigerator. He returned with a Coke for Mordred, and a harsh glare for Cooper. "Don't mind him," he said to Mordred. "That's the way he is. He talks to all of us like that."

"Sir Wankalot doesn't need any help from you," said Cooper. "He's a big boy. If he's got something to say-"

"Shut up, Coop," said Tim. "We're supposed to be playing a game."

"Shall we continue?" asked Mordred.

"Shall we continue?" Cooper mocked him in a nasally voice.

Cooper and Mordred stared at each other.

Tim finally broke the silence. "Coop?"

Cooper looked at Tim, who cocked his head toward Mordred and raised his eyebrows expectantly.

"What, seriously?"

Tim's look of expectation turned to one of exasperated pleading.

"For fuck's sake," said Cooper. "I'm sorry, okay?"

Mordred closed his eyes and offered back a wide, smug grin. "Your apology is accepted."

Julian and Dave exhaled.

"Bite my big black menhir," said Cooper.

Julian and Dave looked at Tim, and the three of them broke into laughter.

Mordred offered an insincere chuckle. His hand was closed in a tight fist around the black bag on the table in front of him.

When the laughter had died down, Tim tried to get the game rolling again. "Okay, so I'm up front getting ready to make a sneak attack. Do the rest of you know what you're doing?"

Dave said "Julian and Cooper are going to jump out the back, and-"

"Not so fast, boys," said Mordred. Everyone stopped talking. Cooper rolled his eyes but said nothing.

"As a sign of goodwill, I've decided to let you roll my special dice." He opened the bag and turned it upside down. Six black, twenty-sided dice clattered to the table. "I'd ask that you be very careful with these, and not roll them until I tell you to." He passed one die to each player.

Tim rolled the die around in his palm. The edges were sharper than the edges of his old, worn-out plastic dice, like it was made of glass. He held it up to the fluorescent light. Either his eye deceived him, or the darkness swirled around inside the die like a storm trapped in a prism. At the center of the storm shone a tiny, barely perceptible red light. It was like looking across a completely dark room at the last ember left glowing in a fire that had otherwise long burnt out. Concentration made the light grow in intensity, but not in size.

"Where did you get these?" Dave's question sounded as though it had been filtered through water.

"They were a gift," said Mordred, cracking open his Coke.

The sound brought Tim out of his trance.

"Okay, everyone roll at the same time. Ready-"

"Wait," said Tim. "Aren't we still in the wagon? What are we rolling for?"

Mordred hesitated, thought, and then said, "It's a saving throw versus magic."

Tim shrugged. "Okay."

"Ready?"

Everyone nodded. Cooper's nod was paired with some eye rolling and a 'let's hurry this shit along' twirling gesture with his hand.

"Ready... steady... roll!"

They released their dice simultaneously. Tim, Dave, and Cooper's dice all rolled on the table at the same time. Julian's die rolled off the side of the table. While his die was busy bouncing off of a chair and on to the floor, the other three dice all came to an abrupt stop on the number 1.

"Wow," said Cooper. "What are the odds of-"

The world went dark.

Chapter 3

Spears of light pierced through Tim's eyes and straight into his brain. He raised his arms to block the light and shut his eyes as tightly as he could.

His ears were assaulted by a roar like a lion getting raped by an elephant. Whatever made that sound was right in front of him, but he couldn't force his eyes open. The roaring continued. The air around Tim vibrated with sound, and he could feel the warmth of breath on his face. He scooted back in his seat.

Slowly, the muscles in his eyelids started to relax, and he was able to crack his eyes open. He wished he hadn't. Sitting directly across from him was some kind of man-beast. A monster. Not some dude in a costume – a real fucking flesh-and-blood monster, and it looked pissed.

Its right arm, which might have been as thick around as Tim, reached across its massive chest and behind its left shoulder.

Tim tried to get to his feet and run, but his feet couldn't find the floor.

The monster yanked something out of the back of its shoulder with a wince. An arrow. The front half of the shaft was coated in black blood, which dripped from the barbed tip.

"Wharrapuck?" said the monster. It dropped the arrow and looked at its clawed hands.

Two new screams pried Tim's attention away from the giant monster in front of him. He wasn't alone in here with the creature. There was some small comfort in that, but who the hell were these people? A short, stout guy with a thick red beard and metal armor sat next to the beast. His feet barely touched the floor. Tim thought of Humpty Dumpty. The other guy was dressed in a long white nightshirt and looked suspiciously like... "Julian?"

"Huh?" said the monster, looking up.

The squat, bearded guy jumped to his feet and ran across the floor of the... where the hell were they? This wasn't the Chicken

25

Hut. He ran through a canvas flap of a doorway and fell forward and out of sight. Judging by the sound of the "Ugh" shortly afterward, it hadn't been a far fall.

"Hold your fire!" came a voice from outside.

This can't be real. We couldn't actually be...

The giant monster turned to look at the guy in the white pajamas. "Jhurian?" it said. It went into a fit of coughing – loud, wet, hacking coughs – and spat a gob of bloody phlegm on the floor.

Pajama guy yelped, jumped to his feet, and ran out the door. He must have landed on the bearded guy, as Tim heard another grunt from below. Pajama guy's torso was still visible as he stumbled forward a couple of steps.

"Hands where we can see them, magic user!" said the voice from outside. The guy in the pajamas raised his hands. His head pivoted left, then right, and he turned around to face the wagon. He didn't look any less frightened than he had in here with the monster.

"You have five seconds to send out the orc, or the wizard dies!"

The monster turned to Tim. The fury was gone from its face. If Tim had to guess, he'd say he was looking at confused desperation. "Thrighm?" it said.

"Cooper?" said Tim. Why was his voice so high? He put a hand to his throat and tried to clear it, but there was nothing to clear.

"Four!"

"Whashgoingon?" said the monster.

"I think we're –"

"Three!"

"We're in the game, Cooper!"

"Two!"

"Shit!" said Tim. "Those guys are about to shoot Julian!"

"One!"

"Wha?"

"On my command, shoot the elf," said the voice outside. "The rest of you keep your eyes on the wagon."

Tim shifted in his seat to get a better view. A soldier on horseback held a crossbow on Julian. A fly buzzed around the soldier's face. His horse stomped its hooves nervously.

"This is your last warning," shouted the voice from outside.

"You either surrender the orc, or else I will have no choice but to..."

The fly landed on the nose of the soldier who was covering Julian. He went to swat it away, and his finger slipped on the trigger of the crossbow. He fired a bolt right into Julian's chest.

"Ow!" Julian looked down at the bolt sticking out of his chest. "What was that—"

Cooper let out a thunderous roar as he got to his feet, tearing the canvas roof apart from the frame. In an instant, he was out of the wagon. His first step landed on Dave. It only took four more, and half as many seconds, before he had run straight past Julian, who stood frozen in fear.

Cooper pulled Julian's assailant off of his horse by the shoulders and swung him around like a drunk uncle swinging a toddler. He made two full rotations before connecting the soldier's boots with the torso of the one who had been shouting the orders. The commander flew backwards, landing on his back a good five feet behind his horse. Cooper made one more rotation and released the soldier he had been swinging. The man spun through the air like a limbed Frisbee. Cooper looked for something else to smash.

A crossbow bolt whizzed by Cooper. A second one struck him in a bicep. He ran at the two soldiers who had fired at him. Their horses stomped the ground frantically, and the riders could barely keep them under control. Cooper grabbed each of them by the throats, smashed their helmeted heads together and threw them to the ground.

The fifth rider bade his horse to move, and the horse seemed happy enough to acquiesce.

Cooper roared after him, but that only seemed to increase his speed, as if pushed into a faster gallop by the force of Cooper's voice.

Dave started to push himself up out of the dirt but collapsed again as Tim hopped out of the wagon.

"Are you guys all right?" said Tim. He tried to clear his throat again. "Cooper? Is that really you?"

Cooper grunted, and a wad of brown snot flew out of one nostril, landing on the ground next to Tim. He winced as he pulled the bolt out of his arm. Dark blood trickled out of the wound, but he didn't appear to be seriously harmed.

"Jesus, Cooper. Are you okay?"

Cooper bent his elbow a couple of times and opened and closed the fingers on his left hand. He grunted an affirmation.

"Where are we?" asked Julian. He hardly seemed to notice the bolt sticking out of his chest.

Dave finally lifted himself out of the mud. "What's going on?"

"I think we all know the answer to those two questions," said Tim.

"Do we?" asked Dave. "Do we really? Maybe you should enlighten the rest of us. Because I, for one, don't know why we're all dressed up in gay renaissance fair costumes, why I'm suddenly only four feet tall and sporting a Grizzly Adams beard, and why you look and sound like a prepubescent girl."

"I didn't say I knew the 'why'," said Tim. "Or the 'how', for that matter. I'm not even sure if 'when' applies. But the 'where' and the 'what' are pretty obvious. We're in the game."

"This game fucking rules!" said Julian. "You guys have seriously been doing this shit since middle school?"

"Not this," said Dave. "This isn't the game." He ran his hand through his gigantic bushy beard. "Well, I suppose it is, but –"

"No," said Tim. "It isn't. We're supposed to be inside the Chicken Hut rolling dice and drinking beer. That's the game. This is... I don't know what this is, but it's not supposed to happen."

"Borghid," said Cooper. Everyone turned to look at him. He was moving his lips and tongue around. "Bo... Mo.. Mor.. Morghid... Morgdid..."

"Mordred," said Tim. "I think he's right. That must be it. What's the last thing you remember before... well, before this?"

"Cooper pissed off Mordred," said Dave. "And we all laughed at him."

"After that," said Tim.

"He pulled out those black dice."

"Those dice," agreed Tim. "Those black fucking dice."

"Magic dice?" asked Julian.

"What else could it be?" asked Tim. "Fucking look at us!"

"Mordred!" Dave stood up on his stubby legs and shouted at the sky. "What the fuck, man? This isn't fucking funny!"

One of the soldiers' horses which had stuck around started to whinny, and it clearly sounded like a laugh. Cooper punched it in the side of the head, and it collapsed to the ground.

"Cooper!" shouted Tim. "Dude! What the fuck?"

"Morghdid," replied Cooper. "Horsh."

"Mordred isn't the fucking horse," said Tim. "He's the CM. He's everything you see. We're inside his imagination or something."

"Then where are all the girls who think his cape is sexy?" asked Dave.

Tim and Julian chuckled in spite of their confusion and fear. Cooper snorted a laugh that shot a couple more snot wads out of his nose.

The wagon backed up a foot, pushing Dave face-first into the dirt again.

Cooper doubled over and laughed so hard, he coughed up a huge glob of brownish yellow phlegm.

"Dude," said Tim. "That's seriously fucking gross. What is going on with your..." He stopped talking. A thought occurred to him. "He can hear us."

"Who?" asked Julian.

"Mordred," said Tim. "He's still there in my fucking Chicken Hut, drinking my fucking Coke, and laughing his balls off at us." He looked up into the same patch of empty blue sky that Dave had shouted at. "Aren't you, mother fucker?" he shouted.

One of the two soldiers whose heads Cooper had smashed together started to stir.

"Um... Tim?" Julian said. "These guys are starting to wake up. What should we do?"

"How should I know?" asked Tim.

"Well what would you have done if this happened in the game?"

"Kirrum," Cooper grunted.

"We're not going to kill anyone," said Tim. "Just kick them in the head or something, and move their weapons away."

Julian shrugged. "Okay."

"Do we have any rope?" asked Dave, standing again, and brushing the dirt from his knees.

"If we do," said Tim, "my char – " he sighed. "I mean I have the Rope Use skill. I can tie them up."

"Did you buy any rope?"

"I don't think so."

Julian had two crossbows tucked under his left arm, and a third one in his right hand. He kicked the stirring soldier in the head, just hard enough to let him know that he should stop stirring. "Why don't you look in the cart?"

Tim grabbed the edge of the wagon and hoisted himself into it with a surprising amount of grace. He went deeper into the wagon, and then emerged again, dragging two bags behind him. "Dave, Julian, I think these are yours."

"How do you know?" asked Dave.

"Because I recognized my own, and Cooper's is pretty hard to mistake for anyone else's."

Cooper's bag looked to have been hastily stitched together from the hides of at least six different animals. Tim guessed he could probably fit at least three of himself inside it. He put his back up against it and bulldozed it to the edge of the wagon.

"Yar," said Cooper. "Thatun's mine." He grabbed the bag as if it were no heavier than a child's backpack and looked inside. He yelped, and a stream of yellow liquid shit squirted down from beneath his loincloth.

"Oh for fuck's sake, Cooper!" shouted Dave.

"What's wrong?" asked Julian.

Cooper tossed his giant bag to the ground, and a human head rolled out of it.

They all stared, mouths hanging open, at the head. The head stared back, its own mouth ajar.

"Whose head is that?" asked Tim. "And why was it in your… shit."

"It was the guard we – " Dave started, and then corrected himself. "The guard Cooper killed at the town gate."

Tim grabbed his own bag, hopped down from the wagon, careful to avoid the steaming yellow puddle of Cooper shit, and joined the others surrounding the severed head. They stared.

The lifeless eyes of the head grew bright. It wasn't a physical change, and Tim wasn't even sure it happened just yet. He peered down at it with the uneasy feeling that it might not be as dead as it was letting on. When it blinked and smiled at them, everybody screamed. Tim grabbed Dave around the waist. Dave grabbed Julian around the leg. Julian made a move to grab Cooper, but changed his mind just before making contact.

"You boys fucked with the wrong Cavern Master," said the severed head. It started to laugh. Tim, Dave, and Julian screamed, and Cooper kicked the head toward the forest. It kept laughing until it hit a tree. "Ugh," it said as it bounced off the tree and rolled to a stop on the ground, where it resumed laughing.

"That's fucked up," said Julian.

"What are we going to do?" asked Dave.

"Let's see what else we've got in our bags," said Tim. "Provided they're not stuffed with body parts, we might find something we can use. Dump out your bags, preferably somewhere that Cooper hasn't shit all over the place."

"Fark you," said Cooper.

"Seriously, dude," said Dave. "I know you're scared and confused. I mean, we all are. But most of us are able to keep our bowels under control."

"Rethsheehowr...shith. Fark you, Dabe," said Cooper. "Ish my Charithma Score."

Tim shook his head. "How low did you roll for Charisma?"

"Sixth."

"Six?" said Tim. "That's not too bad. I mean yeah, it's low, but it's not pants-shittingly low. A Charisma score of six is how I imagine that guy from Friends. You know, the annoying one. What's his name?"

"Any of them?" asked Dave.

"Yeah, that's the one."

"Ima harf-orc," Cooper explained. "I rost two pointsh of Charishma and Inter... Interr... Intelligence."

"Well that explains it, then." said Tim. "You've got a modified Charisma of four. You are almost completely unlikable."

They walked over to where the soldiers were still lying on the ground and opened their bags.

Resting neatly on top of everything else packed in their bags, they each found a metal tube with a screw-on top.

"What is this?" asked Dave, picking up his tube.

"Pipe bomb?" asked Cooper, with only a slight trace of impediment in his speech.

"Not likely," said Tim. "They look like scroll tubes. Did anyone buy scrolls?"

Everyone shook their heads.

Tim shrugged and opened his. "You're not going to believe this," he said.

"What is it?" asked Dave.

Tim smiled. "My fucking character sheet."

Everyone opened their tubes. Sure enough, they each stood looking at the paper version of themselves.

Julian was the first to stop ogling his character sheet and look deeper into his bag. "Oh, look!" he said. "I bought some rope. Silk!"

The other three looked up at him, and instead of noticing the rope he held up, their attention was focused on the wet and sticky red circle on his white robes, expanding from the place where a crossbow bolt still stuck out of his chest.

"Dude," said Tim. "Are you going to pull that out?"

"What?" said Julian, looking down. "Oh yeah, I forgot about that." He laughed.

"How could you forget about that?" asked Cooper. "I'm a Barbarian, and my wounds hurt like a sonofabitch."

"I wasn't hit that hard," said Julian, "and I've got like four hundred hit points."

"You've got what?" asked Dave and Tim together.

"Let me see that!" said Cooper, snatching away Julian's character sheet.

"You don't remember?" asked Julian. "Mordred gave them to me for good role-playing.

"You dumb fuck," said Cooper, looking at the sheet. "Those are experience points."

Cooper handed the sheet to Tim and put a hand on Julian's shoulder. He wrapped his other hand around the bolt. "This might hurt a little." He plucked the bolt out of Julian's chest.

Julian winced, but didn't cry out. After a couple of breaths, he said "That wasn't so bad."

"Hey guys," said Tim. "We might have a little problem." Julian's hit points were disappearing from the paper, swiped away in big chunks.

"What's wrong?" asked Julian.

"I think Mordred is fixing your character sheet."

"Shit," said Cooper. "You might um… want to lie down or something. This is most definitely going to hurt."

"Seriously guys," said Julian with a note of panic in his voice. "I feel fine. In fact, I don't remember the last time I felt quite so –" His eyes widened, and he looked down at his wound. A torrent of blood sprayed out of his chest like a fire hose, covering Cooper's loincloth. "Ohmygodithurts!" he screamed, collapsed to the ground, and passed out.

Tim looked down at Julian's character sheet. In the instant he glanced at it, the number in the box labeled "Current Hit Points" changed from -1 to -2.

Chapter 4

"What did you do to him?" shouted Dave.

"I didn't do anything!" Cooper shouted back. "It's fucking Mordred." He looked down at Julian, who was sprawled out flat on his back. Blood poured out of the hole in his chest in increasingly smaller spurts.

"He's bleeding out," said Tim. "He's not going to make it much longer."

Cooper knelt beside him. He tried to put pressure on the wound with his palm.

"You're only going to make it worse, Cooper," said Tim. "Your hands are filthy."

Cooper did not let go. "If you've got any better ideas," he roared, "now is the time!"

Julian's head fell to the side facing Cooper. For a second, it looked as though he might say something, but all that came out of Julian's mouth was a stream of blood down his cheek.

Dave buried his hands in the shaggy hair on top of his head. Tears began to well up in his eyes. "Did anyone take the Heal skill?" His voice cracked hopelessly.

"No," said Tim, forcing himself to remain calm and think. "We didn't need to, because we had a –" He whipped his head sharply around at Dave. "What the fuck are you doing? Get in there and heal him. You're a fucking cleric!"

Dave stood still, hands still buried in his hair. "Well, I'm not really a cleric. I can't—"

"Go fucking heal him!"

"Okay okay!" shouted Dave. He waddled over to where Cooper's hand swam in Julian's blood. "Back off," he said to Cooper. "I'll need some room." He pulled on his beard with both hands. "God I hope this works. I don't know what to do."

Cooper stood over him, more like a building than a man. "Whatever it is, just fucking do it." His tone promised that there would be consequences for fucking it up.

"Dude!" shouted Tim. He had picked up Julian's character sheet. "Whatever you're going to do, do it now! He's at negative nine! One more point, and he's—"

"I heal thee!" shouted Dave, slapping his hand down on Julian's chest. Blood splattered in every direction.

Cooper picked up Dave by his upper arms. "I heal thee?" he shouted into his face. "Is this some kind of fucking joke to you?"

"I didn't know what to do!" Dave protested. His eyes showed a combination of grief and terror, each fighting for dominance. "What to say! I was trying—"

"Guys!" Tim shouted. His voice was phlegmy and excited. Cooper and Dave looked down at him. "It worked! He..."

He couldn't say any more. The tears started going, and he let them go. He was panting between sobs, and it was all he could do to hold out Julian's character sheet for them to see.

Cooper dropped Dave and took the paper. The number in the box labeled Current Hit Points read -7. He stared at it for a few seconds, and it didn't appear to be changing at all. "So what does that mean? Is he okay?"

Tim knew he was going to have to collect himself and get the rest of the excitement out of his system the best way he knew how. He'd throw up.

Once he decided he was going to do it, his body took over. He dropped down to his knees, palms down on the ground, and let it out. His head hung down for a few seconds while his body sorted out whether or not it was going to make one more go. Once, however, seemed to be enough.

He closed his eyes and breathed deeply in and out. When he opened his eyes, he saw the puddle below his head. What had his character eaten that day before he took over? Shit. Thinking about that was a mistake. His guts turned inside him, and his body gave one more try, but all that came out this time were strings of spit and bile. He stood up and wiped his mouth with one sleeve and his eyes with the other. No point in trying to keep clean right now.

"You all right?" Dave asked.

"Yeah," said Tim, looking down at Julian. "Better now. How's he?"

"I don't know."

"Any change on the sheet?" Tim asked Cooper. Cooper shook his head.

Tim walked up to Julian, who continued to lie as still as he had since he fell there. He peeled up the bottom of Julian's shirt, and rivers of blood flowed down the sides. Underneath was just more blood. Tim ran a finger through it to reveal a line of pale white skin on Julian's belly, just to confirm that there was something under all that blood after all. He peeled back the shirt some more, all the way up past the wound. More blood ran down each side of Julian's neck.

Tim smeared a palm across the area where he guessed the wound to be. In the pink smear across Julian's chest was a small red circle, no bigger than the circumference of a pencil. He stared at it, waiting for more blood to pour out, but none did. To Tim, this meant one of two things. Either Dave had managed to stabilize him, or Julian had just simply run out of blood and was lying there dead in front of him.

Looking around at all of the blood – holy shit it was everywhere – either scenario was plausible. Tim put his ear to Julian's chest, hoping for just a hint of a heartbeat. Surely if Julian had any life left in him at all, it was going to be faint. But the sound that reached Tim's ear was that of a booming drum. He pressed his ear harder into Julian's chest, not bothered at all by the fact that half of his face was getting covered in blood. He relished the sound. He stayed that way for thirty seconds, before getting up and grinning from ear to ear.

Cooper was twice as tall as Dave was, but they were both built as wide as city buses. In spite of their size, they both took a step backward with a look of fear in their eyes.

"What?" asked Tim, and then realized how he must look with half of his face covered in blood. "He's going to make it."

Dave and Cooper's expressions relaxed, and they smiled back at Tim.

"You heard his heartbeat?" asked Dave.

"Heard it?" Tim shouted back ecstatically. "It nearly blew my fucking ears out!"

Dave frowned. "Should it be beating that hard? Is that healthy?"

"I don't think it's his heart," said Tim. "I think it's my ears. I can hear like a motherfucker." He pointed at a cluster of trees about fifty yards away from where they were standing. "I can hear exactly four squirrels running through the trees way the hell over there. I can hear a stream running about forty yards into the forest. I can hear..." He stopped. His eyes widened with fear.

"What?" asked Dave. "What is it?"

"I hear horses," Tim said, turning his head back in the direction of Algor. He looked back at his friends. "Lots of them, and they're coming this way."

"How long?" asked Cooper.

"I don't know," said Tim, panicking. "I mean, the way it sounds to me, they should just be about fifty feet away, just about to trample over us. But I can't see them. Can you?"

Cooper craned his neck up and looked in the direction Tim had indicated. "No. Not yet."

"Well we have to get out of here," said Tim. "We should hide in the forest."

"What about them?" asked Dave, pointing to the soldiers who were still lying on the ground. They might have still been unconscious. More likely they were faking it, so as to not be kicked in the head again.

"I'll tie them up," said Tim. "You grab Julian and start heading into the forest. Cooper and I will catch up."

"We should stay together," Dave objected.

"You are slow as shit," said Tim. "You have a Base Movement Speed of twenty." He saw that Dave was not fully appreciating the unconventional nature of the argument. "Look at your stubby fucking legs!"

"Look at yours!" Dave shouted back at him, but he was already picking up Julian's limp body.

Tim grinned at him. "I don't plan on walking there. I've got a huge fucking moron to carry me." He looked at Cooper, who grinned back at him with pointed, yellow teeth. Then back to Dave. "Go!"

Dave made his best attempt at a run, but it wasn't easy going with Julian slung over his shoulder. Julian's hands dragged on the ground behind him. The trees were too close together here for the horses to be comfortable pulling the cart any further, but it was a far cry from dense woodland. The ground was still thick with grass, and there wouldn't be anywhere to hide. A single horse with a rider would easily be able to maneuver through the trees until they got deeper in.

Tim grabbed Julian's rope and tied the hands and feet of the soldiers. If they were awake, they showed no signs of it. Being tied up would have to be better than being killed, especially when help was on the way. "Grab all the shit you can carry!" he shouted to Cooper.

Cooper tore the canvas roof the rest of the way off the wagon and started throwing stuff onto it. All their bags, all of the weapons that no one had thought to use during the fight, even the weapons the soldiers had carried.

Tim relieved the soldiers of their purses as he tied them up. The hoofbeats were getting closer.

"They'll be coming over that ridge any second now," said Tim.

"You ready?" asked Cooper. He was holding all four corners of the wagon's roof in one hand.

Tim looked ahead to see what progress Dave had made. It wasn't much. They were still only about thirty yards away, and he had stopped.

"What the hell does he think he's doing?" asked Tim.

Cooper looked over at Dave, who was putting Julian's body down on the ground. He huffed angrily, and a ball of snot shot out of his nose. He started to move in that direction.

"There's no time," said Tim. "We'll need some of this shit, and we've got to go now. We'll deal with Dave when we catch up to him. Let's go." Tim hopped on top of the makeshift canvas sack and steadied himself. He slung a quiver of arrows over his shoulder and readied his shortbow in one hand. He sat facing backwards, ready to fire if it came to that.

Cooper started pulling, and Tim did his best to keep his balance. He sincerely hoped that he wouldn't need to fire any arrows while riding like this. It seemed a lot easier in his imagination. On the horizon, a cloud of dust rose into view over the ridge. It would soon be replaced by God knew how many men on horseback, armed to the teeth and thirsty for blood.

"Hurry up, Coop! They're coming!"

Cooper grunted and heaved. Tim peeked around Cooper's flank and saw Dave kneeling down over Julian. He hoped he was mistaken, but Dave appeared to be beating on Julian's body and shouting at him.

"Dave!" Cooper roared. "What the hell are you doing?" He pushed forward.

When he was nearly on top of them, Tim heard something he didn't expect. Julian was screaming in terror, and it was the sweetest sound Tim had ever heard. Julian scrambled up onto his elbows. Dave silenced his screams with a slap in the face, and said something to him. Julian jumped to his feet and looked back toward Cooper and Tim. Cooper grinned and waved, still running. Julian smiled awkwardly, gave a small wave back at him, and then looked past him. The smile left his face immediately.

The cloud of dust was growing thicker on the horizon. Cooper kept running, and Julian soon got the hint that he should be doing the same. Julian didn't run like a man who had just lost most of his blood through a hole in his chest. He easily outran everyone, bolting deeper into the forest like a coked-up hooker fleeing a crime scene. The trees here grew more closely together. The grass gave way to dirt, and undergrowth was visible just up ahead.

The canvas sack left a trail of flattened grass behind them. Tim hoped to gain a little time when the oncoming army stopped to question the soldiers he had tied up. How much time that bought them would depend on whether or not they had been faking their unconsciousness. Either way, they wouldn't be able to count on much more of a head start than what they had now, and their trail would be easy to follow. He hoped they would at least have time to-

Something caught his eye. He hopped off the bag.

Cooper stopped. "Tim!" He tried to whisper, but that only brought his voice down to that of a normal person's.

"Keep going!" said Tim. "I saw something I think we might need." Cooper looked at him doubtfully. "I'll catch up," Tim reassured him. "I'm sneaky."

Cooper kept going, and Tim crouched behind a tree. There were enough trees blocking his view so that he couldn't make out what the new group of soldiers were up to. That was good. His friends should be out of view by now.

From where he crouched, Tim couldn't make out any of the new set of riders, but he guessed by the slowing of the hoofbeats that they were now approaching their bound and sleeping comrades. He also guessed that he wouldn't have to climb far up the tree he was hiding behind before he'd get a good view of them, and they of him.

He hadn't come here to climb, though. His target was on the ground, about thirty feet away. If Tim didn't know any better, he would have thought it was staring back at him. No, he decided. He didn't know any better. How could he, after everything they had all just been through in the past half hour? In fact, that was the whole reason he was preparing himself to step out into danger to grab that stupid head. And now the fucker was smiling at him. Grinning even. He was sure of it. It was daring him to come out into the open and retrieve it. He gave it the finger, and while he couldn't see any perceptible movement, he had a strong feeling that its grin widened.

Tim closed his eyes and tried to take in his surroundings through his ears alone. The horses had stopped, and men were shouting at one another. He was close enough to have heard that much even through human ears. His own group had also stopped, which he hoped meant they had found a decent place to hide. That would be good.

"Look at the state of this place!" said one of the new riders as he dismounted his horse.

"By the Gods, man!" said another. "There are puddles of shit and vomit everywhere. What manner of... oh the smell!" He wretched, and then made his own contribution to the field where grass would never grow quite the same again. He wasn't alone. Tim heard at least three other men spill their breakfasts. He'd never have a better opportunity than he had right now.

"Sir," called a third voice in a desperate plea. "They clubbed one of the horses in the face. The poor thing's lucky to be alive! What kind of barbarians would do such a thing?"

"Barbarians indeed," replied the first voice, the voice of authority. He spoke softly, but his voice carried on the wind to Tim's sensitive halfling ears. "The evil kind," he spoke more loudly in response to the question. "The mongrel orcish kind, as well as the band of freaks that travel with it. The kind we hunt!"

Tim took a deep breath. Four ranks in Move Silently, and a plus two bonus for being a halfling. He crept out from behind the tree, hunched over as low as he could while still remaining on two feet.

"You there!" shouted the voice that Tim had decided belonged to the leader.

Tim froze in his tracks. If he had had any piss left in his bladder, he surely wouldn't now. What had gone wrong? He hadn't taken but a single step away from the tree. Perfectly silent. His eyes were fixed straight ahead on his target. One of its eyes winked and then both of them moved twice in the direction the shout had come from, as if to gesture that Tim should do the same. Tim looked, and saw that the shout was not directed at him. It continued. "You four sorry sacks of dog shit! Wake up!"

"That was lucky," said the severed head twenty feet in front of Tim.

"Shut the fuck up," Tim said back in a harsh whisper. His tiny heart was beating hard enough to send the blood through Cooper's enormous body. He tentatively took a second step, and heard a sound that, to him, sounded like the trunk of a tall pine snapping in a hurricane. He looked down and saw a twig under his foot that he was sure hadn't been there a second ago. He whipped his head back up to look at the head on the ground.

The head made a mockingly apologetic face. "Sorry, dude. You rolled a 1 on your Move Silently check. Of all the times to roll a-"

"I am going to find you, Mordred," Tim whispered, "and I'm going to murder the shit out of-"

"There's one of them!"

Tim turned his head, and for an instant his stunned eyes met the cool, satisfied gaze of the man who Tim assumed everyone was calling 'sir'. He turned and ran as fast as his tiny legs would carry him. As it turned out, that wasn't very fast at all.

"Take him alive!" shouted the captain, and that offered little comfort to Tim.

As he ran, Tim kept his ears alert. Men shouting, boots climbing into stirrups, and horses stomping the ground excitedly, ready to be taken for another gallop.

When those hooves started to move, Tim knew he didn't have much time left. Why was he running? What did he hope to accomplish by it? There was no way he could outrun a horse, not even a one-legged horse pulling a wheel-less cart full of lead bricks. Running wasn't what he'd been made for. And when, after a full minute if he was lucky, they finally caught him, crying like a little girl, would he suffer the further indignity of being caught while trying to run away? Fuck no! He was a halfling, goddammit, and a rogue as well. When he was caught, it wouldn't be because he failed to outrun them. No. When he was caught, it would be because he failed to adequately hide from them.

Tim's hiding options were limited to an open meadow sparsely dotted with trees. He made his best effort to disguise himself as a pile of leaves at the base of a tree, and was discovered immediately.

"Um, sir?" said a young soldier. Streaks of vomit stained the front of his leather armor. "I think I found him." His eyes were locked with the one eye that Tim hadn't the time nor the leaves to properly cover.

The captain trotted into Tim's field of vision, and Tim refocused his unobscured eye to meet his gaze. That gaze met him with a smile. It wasn't a warm let's-just-put-this-whole-mess-behind-us smile, either. It was more the sort of smile a man might have after trying unsuccessfully to swat a particularly elusive fly all day, and then later finding said fly having gotten itself caught between the window and the screen. It was a now-I've-got-you-and-there's-absolutely-no-possibility-of-you-getting-away smile.

"Are you attempting to hide?" asked the captain. "Or are you just very, very dirty?"

Tim was certain he'd been caught, as there was now a crowd of men staring right at him, one of whom was talking to him. But until he was threatened with violence or forcibly grabbed from his hiding place, he would maintain that he was hiding successfully and they were playing some mind game to lure him out.

"Stand up, boy," said the captain. "If I have to have one of my men force you to obey, I promise it will be far more fun for him than it will be for you."

Tim decided that this fell in line with his criteria for breaking his cover and complied.

"Well well," said the captain. "It's not a boy after all. It's a halfling." He looked genuinely impressed. "You're quite a long way from the Shire, aren't you lad?"

The Shire? Am I really from The Shire? Mordred, you unimaginative bag of come.

"My name is Righteous Justificus Blademaster, son of Eldor,

Captain of the Guard, and Chief Peacekeeper for the city of Algor and the surrounding principality."

Tim's mind raced, trying to milk all it could from the scant information it received. Subtlety, evidently, was not Mordred's strong suit. With a name and title that long and ridiculous, this guy was probably someone that Mordred wanted to keep around. Probably a third or fourth level fighter. Even if his friends were with him, this wouldn't be a group they could take down at level one. He was stuck.

"What is your name, runt?" All the pretense of good humor was gone from the Captain's voice.

Tim remained silent. As long as he was doing so, he tried to make it look like he was being defiant. But the truth was that he was too scared to form coherent words, and that he had overlooked giving his own character a name in his haste and eagerness to get the game going.

"Diego!" Shouted the captain, not taking his eyes off Tim's.

"Sir!" the soldier behind him shouted in response.

Shit. Another guy with a name. He had to be at least level two.

"The little fellow seems to be at a loss for words. See if you can't jog his memory a bit."

"Very good, sir," said Diego, dismounting his horse.

"Diego," the captain spoke more softly. Diego paused. "Jog it softly for now. We may need him alive."

"As you wish, sir."

Tim wanted nothing more than to give the men his name and avoid having the shit beaten out of him, but his mouth just refused to form the words.

Diego dropped to one knee, relieved Tim of the bow he had forgotten he was holding, and of his belt, which had a dagger sheathed in one side of it, and his rapier sheathed in the other side, and tossed the weapons aside. He put one hand on Tim's shoulder. "Come now, my boy," he said gently. "You don't want to make this harder than it has to be, do you?"

Tim shook his head. The hand on his shoulder tightened around the back of his neck, and Diego's other hand punched him in the gut.

"Then answer the question!" shouted Diego.

Tim doubled over and tried to vomit, but his body was all out of fluids. Diego's hand loosened its grip, and Tim collapsed to the ground. He remained on his hands and knees, head slumped down between his shoulders. Diego kicked him in the ribs with the hard, cold steel of his boot, making the punch to the gut feel like a moderately heavy blow in a pillow fight. Tim rolled over on his back, still unable to make any articulate sounds, but he was able to raise one finger.

The finger he raised was not the one he wanted to, which would have all but guaranteed him getting kicked to death, but rather his forefinger, in a gesture that was meant to convey that if they stopped kicking him for a moment, he would give them the information they required. Diego motioned to give him one more kick just the same.

"Stop," said the captain, without much enthusiasm, but with enough declaration in his voice to make it an order. Diego planted both feet on the ground. "I think the young halfling has finally found his tongue."

Tim had indeed found his tongue. It turned out that getting the shit beaten out of you was a solid cure for being tongue-tied after all. "Tim," he said. "My name is Tim."

"I don't suppose, Mr. Tim," said Captain Righteous in a calm voice, "that you would like to tell me the likely whereabouts of your associates, would you?"

"I don't know where they are," said Tim weakly.

"I figured as much. Very well. Diego, he can ride with you."

"And what of the others, sir?"

"They're long gone by now. We'll throw this one in a cell and let the lord decide what to do with him."

Tim didn't know whether the captain was referring to 'the lord' as in the governing figure in the town of Algor, or as his personal lord and savior Jesus Christ, and wasn't sure which he would have preferred determining his fate.

Captain Righteous Justificus Blademaster smiled down at Tim. "I suspect that after a night in the dungeon, he'll be more than willing to give up the location of his friends."

Diego kicked Tim in the face, and Tim obediently lost consciousness.

Chapter 5

Cooper trudged deeper into the forest. The trees grew closer together, and the undergrowth now came up past his knees. He had lost sight of his friends, and was only guessing at the direction they might have gone when he heard his name whispered.

"Cooper!" It was Julian. Cooper stopped and looked around.

"Over here!" Julian was peeking out from behind a tree, waving an arm. He was surprisingly difficult to spot. If they all had made it this far into the woods, they might have had a good chance at evading the soldiers. He lumbered through the brush, barely noticing the thorns trying to tear into his thick, gray skin.

"Where's Tim?" asked Julian.

"I don't know," said Cooper between pants, dropping the corners of the wagon cover he had been dragging. The canvas had fared a little worse against the thorns than his skin had. "He hopped off. Said he needed to go back for something."

"Shit," said Dave, who was sitting on a rock, still catching his breath. Apparently, he hadn't beaten Cooper here by much. He looked at Cooper accusingly. "And you just let him go?"

"What was I going to do?" asked Cooper. "He told me to keep going, and that he would catch up."

"What a fucking hero," said Dave. He stood up as tall as he could and looked Cooper in the face. "You're the reason we're in this mess, and you leave him alone out there, trapped in the body of a little kid, and —"

"How is this my fault?" Cooper shouted.

"You had to go and chop that guy's head off."

"Oh fuck off! You would've done the same thing if you could have. That was back when we were still playing a game, before Mordred... before Mordred did whatever the fuck he did."

"Who provoked him? You couldn't just keep your big mouth shut, could you?"

"Fuck you, dude. You were laughing your balls off."

Dave sat back down on his rock and sighed. "Fucking Mordred."

"Guys, shut up!" said Julian excitedly.

"Fuck you," said Cooper.

"Shut up," Julian repeated insistently. "I think I hear something."

Cooper tried to concentrate on whatever it was that Julian thought he heard. His patience, already thin at the best of times, was close to snapping.

"I don't hear anything," he grumbled.

"Those guys reached the wagon," said Julian. "You seriously can't hear them? They're practically shouting."

"You're an elf," said Dave. "You've got super elf hearing or whatever. We already went through this with Tim while you were dying."

"Sweet!" said Julian.

"Well, what are they saying?"

"I can't hear them perfectly, but I think they're complaining about all of the shit and puke on the ground."

Cooper busied himself spreading out the remains of the makeshift canvas sack, exposing the party's inventory.

"Dude," said Dave. "Keep it down. He's trying to listen."

Cooper found and picked up his enormous axe. The blade was a massive chunk of iron, fanning out on each side like the wings of a huge, head-severing butterfly. The shaft was thick and wooden, twice the length of one of the blades. He swung it back and forth in his hands a couple of times to get a feel for the weight. Running his thumb along the edge of the blade, he understood how easily this could take a man's head off.

"If we need to get out of here in a hurry, I'm not going to be able to drag this shit behind me anymore."

"Fair enough," said Dave, and grabbed his own pack. He picked up his mace and shield. The mace looked like a solid metal, thick stemmed rose in mid-bloom. Dave waved it around like he'd been doing it for years.

Julian stepped out from the cover of the tree, stopped abruptly, and ran back. He looked through wide eyes at Cooper and Dave, who had stopped waving their weapons around and were looking back at him for some kind of explanation. "You didn't hear that?"

They shook their heads.

"Someone just shouted 'There's one of them!'"

"Well they weren't talking about us," said Dave. "That only leaves..."

"Tim," Cooper grunted.

"What do we do?" asked Dave.

"We go get him," said Cooper as if it was perfectly obvious.

"There's like half a dozen armed men!" said Dave.

"Actually," said Julian, "It's closer to a full dozen."

"They'll kill us!"

"And if we sit around here and do nothing, they'll kill him. Look, I took out those first five guys without any weapons. Look at this axe. Hell, look at that fucking mace you're holding. We can take these guys down with no problem. We'll get Tim back, run back here into the woods, and figure out a way to get out of here."

Dave looked at Julian. Julian shrugged.

"Alright," said Dave.

Cooper grabbed Julian's backpack and started to toss it to him.

"Stop!" said Julian. Cooper stopped, puzzled. "There are a bunch of oil flasks in there."

"Oh, right," said Cooper, and handed the bag to Julian as delicately as he could. "Do you want to bring your tent?" he asked, half mockingly.

"Nah," said Julian. "If we end up having to sleep in the wilderness, here is as good a place as any."

Each of them picked up a crossbow, and a handful of bolts for it. Cooper grabbed Tim's backpack, and an extra crossbow for him, in case he needed it. They were about to head in the direction they had come from, but Julian changed his course and walked as quickly as he could manage through the thick undergrowth. Dave and Cooper followed close behind him.

After less than a minute of walking, the sound of galloping trickled down to a trot, and then to nothing. Julian stopped and held up a hand behind him.

"Something's wrong," Julian whispered. "They've stopped. If they found Tim, shouldn't they be shouting, or fighting, or something?"

"Maybe he got away," said Dave doubtfully.

"Maybe you misheard them, or they made a mistake and didn't

see him after all," offered Cooper.

Julian strained his long, pointed ears, but then shook his head. Hesitantly, he began moving forward again. The moving was easier outside the thickest part of the forest.

"Then answer the question!" came a voice that Cooper had no trouble hearing, even without the aid of Julian's freakishly big ears.

Cooper guessed that source of the voice was coming from just beyond the crest of the next hill they were facing. They all stopped and listened.

"They're interrogating him!" Dave whispered.

"If he's smart," said Cooper, "he'll tell them just enough to keep them interested. If they think he's told them everything he knows, they're as likely to kill him as they would be if he didn't say anything at all."

"How do you know?" asked Julian. "Is that actually in the rulebook?"

"No, but I watch a lot of TV, and I suspect Mordred does as well."

"Is he smart?" asked Julian.

"Mordred? How the fuck should I know?"

"No, Tim."

"I guess," said Cooper. "He got better grades in high school than I did. But then, he put in considerably more effort than I did as well."

"I mean, in the game. What's his Intelligence score?"

"Good question. I'll look." Cooper opened Tim's bag, and pulled out the tube containing his character sheet. "He's got a 17."

"That's pretty smart, right?"

"That's really fucking smart."

Dave stood back while the other two looked over Tim's character sheet. "What's his Wisdom?"

"What difference does that make?" asked Cooper.

"This isn't a matter of what he does or doesn't know. This is a matter of how savvy he is in choosing what to reveal. I think that falls under Wisdom."

"It's an 8."

"8 is low?" asked Julian.

"A little below average," Cooper said distractedly.

"Oh my God!" said Julian. "Look at his Hit Points! He's only got two left!"

"Keep it down," Cooper growled. "That's nonlethal damage. They're probably just kicking the shit out of him. He'll get it back."

"What the hell does that mean?"

"If you want to hurt someone, but not actually kill them," Dave explained, "say like in a bar fight back home." He paused for a moment. "That is, a bar fight in which the parties involved don't actually want to kill each other."

"Okay."

"You can choose to do nonlethal damage. It will hurt, but the worst it's going to do is knock you unconscious. You won't die from it, and you'll get it all back after a few hours."

"Still, we should go and get him. We can't just stand here and let them kick the shit out of him."

"No," said Dave. "If they're only doing nonlethal damage to him, that means they probably want to keep him alive. That's good news. We can creep up a little closer, and attack if we see an opportunity, though it's probably best if we don't."

"Why not?" asked Cooper.

"Because none of us have killed anyone before. We can argue all we like about whether it's justified or not, but when it comes down to it, are any of us actually prepared to do it? What if we freeze up? You think these guys are going to hesitate for one second before opening fire on us?"

Julian, Cooper, and Dave crept closer toward the party of soldiers, hiding behind trees as well as they were able to, until Julian signaled he was close enough to hear the conversation.

"They're asking him about us," said Julian.

"What's he saying?" asked Dave.

Julian listened. "He said he doesn't know where we are."

"Fuck this," said Cooper. "If they don't think he has any information to give them, they might just kill him." He gripped the handle of his greataxe and stood up.

"They aren't going to kill him," said Dave. "Those are soldiers. They aren't thugs or gangsters."

"What the fuck do you know about who these guys are?"

"You two shut up," Julian hissed. "Let me listen." He glared up at Dave and Cooper.

49

"Well what did they say?" asked Cooper.

"I couldn't catch it all," said Julian. "Something about a dungeon, I think." He ducked suddenly. "Get down!"

Julian, Dave, and Cooper hid behind trees and listened to the fading sounds of horses galloping back to the city.

Chapter 6

Julian sat on a rock, reorganizing the items in his bag to keep his mind off of Tim. It wasn't working. He walked over to where Cooper and Dave were talking.

"So now what do we do?" Cooper asked Dave, his face and voice carrying the unspoken message that he had damn well better have a plan in mind.

"You heard Julian," Dave said without much confidence. "They have no intention of killing him. They're keeping him alive for information on us."

"And what if he gives it to them, then what? Tim's a good friend, but he's never spent a night in a dungeon before."

"What's he going to tell them?" Dave asked. "Where we are? What our plans are? They are working under the assumption that we have a plan and a secret base of operations or something. We have the advantage of having no idea where we are or what we're doing."

Julian struggled to find any advantage in what Dave had said. He spoke up. "So what do you propose we do?"

"We'll sneak into town and bust him out of there. Classic C&C adventure."

Cooper held out his hands, palms up. "All right then, let's go."

"We can't go right now," said Dave.

Cooper put a finger over one nostril and blew a wad of dull brown snot from the other. Dave gagged at the squishy smack it made when it hit a nearby tree. "Why not?" Cooper asked.

"He'll have to tough it out in there for one night. We need to rest."

"Oh, I'm sorry," said Cooper. "I'll tell you what. I'll run off and find a goose. We can make you a nice pillow. Tim can wait in his little dungeon until after you've had your beauty sleep."

"That's not what I meant," said Dave. "Look, we've got to make use of every advantage we have. You're injured. I'm out of healing

51

spells, and Julian hasn't memorized any of his spells. He's next to useless if we get into a scrap. All he has to defend himself is a stick, and a crossbow that he doesn't know how to use."

"I can use a bow," said Julian. "We went through this. Elves can use bows."

"Not crossbows."

"How hard could it be?" asked Julian. "You just point it at something and pull the trigger, right?"

"Fine," he said. "If it's so easy, see if you can shoot that tree from here."

"That little one, way over there?"

"If that was a guy running at you with a sword, he'd be a lot smaller and harder to hit," said Dave, "And you'd want to hit him while he was much farther away than that."

Julian raised his crossbow with both hands, peered down the length of the shaft, and lined up his target tree. Dave started to say something, but Cooper put a hand on his shoulder and shook his head. Julian cleared his mind. Just him and the tree. One, two, three. He pulled the trigger. A flash of white and a stab of pain shot through his face, radiating from a point just below his right eye. The world spun around once, and lights danced in his periphery. He staggered around and dropped to one knee. Through a haze of pain, he could hear Cooper and Dave laughing. He let the crossbow drop from his hand. A smudge of red darkened the butt.

"Fuck you guys," said Julian. "That hurt." He ran a finger over the spot where he'd hit himself, and looked at his fingertip. "Look!" he shouted, holding up his finger for the others to see. "I'm bleeding!"

"Grow a dick," said Cooper. "You're covered in blood anyway. I don't think that little scratch is going to amount to any hit point loss.

"Where's my bolt?"

"You know that tree you were aiming at?" asked Cooper.

"Yeah."

"Well it's nowhere fucking near there."

Julian gave him the finger.

"I think it landed in the grass over there," said Dave.

"Well I'm going to go get it," said Julian. "We only have a couple dozen of these."

"Good idea," said Cooper.

He ran toward the bolt, but something he saw on the ground made him stop. "Hey guys!" Julian shouted. "Get over here!"

"What now?" said Dave.

"Probably stepped on a pebble and wants to be airlifted to a hospital," said Cooper.

"You know," shouted Julian. "I can still hear you guys."

"Fuck," said Cooper. "Sorry."

Cooper stomped through the trees toward him, Dave waddling behind.

"What did you want?" asked Cooper when they had nearly reached him. When Cooper looked down and saw what Julian had found, he had to grab hold of a tree to remain standing. Julian was sure Cooper was going to vomit or shit himself again, but he managed to hold it in at both ends. He blew some snot from his nose to his upper lip.

Julian winced. "Dude, do you have a cold or something?"

"It's not my fault," said Cooper, wiping the snot away with his forearm. "I'm a half-orc with a Charisma score of 4. I'm nearly as unpleasant to be around as a person can possibly be."

Dave, who was walking more slowly on his significantly shorter legs, caught up with them. "What are you guys... oh, it's him again."

The three of them looked down at the severed head lying face up, expressionless, on the ground.

"Do you suppose that's what Tim came back for?" Julian asked.

"Why would he do that?" asked Cooper.

"Mordred spoke to us through it once. Maybe he thought we could communicate with him through this head."

"He's the CM," said Cooper. "He can talk to us through whatever he wants to." He pointed to a tree. "If Mordred wanted to communicate with us through that tree, he could do it." One of the tree's main branches bent down, and several of its smaller branches curled into a bunch, leaving one in the middle standing straight up. "See?"

"That's unbelievable," said Julian.

"Fuck you, Mordred," said Cooper, and shot the tree with his crossbow. The bolt hit the trunk of the tree dead center. The branch remained where it was, as if that had been the way it had grown naturally.

"Okay," said Julian. "I see your point, but maybe he thought this head would be a better... what's the word I'm looking for? I want to say container..."

"It wouldn't be a good container," said Dave, looking at the head disapprovingly. Too many holes, and it's already full."

"No, that's not it. Condition... conductor..."

"Conduit?" asked Dave.

"Conduit!" shouted Julian. "Maybe he thought it would make a good conduit. Like if we needed to ask Mordred something, or he wanted to tell us something, it would be easier to do that through a face than it would be through a tree."

Dave shrugged and pointed a thumb back over his shoulder. "I think he just told us pretty much all he wants to tell us through that tree."

"Maybe," said Julian. "But what else would Tim have come back here for?"

Dave stroked his beard and Cooper picked his nose in silent contemplation, but neither of them came up with any answers.

"Well someone should probably carry it then," said Cooper. Dave and Julian looked at him. "Yeah yeah, fine," he said. "I cut it off. It's my responsibility." He picked it up delicately with his thumb and forefinger by the hair, and held it out at arm's length. "Well how about it, Mordred," he said. "You in there or what?"

The head's eyes came alive and looked into Cooper's. It pulled back its lips, bared its teeth, and hissed.

"Bwaauugghhh!" shouted Cooper. He flung the head to the ground. A clump of hair remained in his hand. He shivered and brushed it away on his loincloth.

"Dude," said Dave. "Be careful with that. It's not going to do us any good if you smash it to pieces."

"Did you see what it just did to me?" asked Cooper.

The head had landed upside down, still facing Cooper. "You should see what I did to your mom last night," it said.

Cooper pulled back a leg to kick it, but then stopped, and put his foot firmly back on the ground. "You don't want to play the mom game with me, fucker."

"Just put it in your bag," said Dave.

"Fine," Cooper said. He gave the head a little kick to roll it over, and grabbed it by a different patch of hair. He addressed it one more time. "You'll like it in there," he said. "It's dark, lonely, and smells like your mother. Just like home."

"Your mother smells like-" the head began, but whatever it meant to say after that was muffled by it being shoved face first into the bag. Cooper put the bag on the ground and squatted over the opening.

"What are you doing?" asked Dave.

Cooper looked up and grinned. "I'm going to fart in the bag, and then close it up real quick."

"Are you, um…" Julian said. "Are you absolutely certain that you're going to fart?"

Cooper's lips pursed, and his huge brow furrowed. "No," he said. "You're right. It could just as easily be a shit. Let's go." He stood up.

"Where are we going?" asked Julian.

"Back to where we left your tent, I guess." He looked at Dave for confirmation. Dave nodded. "I think Dave is right. We'll need everything we've got to get Tim back, and we'll need the time to come up with some sort of plan."

The ease with which they found their belongings prompted Dave to suggest that they look for a better place to set up camp. They found a small stream, and laid their belongings on the bank of it. Julian walked in and sank into the cold water. He'd never seen as much blood as he was now covered with, and he wanted to get rid of as much of it as he could. It was enough to taint the color of the water for a few seconds, but some of the blood had set into the fabric. Until he found a place to buy some new clothes, he'd have to be content wearing faded rusty brown.

Cooper got in the water downstream from him. A good five or ten minutes of scrubbing revealed his skin to be smoother than he thought it was. There were shiny hints of pink in the gray, and the scars were more plentiful and much better defined. He probably lost about fifteen pounds of filth.

Dave only cupped some water in his hands and splashed it on his face. His expression was all the grimmer when he rubbed the water out of his eyes.

"What's wrong?" asked Julian, sitting up in the stream.

"I thought that might wake me up," said Dave. "I thought that after I opened my eyes, we might be back at the Chicken Hut, shooting the shit and drinking beer."

They made their camp on the other side of the stream. Dave and Cooper argued about how to build a fire for about twenty minutes, but the ground was damp and neither of them were able to produce so much as a spark with either rocks or sticks. Julian set up his tent, which would accommodate both himself and Dave. Cooper made a crude shelter out of the remains of the canvas wagon cover.

"I'm hungry," said Julian. "Do either of you have any food?"

Dave rummaged around in his bag. "I think I bought a day's worth of rations." He produced a small pouch and looked inside. "Ooh, jerky. Want some?"

"Yes, that would be very-"

"I think I bought five days' worth of rations," said Cooper, looking in his own bag.

Dave retracted his arm, and with it the offer of his food. "Good," he said to Julian. "Eat some of his."

"I don't want to eat his. He's got a rotting head in his bag, and it's bound to taste like fart. No offense, Cooper."

"Fuck you, dude," said Cooper, happily munching away at his own bag of dried meats and fruits. "Tastes great to me. If you'd rather starve to death, be my guest."

Julian's stomach rumbled, as if to tell him to quit moaning and put something in it. "Fine," he said. "I'll eat your fart rations."

"Don't do me any favors," said Cooper. "Dave, do you remember the last time you had such good jerky?"

"That would have to be," Dave paused to think. "Hmm... sometime around..." Another pause. He scratched his head. "Never. Have you tried the dates?"

"Delectable!" said Cooper, holding one in front of his face to look at it fondly before popping it into his mouth.

"Screw you guys," said Julian. "Come on, Cooper. Just give me something to eat."

"You didn't say the magic word."

"Fuck you."

Cooper tossed him a bag. "That's actually the magic word I had in mind. I was going to hold out until you said it."

"What a big surprise," said Julian, and tore away a chunk of meat with his teeth. The taste of fart was present, but not overpowering.

"So," said Dave. "What's the plan?"

Cooper shrugged his massive shoulders. "Bust in. Get Tim. Bust out."

"That isn't a plan."

"It's the only one that's been proposed so far."

Julian carefully removed the remaining contents of his bag. "Let's see what we've got to work with." He had a waterskin, nine flasks of oil, and ten torches. "I wouldn't mind making use of a few of these torches. They're really bulky."

"We could burn down the outer wall," suggested Cooper.

"How do you propose we do that?" asked Dave. "We couldn't even get a campfire going."

"What do you guys have in your bags?" asked Julian.

"Not much," said Dave. "I spent most of my gold on weapons and armor. The rest of it I spent on the bag itself, and this food."

Julian looked at Cooper.

"Same here," said Cooper. "Barbarians travel light. I've got a dude's head, and some more food."

"Nobody really has a good idea what we look like, do they?" asked Julian.

"I don't know," said Dave. "I'd say quite a few people could pick Cooper out of a lineup after seeing him cut that guy's head off."

"That's right," said Julian thoughtfully. "They'd know him. In fact, they'd probably just kill any half-orc who turned up. But until we hopped onto that wagon, there was only one person who would have given me or you a second glance, and his head is in that smelly bag."

"You don't think anyone saw our faces?"

"Not enough to recognize us, I wouldn't think. I mean, they know to be on the lookout for a dwarf, an elf, and a half-orc traveling together, but if you and I went in separately, I don't think we'd run into any trouble. Cooper would have to stay here of course."

"All right," said Dave. "I see where you're going with this."

"To what end?" said Cooper.

"What do you mean?"

"Okay, let's say you get through the gate and into the town.

What are you going to do then?"

Dave frowned. "We'll get a layout of the land. Scout out the location of the prison. Look for weaknesses in the security. Inquire about-"

"Fuck all that. Tim doesn't have that kind of time."

"So what do you suggest?"

"Burn that shit down!" said Cooper, who sounded exasperated at having to repeat himself.

"Oh," said Dave. "You were serious about that?"

"Fuck yeah, I'm serious. Do you see any obvious flaws in the plan so far?"

"Aside from us not being able to start a fire?"

"Yes. Aside from that."

"Well," said Dave in mock thoughtfulness, "There's the small point of burning down a fucking city."

"I'm not talking about lighting up a church full of children. Just part of the outer wall. It's a fucking fence. They can build it back in a day or two."

"Fine. After we call massive amounts of attention to ourselves, provided we're able to start a fire of course, and we're staring at a burning wall, then what do we do?"

"I'm still working out the details," admitted Cooper. "Anyway, it's more than you've come up with."

"I'm working on something," said Dave defensively. "I just haven't fleshed it all out yet."

"Let's hear what you've got so far."

"All right," said Dave. "How about this? We go up the road leading out of town a bit and hijack a wagon. Cooper and I hide in the back, and Julian drives it into town."

Cooper nodded silently.

"Why do I have to drive the wagon?" asked Julian. "I'd much rather be hiding in the back."

"Somebody has to drive the wagon."

"Well, we're hijacking it. The odds are good that it will already have a driver."

"Do you want to trust our lives to someone we just stole a wagon from."

"No."

"Look," said Dave patiently. "You've got the highest Charisma score of any of us. And you've got the Diplomacy skill. If anyone is going to get us through the checkpoint, it's you."

"But I've never played this game before," said Julian. "I don't know how to use the Diplomacy skill."

"It's not like setting the timer on a microwave," said Dave. "It's just a skill you have. Something you're naturally good at. Some people are good at juggling, or knitting, or playing the piano. You are good at talking to people, getting them to do what you want."

"Right now," said Julian, "I'm trying to talk you into not making me drive the wagon. How am I doing with that?"

"You're failing miserably," said Dave, smiling. "But you make a fantastic argument. The very fact that I nearly considered it is proof that you are indeed a skilled diplomat. Cooper, what do you think?"

"I'm with you, Dave," said Cooper. "He has me almost entirely convinced that he's going to fuck this whole thing up. That's skillful diplomacy if I ever saw it. I have every faith in him."

"Why do I feel like I've just been-" Julian's eyes widened. "What was that?"

"What was what?" asked Dave.

"I thought I heard something."

"It was probably just a-" Dave disappeared in a flash of spotted yellow fur baring sharp white teeth. He was just able to get his arm up in time to give the creature something other than his face to bite.

Cooper and Julian jumped to their feet.

"Mother fucker!" shouted Cooper.

"What's going on?" shouted Julian.

"Random encounter," said Cooper. "Just a leopard. Shouldn't be a problem."

"Get it off me!" shouted Dave. He lay on the ground with one bleeding arm caught firmly in the leopard's mouth. Its teeth had torn through the metal scales of his gauntlet, through the padding underneath, and through at least enough flesh to bring forth a disturbing amount of blood. Its forepaws raked over his armor on his chest, searching for somewhere to take hold. Dave's other hand groped around on the ground in search of his mace.

Cooper roared as he brought his great axe down, swiping the leopard across the back, knocking it off of Dave entirely. Leopard blood splattered all over Julian. Dave backed away from it on hands and feet, like a crab.

The great cat snarled and growled at the trio. Its face was caked and dripping with Dave's blood, and it had an axe wound in its back that looked like it should have more than severed the beast's spine.

"How is it still moving?" asked Julian.

"It's still got at least one hit point," said Cooper. "It can keep fighting until it reaches zero."

Julian drew his sword and held it toward the leopard. The blade shook in front of him. "Now stay back!"

The leopard let out a high feline scream and charged at Julian. Julian dropped to the ground just as the leopard jumped into the air to pounce on him. He thrust his sword upward and caught the cat in the belly. It gave out one last cry of pain as it collapsed. Its eyes glazed over and the last of its life gurgled out into a red puddle around it.

"Dave, are you okay?" asked Cooper.

Dave shivered as he attempted to remove what remained of the gauntlet from his lower arm. He clenched his teeth and pulled it away in one go. "Yeeaaaaooow," he said, tears suddenly squirting out of both eyes and running down the sides of his face. He tossed the shredded metal glove away. It had done him all the good it was going to do. "No, I'm not fucking okay! Look at my arm!" The space just below Dave's elbow and above his hand was a bloody, fleshy mess.

"How bad is it?"

"I don't know, Cooper," he said. "I'm not a doctor, but on a scale of one to ten, I'd rate it pretty fucking bad."

"Score one kill for the wizard!" said Julian. Having already stood at Death's Door earlier in the day, he wasn't all that worked up about Dave's arm. He pulled his sword out of the leopard's body.

"No way, dude," said Cooper. "That kill belongs to me. I dealt a shit ton more damage with my axe than you did with your faggy little sword."

"He was still fighting after you hit him with your axe," Julian argued. "This faggy little sword of mine eviscerated that motherfucker."

"Fuck you guys," said Dave.

"What do you reckon leopard tastes like?" asked Cooper.

"I wouldn't think it'd be very good," said Julian. "I read that carnivore meat doesn't taste very good at all."

"Still, might be worth a try. Who knows when you'll get another chance to eat leopard?"

"Let's get Tim back first," said Julian. "If this is still here after we come back, and it isn't riddled with maggots or anything, we'll all have a good old-fashioned leopard cookout."

"Fuck that," said Cooper. "I'm at least going to take its skin off now."

"What are you going to do with its skin?"

"I'll make something out of it."

"Like what?"

"I don't know. A new bag, or a new loincloth. Maybe both if there's enough skin."

"Do you know how gay you would look with a matching leopard skin bag and loincloth?"

Even Dave's grimace of pain broke into a laugh. He looked really bad. Sweat covered his forehead, and blood dripped rapidly from his wound into a puddle below where he held his arm up.

"I've got an idea," said Cooper. "Do you have a dagger?"

Julian shook his head. "I couldn't afford one."

"Dave, you got a dagger?"

Wincing, he jerked his head backwards in the direction of his bag.

"What do you need a dagger for?" asked Julian.

"Leopard skin," said Cooper.

"F..fff...fffuck you!" said Dave.

"Seriously man," said Julian. "That's not cool. He's in pain."

"It's for him," said Cooper. He looked over the carcass, grabbed one of the forepaws, and held it up. He looked back at Dave, and then down at the paw, nodded to himself, and then jabbed a hole as close to the shoulder as he could. Blood ran slowly and smoothly from the puncture. Then he sawed at the hole, cutting all the way around the leg. He pulled it down over the leg like a sock turned inside out. Julian closed his eyes and breathed deeply until the urge to vomit passed. He went and sat next to Dave, whose arm still had at least some skin left on it.

Dave took in a deep breath, held it, and then spoke. "What is Cooper doing?"

"I don't know," said Julian. "As far as I can make out, he's just mangling that leopard corpse."

Cooper made another puncture in the skin, and cut around the circumference of the joint just above the paw. He sawed away until he had completely separated the tube of flesh from its former owner. He dipped it in the river, and wiped away the blood. Then he turned the tube inside out, and gave a self-satisfied nod to the finished product. He walked back to where his friends were sitting.

"Hold him still," said Cooper. Dave closed his eyes tight, continuing to hold out his injured forearm, and Julian held it steady by the elbow.

"This may sting a bit, Dave," said Cooper. And without another word, he shoved the leopard's leg skin as hard and quickly as he could over Dave's fist, down his arm to the elbow.

"Aaaauuuugggghhh!" Dave screamed.

"How does it feel?" asked Cooper.

"It hurts like a bastard."

Cooper frowned. "Oh."

"But it's not half as bad as it was before." The spotted, furry skin fit snugly down the length of his forearm. He opened and closed his hand, just to make sure that he could, and looked at his forearm muscles move under his new sleeve. "Thanks, Cooper."

"It looks bad ass," added Julian.

"Do you think it's really okay?" asked Dave.

"It's skin, ain't it?" said Cooper. "All it needs to do is keep your blood from leaking out until tomorrow morning, and then you can heal yourself."

"Why does he have to wait until tomorrow morning?" asked Julian.

"He has to pray for his spells every day," Cooper explained.

"Why can't he pray for some spells right now? It's not like we're busy."

"He needs to choose a certain time of the day to pray. He chose dawn."

"You mean he has to schedule an appointment with God?"

"Something like that," said Dave. "Look, I know it's only midafternoon, but we ought to see if we can't get some sleep right now. I'm pretty sure I'll be able to sleep. The sooner we sleep, the sooner we can go after Tim."

"I'm fucking knackered," said Cooper.

"I'm not actually tired at all," said Julian. "Well, that's not exactly right. I am tired, very tired as a matter of fact, but not what you'd call sleepy."

"Good," said Cooper. "You can take first watch."

"What should I –"

"Just stay awake and keep your eyes open for leopards and shit. If there are any problems, wake us up."

"Oh, all right. I can do that."

Dave fell asleep almost immediately.

Cooper stayed up for a while with Julian. He tried to skin the rest of the leopard, and had better success with some parts of it than with others. He left behind a mutilated carcass that neither of them cared to look at. Then he cleaned the bits of skin he thought were salvageable, and threw the carcass into a clump of undergrowth.

"Do you think we should take a look and see how bad he's hurt?" asked Julian.

"Christ, no," said Cooper. "Let the guy rest. You think he's going to be able to sleep if we try to pull that leopard skin off his arm?"

"I wasn't talking about looking at his arm."

Cooper looked at him quizzically.

"I meant maybe we should take a look at his character sheet."

"Oh, right," said Cooper.

"I mean, if that's okay. I don't know the rules. Are you supposed to look at one another's character sheets?"

"We're beyond the game. And beyond the rules of etiquette. We should take a look at Tim's as well. See how he's holding up."

Dave's sheet revealed that he had lost a total of six hit points.

"That's not so bad, is it?" asked Julian.

"Well, it's more than half of his life for an arm wound."

"Sounds worse when you put it that way. How's Tim doing?"

"Not so hot. He's at two points below zero."

"Does that mean he's-"

"No," said Cooper. "It's still all nonlethal damage."

"But I thought he was supposed to gain that back over time. He's worse off now than he was before."

"Yeah. He probably woke up, and they kicked him again or something."

"That's not good," said Julian, not at all comforted by Cooper's speculations of what Tim was going through.

"If they've kept him alive this long without doing any real damage to him, he should be okay until we can get to him. It's probably better for him to sleep through as much of that as he can."

There was a certain logic to that, and Julian guessed it was better to think about things that way than to worry, considering the amount of good either option was going to do for Tim.

"Hey!" said Cooper in an unexpectedly bright tone of voice. "I just thought of something."

Julian looked at Cooper expectantly.

"We just fought a leopard!"

"Well done," said Julian. "I seem to have a vague recollection of that myself. You say you only just thought of that?"

"Fuck you," said Cooper, much to Julian's relief. He was still Cooper. "We should look and see if we got any experience points from it."

Cooper and Julian each looked at their own character sheets.

"I've got 875 points," said Julian. "Is that good?"

"Yeah," said Cooper. "That's pretty close to second level. "I've only got 725."

"Why do you have less than me?"

"Because you had your nose up Mordred's ass at the beginning of the game."

"Oh."

The afternoon was beginning to fade into evening. Cooper stretched out his huge gray arms, and thumped himself on his broad, bare chest. "Well, I'm going to turn in. Go ahead and wake me up if you get sleepy. Let Dave get as much rest as he can. If you hear anything out of the ordinary, though, wake us both the fuck up right away."

"Okay," said Julian. "Good night."

Julian walked around the camp, looking for something to occupy his mind with, and came up short. He sat down on a rock and his eyes fell upon his bag. Maybe there was something in there worth looking at. He looked inside and found a large book and a small draw-string leather pouch.

He opened the pouch. It was full of something that looked like birdseed. Was that some food that he had forgotten buying? He took out a pinch of it and put it in his mouth. He spat it out immediately. He had never tasted birdseed before, but always imagined it would lean more toward bland than outright offensive to the tongue.

Hopefully the book would offer more in the way of time-killing opportunities. He took a seat on the ground under a part of Cooper's canvas shelter. As if he had his own personal alarm system, Cooper farted at him. Julian's eyes stung and watered, but he was determined that he was going to have a look at this book. It might be something important. He opened it and found a bunch of hieroglyphs on the first page.

"Great," he said glumly. "A bag of shitty tasting birdseed and a book I can't read." He looked back down at the page, and found that the glyphs weren't entirely unfamiliar to him. The longer he stared, in fact, the more familiar they got. He stared for about a full minute before he was able to start forming words in his head. It was an instruction manual of some kind, but the instructions themselves looked far too complicated to remember and follow. It was full of words he wasn't sure he'd be able to pronounce properly and gestures that he was almost certain he would never be able to do. At least not right now. He was too tired for this shit right now. He'd have another look at it in the morning maybe. He closed the book and walked back over to his bag. Just birdseed now.

Julian jumped when he heard a muffled noise come from Cooper's direction. Something moved in Cooper's bag, like a small animal was stuck in there. Poor thing. Bad enough to be stuck in anything belonging to Cooper, but when you consider what he was keeping in there, a... Shit! That's what was moving. The soldier's head. Mordred?

He opened Cooper's bag and picked up the head by one ear. The face didn't look happy. It took a deep breath in. Into what, Julian had no idea. It wasn't connected to any set of lungs that he could see. Its eyes darted back and forth until they met Julian's. "Scratch my nose?" it said.

Julian punched it in the nose. He couldn't get a lot of force behind the punch without risking either losing hold of the ear or ripping it off entirely. But he got his point across.

"I suppose you think I deserve that," said Mordred.

"What do you want?" asked Julian. He considered demanding that he bring them back home, but suspected he knew what kind of answer he was likely to get, and didn't think he'd be able to resist smashing this head into an unrecognizable pulpy mess upon getting it.

"Just want to help a bit," said Mordred. "You being new to the game and all, I thought you might have some questions." -

Julian couldn't resist. "When are you going to let us come home?"

"Uh-uh," said Mordred. "I mean game-related questions."

Julian considered punching Mordred in the head again, but decided that he'd better take whatever kind of help he could get. To avoid any further temptation, he placed the head in a tree, where a branch forked upward from the trunk.

"Fine," said Julian. "How do we get Tim back?"

"That's up to you."

"Well then fuck you."

"Nothing else you'd like to know?"

"Like what?"

"Like what's in that little pouch, for instance?"

Julian looked back at his bag, and then at the head in the tree again. "The birdseed?"

"Did you buy birdseed at the beginning of the game?"

"No."

"Then why do you think you have a pouch of birdseed?"

"Because I fucking looked at it, shithead."

"What did you buy at the beginning of the game?"

Julian thought. "I bought a longsword, and a tent-"

"Yes," said Mordred. "Go on..."

"And a backpack, and some arrows."

The head in the tree rolled its eyes. "Yes, of course. Mustn't forget the arrows. Where would you be now without those arrows? What else?"

"Nothing else," said Julian. "I couldn't afford anything else. I was so broke that you just went ahead and gave me-"

The head smiled. "That's right," it said. "What did I give you?"

Julian thought. "I don't remember."

The head sighed. "Why don't you look on your character sheet?"

"Okay," said Julian. He pulled out his character sheet, and looked at his inventory. It wasn't a long list, and he soon ruled out everything but... "Bag of Magical Shit?"

"That's all you wrote down?"

"Yeah."

"Do you remember what it was for?"

"No," said Julian. "But I remember it was supposed to have been expensive. 100 dollars or something."

"Gold pieces."

"Whatever, dude. It's fucking birdseed. What kind of finicky-ass birds do you have around here?"

"Just spread it around on the ground and see what happens."

Julian went back to his bag, grabbed the pouch, and dumped it on the forest floor. He looked over at the head. "There. Satisfied? Have I completed the mission? Can we go home now?"

"Look!" said Mordred.

Julian looked. The pile of seed glowed with a faint green light.

"Shit!" said Julian. "It's radioactive? I put some of that in my mouth. Am I going to be okay?"

"It's not radioactive," said Mordred. "It's magical. Just watch it, all right?"

Julian watched. A chipmunk scurried out from behind a tree, looked at the pile of seed, looked up at Julian, and then back down at the seed, as if he were assessing the amount of danger he would be getting himself into by coming too close. In the end, he decided it was worth the risk. He approached the pile, nibbled a bit, and then ran off. It appeared to have a similar opinion of the taste of the stuff as Julian had.

"It tastes like shit. I figured out that much for myself."

"Shut up and keep watching."

A rat came up and sampled a bit.

"Oh shit," said Julian. "There are rats out here?"

"Don't like rats?"

"No," said Julian. "Who the hell likes rats?"

"Fine," said Mordred. The rat scurried away.

"What do you think about snakes?" As Mordred spoke, a tiny

viper slithered up to the pile, and licked at some of the seed.

"Hate them," said Julian.

"Toads?" A fat, brown toad hopped up to the seed, shot its tongue out, and plucked a little from the pile.

"Ew," said Julian.

The head sighed. The toad convulsed, inflated its neck, and spit out the little bits of seed it had taken in. It hopped off.

"I think I'm going to throw up," said Julian.

A black bird flew down from a tree, landed next to the seed, and stared up curiously at Julian.

"Do you hate ravens too?" asked Mordred.

Julian shrugged. "No," he said. "To tell you the truth, I've never given them too much thought one way or another." He stared back down at the bird.

"Good enough for me," said Mordred.

The raven stepped closer on his skinny black legs, rose its wings up defensively, and let out a small caw. Julian crouched down, enamored with the bird, and hoping it wouldn't fly away. He smiled. "Go ahead, little guy. Give it a try if you want."

The black bird pecked at the seed. To Julian's surprise, it didn't immediately fly away. In fact, it seemed to actually like the stuff. It pecked down again and again. It flapped its wings furiously and buried its head inside the pile.

"Jesus Christ," said Julian. "When's the last time this thing had a meal?"

The bird went on eating and eating, and the pile of glowing seed grew smaller and smaller. It didn't seem possible for it to eat so much food in one sitting.

"It's ravenous!" said Julian. He shut his eyes tightly in a disgusted expression. "Oh my God. Did I just say that?"

"Good one," Mordred chuckled. Julian was glad that he was the only one awake to have heard it.

The raven kept pecking away until every speck of seed was gone. It stared up at Julian with shiny black eyes. Then it fell on its back and started to convulse. It kicked its legs and flapped its wings in a frenzy. The wing-flapping had the additional unnerving effect of throwing its body back and forth on the ground. It cawed sharply and twisted its neck from side to side.

"Oh shit!" said Julian. "It's dying."

"Give it a second," said Mordred.

The bird seemed to calm down after a moment, still twitching here and there, but maintaining enough control to stand upright once more. It spread its wings out and its body shivered. All of its feathers stood up simultaneously. It opened its beak wide, but no sound came out. A couple of feathers flew off of its back into the breeze, and it gave one last horrible convulsion. Feathers flew everywhere. It lowered its head and flapped its wings as hard as it could without leaving the ground, surrounding itself in a cloud of discarded feathers. As hard as it flapped, and as many feathers as it rid itself of, it never seemed to run out of them. It was as if it were growing new ones. Actually, it wasn't just growing new feathers. It was growing... just growing. It grew to half again its previous size. It was more like a black falcon now. It stretched out its wings one more time, opened its beak wide, and burped.

"Feel better now, big guy?" asked Julian.

"Indeed I do, Master," said the bird. "Thank you very much."

Julian jumped. It wasn't exactly the fact that the bird spoke to him that startled him. He had been through a lot in the past couple of hours. A talking bird just seemed par for the course. What threw him off was the way that it spoke to him. It sounded... British?

"Did that bird just..." he turned to look at the head, but fell silent when he saw it. It was as lifeless as one would expect a severed head in a tree to be. Mordred was gone. The head in the tree sat staring through glazed eyes at nothing. Julian gave it a light punch in the nose, just enough to knock it out of its position in the tree and onto the ground. He once again lifted it by the ear and carried it back to Cooper's shelter. His initial intention was to put it back in Cooper's bag, so they wouldn't forget it. But when he considered the likelihood of them forgetting it if he placed it in the line of fire of Cooper's ass, and weighing it against the likelihood of it coming back into being as Mordred just as Cooper was farting, or even having an involuntary shit in his sleep, he was willing to take that risk.

"You can talk?" Julian asked the raven when he returned.

"Of course, sir," responded the raven.

"What's your name?"

The bird gave an ear-splitting caw, followed by two small chirps.

Julian cringed at the sound. "I don't think I'm going to be able to pronounce that."

"I'm yours to command, sir," said the bird. "Call me by whatever name you like."

Julian thought for a moment, but the idea at the forefront of his mind wouldn't cede a runner up. "What do you think of Ravenus?"

"Very clever, sir!"

"No, it's really not," said Julian. "I just thought-"

"No, I get it, sir," said Ravenus. "It's a play on words. I'm a raven, and when you saw me eat all that food, you must have thought I was ravenous. It's brilliant."

Julian lowered his head. "Yeah, it's a stupid pun, but I thought-"

"Not stupid at all, sir. Supremely clever!"

"Thank you," said Julian, not feeling like he deserved this level of praise. "There was that, but I also thought it sounded like kind of a badass Latin-sounding name for a raven. You know, intelligent and fierce."

Ravenus stepped back and brought his wings forward over his chest. "Is that what you think of me, sir?" He looked as though he might stumble and fall over.

"Well look at you," said Julian. "You're bigger than any raven I've ever seen, and as far as intelligence goes, well I think you might be on par with my friend Cooper over there. No offense."

"I can only dream of being the bird you think me, master."

"Another thing," said Julian. "I'd rather you not call me master."

"But sir!"

"Yeah," interrupted Julian. "I don't want you to call me sir either."

"It would be highly irregular, and inappropriate if I may say so, for me to address you as anything but-"

"How does this work?" asked Julian. He thought for a moment. "Okay, how about this? As your master, I command you to not call me master."

"Well played, sir."

"Or sir."

"Shit." Ravenus jerked his head up. "A thousand pardons, sir... I mean..."

Julian laughed. "You'll fit in well here. My name's Julian. Just call me Julian."

He explained their situation to Ravenus as best he could, starting with his transportation to this world, and ending with the leopard fight.

"That is a fascinating story, Julian."

"Thank you," said Julian. "What do you think about our plan for rescuing Tim? Does it sound feasible to you?"

"It's a brilliant plan, sir," said Ravenus. "Completely flawless! I don't see how a single thing could go wrong."

"Who the fuck are you talking to?" asked Cooper, scratching his ass with one hand, and wiping his closed eyes with the thumb and forefinger of the other. He walked over to the tree where Mordred had been perched and lifted the front of his loincloth to urinate on it.

"I'm sorry," said Julian. "Did I wake you?"

"Not so much you," said Cooper, "as some damn squawking bird." He shook his member dry, coughed up some phlegm into his puddle of piss, and turned around to face Julian. "What the fuck is that?"

"This is Ravenus," said Julian. Then, addressing the bird "Ravenus, Cooper."

Cooper blinked his eyes a few times. "Seriously? You called it Ravenus? That's gay as fuck."

"Your mom's gay as fuck."

"So you got your familiar, did you?" Cooper asked Julian.

"I suppose so," said Julian doubtfully. "Is that what you are?" he asked Ravenus.

"I beg your pardon, sir?"

"My familiar?"

"Oh, yes sir," said Ravenus. "And quite proud of it."

"Yeeeaaaggghhh," said Cooper, contorting his face and putting his hands over his ears. "Can you shut that thing up?"

"I would have thought you'd be impressed."

"You've got a big bird," said Cooper. "I'm impressed. But I'm also fucking tired."

"Big?" asked Julian. "That's what you're most impressed by?"

Cooper looked at his friend thoughtfully. "What? Does it do tricks?"

"It fucking talks, you dolt!"

"No it doesn't."

"Sure it does," said Julian. "We've been chatting away for the better part of an hour."

"Dude, are you okay? Was that crossbow bolt laced with something?"

"Ravenus," Julian said, "Please state your name for my friend here."

"Ravenus," said Ravenus.

Julian looked smugly up at Cooper, who was wincing again. "Satisfied?"

"Seriously?" asked Cooper. "How do you get Ravenus out of Bwaaaarrrg?"

"He spoke as clearly as I'm speaking to you now!"

"He just screamed like a car horn."

"You're insane."

"You're the one talking to a bird," said Cooper. "Listen, you can't actually talk to your familiar until you go up a few levels. What you've got now is an empathic link. Maybe that's stronger than I'd always imagined it was, but it's not-"

"He. Fucking. Talks."

"No," said Cooper. "He doesn't."

"Ravenus," said Julian. "What's your favorite color?"

"I'm rather partial to lavender."

Cooper laughed. "His favorite color is SCREEEEEEEEEEECH?"

"He said lavender."

"Fuck, that's worse."

They were interrupted by a loud moan from inside the tent.

"Goddammit!" shouted Dave, crawling out of the tent on two knees and one hand. "Who's raping a cat out here?"

"Julian's got a pet bird," said Cooper.

"Oh yeah?" said Dave. He looked over and saw Ravenus. "Fuckin A."

"Ravenus, this is Dave."

"Pleased to meet you, sir. My name is Ravenus, as I expect you already know from my master's introduc-"

"Aaaahhh!" shouted Dave, covering his ears. "Make it stop!"

"What the hell is wrong with you people?" asked Julian. "He was just introducing himself."

"He thinks the bird can talk," Cooper said to Dave.

"Oh yeah?" said Dave. "What are his vocal cords made of? Chalkboards and forks?"

"You guys are dicks," said Julian. "Go back to bed."

"I'd love to," said Dave. "Just stop stabbing that poor thing so we can get some sleep."

Dave and Cooper went back to sleep. Julian sat down with Ravenus on his arm.

"I don't know what's wrong with them," said Julian. "But I guess we'd better pick up this conversation again in the morning. Get some rest." Ravenus nodded, hopped down onto Julian's lap, and nestled to sleep.

Julian sat with his back against one tree, and faced another. He spotted a beetle crawling up the trunk and stared at it. A few hours later, he was surprised to find that it was completely dark outside. Had he dozed off? No, he could clearly remember the entire span of time. He'd just been staring at this tree. He'd always been a daydreamer, but this was different. He hadn't even been thinking about anything. Just staring. Anyway, he felt refreshed now. He felt like he could take another crack at that book, but not with only the starlight to read by. He could see his surroundings just fine, but it wasn't the sort of light you'd want to read a book under.

Now that the clouds had moved on, the stars were out in full force. In the tiny patches of sky that he could make out through the gaps in the forest canopy, Julian saw more stars than what he thought a full sky might offer on the clearest night back home. He was tempted to make his way back to the edge of the woods and take in the sight of this full sky, but he stayed near his camp. Was this what the sky looked like before smog and electric lights? It hardly seemed possible. Julian thought that it might actually not be. He had no idea where he was, after all, and this world might just have more stars above it than the one he had come from. It might even have a couple of extra moons, or none at all. He scanned few bits of sky for evidence of any moons. The results were inconclusive.

Julian spent the next few hours being bored. After enough time had passed that he thought the other two might have had their full quota of sleep, he considered waking them up. He decided against it. They'd be better off for the extra rest. It was still too dark to properly read, but Julian felt like his head was going to explode if he didn't distract himself with something. He sat down on a rock, and opened the book. He shifted around until a patch of starlight fell on the pages. This wasn't so bad actually. He wished he had done this hours ago.

He flipped through the book to see if anything in particular caught his eye, and was surprised to find that after the first twenty-two pages, only about a quarter of the way through, the rest of the book was blank. He turned back to the first page. The glyphs, at first, held no meaning for him. It didn't take as much concentration this time before they started forming words in his mind. The words, in turn, were also meaningless to him, but as he focused his mind deeper, complete and comprehensible thoughts manifested themselves in his head. This pattern followed with paragraphs, until he found that the whole page culminated in a singular purpose. This particular spell would offer him a small amount of protection, a small edge in the face of certain perils. It looked as though it might come in handy, but from what he could make out in the text, he thought it was likely to fizzle out after about one minute. The payoff hardly seemed worth the amount of effort it would take to memorize all of the complicated gestures and incantations necessary to cast the spell.

He turned to the second page, and found it equally disappointing. It would grant him the power to detect whether or not something was poisonous. A practical skill under the right circumstances, yes. But this wasn't the sort of sort of thing he got into wizardry for.

Julian found that the spell on page three would allow him to read magical writing. Well he was already fucking doing that, wasn't he?

He kept flipping.

Bullshit.

Bullshit.

Boring.

Bullshit.

"Oh hell yeah," he whispered.

As a child, he'd always been fascinated by magic. In more recent years, however, reality started to creep in just a bit deeper with every pizza he delivered. Pizza was real. Magic wasn't. The imagination of his youth had been squeezed out of his soul like toothpaste.

But here he was, a wizard in a fantastic world, looking down at book of spells. The spell he was looking at now put the toothpaste back in his tube. This one would send bolts of energy out of his fingertips, which would make their way unerringly to whomever he cast it at. That's what being a wizard was all about. Practicality be damned. He stood up, set the open book down on the rock he had been sitting on, and started practicing the necessary motions and incantations.

He was so deeply involved in his studies that he didn't notice Dave and Cooper walk up behind him until Cooper spoke.

"What the fuck are you doing?"

Julian turned his head around, his body frozen with one leg up, and his arms positioned in a way that made him look like he was trying to hug an invisible giant. He relaxed into a normal standing position and turned the rest of his body around to face them. "I'll show you what the fuck I'm doing," he said. "Point at something. Anything."

Cooper pointed to Dave.

"No," said Julian. "Bad idea. Pick something else."

"Fuck," said Cooper. "I don't know. That tree over there."

"All right," said Julian with a wry smile. He closed his eyes, shook his arms to loosen up the joints, and brought his hands together. He opened his eyes and stared fixedly at the tree. "Bisulfate!" he shouted, and swung his left arm up over his head. "Ascorbic acid! Azodicarbonamide!" He raised one foot off the ground and stamped it back down.

"No!" Cooper shouted. "Julian, stop!"

Julian didn't stop. He thrust both hands forward, fingers stretched out. "Methylchloroisothiazolinone!" With that, the tip of his right forefinger glowed with a bright white light which grew in intensity until it burst into a glowing arrow. The arrow flew lamely toward its target in a shower of sparks, like a bottle rocket struggling against the counterforce of a small parachute. Julian lowered his arms and watched it fly. Cooper and Dave turned their heads slowly to follow the path of the projectile hobbling the rest of the way through the air into the tree, where it fizzled into a small puff of smoke and slightly charred bark. Julian shrugged and turned to his friends.

"What do you think?" he asked.

"I think you're a fucking idiot!" shouted Cooper. Dave shook his head.

"Well, it was somewhat less spectacular than what I was expecting," admitted Julian. Then he grinned. "Still, pretty cool that I can do that, don't you think?"

"Yeah," said Cooper. "Pretty fucking cool, except that now you can't."

"What are you talking about?"

"You only get to do that once per day," said Dave.

"No way," said Julian, smiling the smile of a man who knows something his adversary does not. "I memorized that shit."

Dave sighed. "Go ahead then," he said. "Try it again."

Julian rolled his eyes and turned back toward the unfortunate tree. "Okay, here goes." He shook his arms again, and brought his hands together. He closed his eyes, and then immediately reopened them. "Shit."

"Uh huh," said Dave. He poked lightly at his leopard skin gauntlet and winced.

"I can't remember a single word of it!" said Julian. "I spent an hour memorizing all that! How can it just be gone like that?"

"The magical energy flows from your mind, or something like that."

"That's bullshit!" shouted Julian. "That's not the way memory works!"

"That's how it works in the game," growled Cooper. "It's in the rulebook."

"My arm's killing me," said Dave. "I'm going to go pray for my spells."

Julian nudged his spellbook off of its rock with his foot, and sat down. "So I've got to spend another hour studying that shitty spell?"

"Not today," Cooper grumbled.

"Why not?"

"Because you're a first level wizard," said Cooper. "And a dumb one at that."

"Watch it," said Julian. "Your Intelligence score is four points lower than mine."

"That's why I'm not a fucking wizard!"

Ravenus flew in and landed on Julian's shoulder. "What's all the fuss?"

"Cooper's mad because I used up my only spell," said Julian.

"What did you use it for?"

"I shot a tree."

Ravenus shifted his weight several times from foot to foot. "Was the tree..." he paused to find the right words. "...threatening you in some way?"

"No," said Julian. "I'd just never casted a spell before, so I wanted to try it out."

"Congratulations!"

"Thanks."

Cooper grimaced at Ravenus. Julian pressed on.

"I don't understand why I can't just study it again," he said to Cooper. "We've got the time, don't we? I mean, Dave's going to need some time to pray or whatever, isn't he?"

"You only get to memorize your spells once per day. At first level, you only get one first level spell. A wizard can get bonus spells based on his high Intelligence score. You, however, don't have a high Intelligence score, which is why I advised against you being a wizard in the first place."

"But I wanted to use magic."

"I told you to be a sorcerer. You have a high enough Charisma score to be a decent sorcerer."

"What does Charisma have to do with sorcery?"

Cooper shrugged. "Not much," he admitted. "I think they just wanted to make another class based on Charisma because nobody wants to be a bard."

"So you're telling me," Julian said, "that if I sit here and study that same spell again, I'll be unable to memorize it?"

"That's what I'm telling you."

"But that doesn't make any sense."

"Game balance," said Cooper, as if that explained everything. Julian only stared back at him. Cooper sighed. "If a wizard can keep casting every spell he knows willy-nilly, then wizards would be far too powerful. As it stands, some people already feel that they are overpowered at higher levels."

"So you mean to say that we're living in a world where the laws of nature, physics, and reality are governed in turn by half-baked rules some guy made up?"

"In a nutshell."

"And game balance always trumps logic?"

"Pretty much."

"So I'm pretty well screwed then? Forever doomed to be a shitty wizard?"

"Nah," said Cooper. He slumped down against a tree. "You can always choose to be a sorcerer when you get to level two."

"You can just switch horses like that?"

"Not exactly. At least some of you will always be a shitty wizard. But you don't have to take any more levels of wizard if you don't want to. If you take a level of sorcerer at level two, then you'll just be a level one wizard and a level one sorcerer. If you find sorcery suits you, you can keep going with it. If not, you can always take a level in something else. I wouldn't recommend spreading yourself out too thin though."

"What do you recommend?" asked Julian. "I mean, I really should do what's best for the group. This isn't a game anymore, after all."

"Go with sorcerer. Dave and I can hold our own in a fight pretty well. Hell, so can you. But we really should have some sort of spellcaster in the party."

"What about Dave?"

"He does clerical spells, and I have a feeling he'll be using a lot of those to heal us. The sorts of spells you use are arcane, and they have a variety of different uses, not the least of which is blasting the shit out of large groups of enemies."

"That's sort of what I had in mind going in." Julian looked over at Dave. "Who is he praying to, exactly?"

"Dunno. Some god or another."

"And this god is just going to up and give him whatever spells he wants?"

"Any of the level one spells."

"To what end?"

"What do you mean?" asked Cooper.

"I mean, I don't see what's in it for the god."

Cooper yawned and pulled a hunk of yellow sludge out of one ear with the claw of his pinky finger.

"I'm sorry," said Julian. "Am I boring you with talk of Dave over there actually communicating with the divine?"

"Kind of, yeah."

"Ravenus," said Julian. "Cooper here just asked me to ask you where you were hatched."

"Really?" said Ravenus. He flapped down to the ground. "Because, you see, it's actually a very interesting story. I was-"

"All right already," said Cooper. "Just get it to stop squawking. What do you want to know?"

"Sorry, Ravenus," said Julian. "I was just kidding. He doesn't really want to hear your story. Myself, I'd love to hear it. We'll swap stories later."

"Very good, Julian."

"Why don't you go fly around and tell us if you spot anything alarming or interesting?"

"Of course," said Ravenus, and flew away into the trees.

"It's really starting to creep me out how you keep talking to that bird."

"So tell me more about Dave," said Julian. "He's a priest or something?"

"He's a cleric," said Cooper. "Like a holy warrior. He fights for his god. Think of him like a knight in the Crusades."

"Fights against whom?"

"Anyone whose alignment opposes his god, I guess."

"Alignment?"

"Good, evil, law, chaos, that sort of thing."

"What alignment is Dave's god?"

"I don't know," said Cooper with a hint of desperation in his voice. "You really should be asking him these questions. I'm a fucking barbarian. I can't read. I barely know my own name."

"You can read your character sheet," Julian argued.

"I think that works differently."

"How so?"

"I don't think those character sheets are of this world. In fact, I don't think the conversation we're having right now is of this world."

"I don't understand."

"For example," said Cooper. "Right now we are having a fairly intelligible conversation. Am I right?"

"Okay."

"My character would be unable to have this conversation with someone of this world. I'm a fucking moron."

"So why can you talk like this with me?"

"Because when we're just alone together, part of us is still us. When we interact with anything in this world, we are strictly our characters."

"I still don't understand."

"Let's do an experiment," said Cooper.

"Okay."

"Take this stick, and write a word in the dirt. I'll try to read it."

Julian pursed his lips, took the stick from Cooper, and wrote the word 'cat' on the ground. When he was finished, he looked up at Cooper. "Well?"

"I have no fucking idea what that says."

"Honestly?"

"No," said Cooper. "I was lying because I thought my lack of literacy might impress you."

Julian took his character sheet out of its tube, scanned through the spells listed on the back of it, and then held it up to Cooper, pointing to a word. "What does this say?"

"Prestidigitation," said Cooper unhesitatingly.

"That's amazing!" said Julian.

"Not really," said Cooper. "It actually kind of sucks. It's just a spell for performing little tricks, like at a kid's birthday party or something."

"No," said Julian. "It's amazing that you can read 'Prestidigitation' on my character sheet, but you can't read 'Cat' when I write it out on the ground."

"You know, I was being sarcastic before when I said I was trying to impress you with my illiteracy."

"Let's see how you do with math," suggested Julian. "What do you get when you multiply..."

Chapter 7

Tim's body was bouncing up and down when he woke up, surrounded by the sound of galloping hooves. His whole body ached, but his face was absolutely throbbing with pain. The taste of blood was thick in his mouth. One of his eyes was swollen shut. The other one might have been as well. It felt like it was opening, but no light was reaching it. He was in the dark. He noticed his hands were tied behind his back. There was only one explanation. He was lying face down on the back of a horse with a bag tied over his head.

Shit.

He moved his bound wrists together to get a feel for the rope, and grinned inside his bag. He would be able to get his hands free in a matter of seconds when he chose to. Not yet, though. Not at this speed. He didn't know what kind of damage he'd take from falling off a horse at full gallop, but imagined he could survive it. It was the other horses he heard right around him that he thought he probably wouldn't survive. They'd just trample right over him. Best to lie still until they slowed down. In the meantime, he would work out the rest of his escape plan in his head.

His circumstances didn't allow for a whole lot of complexity. He'd free his hands, take the bag off of his head, hop off the horse, and... No. He would be spotted as soon as he freed his hands. He'd have to hop off the horse before he took the bag off of his head. It was risky, but he'd need as big a head start as he could get.

The horses pounded the earth beneath their hooves for what seemed to Tim like a very long time. But then, time tends to pass more slowly when one is tied up with their head in a bag. He went over his plan again and again in his head. Each time he re-visualized it, it seemed more and more plausible. By the time the horses actually slowed down, it seemed foolproof. He was a rogue. This was the sort of thing that rogues do. He had taken the Escape Artist skill, and the Stealthy feat. Also, he had the added stealth that came naturally with being a halfling. He was quick and nimble and hard to hit. Everything was working in his favor.

"Ho, there!" shouted the captain, and the gait of the horse he was riding on made the transition from gallop to trot to walk in less than ten seconds. Now was the time. He freed his hands with as little effort as he had expected to, and pushed himself backwards from the animal's back. He barely had the time to register the feel of his feet hitting the ground before he felt someone else's foot kick him squarely in the temple. Stars flashed inside the darkness of the bag, and then he once again entered the realm of complete darkness.

The next time he woke up, it was due to a splash of water on his face. It tasted like someone forgot to flush. He was unable to wipe it away, as he discovered that each of his arms was being held by a soldier on either side of him. His vision swam through the dirty water and focused on the bucket that it had presumably come from. The bucket was being held by a short, bald humanoid creature with dark yellow skin and rusty red eyes. He had a face like a bat, complete with a broad, flat, and turned-up nose, and giant pointed ears. He grinned at Tim, exposing a mouth half full of once-pointy teeth that had opted to just rot away rather than fall out like the other half had done. He was very short by human standards, only a little bit taller than Tim. The man behind him towered over both of them. It was Captain Righteous Justificus Blademaster. Nice to see a familiar face.

"Check him for hidden weapons," ordered the captain. "Look closely for thieves' picks." Tim had nothing on him that they hadn't already taken away.

After a very thorough search of his person turned up nothing of interest, the guards pushed Tim into a cell with a tiny barred window on the rear stone wall near the ceiling, presumably to remind the occupant that there was still a world full of sunshine outside which they would never be a part of again, and a small hole in the far corner carved through the stone floor, presumably for the occupant to shit in. His latter presumption was based on the corona of brown-stained stone surrounding the hole.

The iron-barred door clanged shut, and the little creature with the bat face turned a comically large key in a lock that Tim reckoned he could probably pick with a ship's oar. He then slunk down the hall and out of sight. Captain Righteous gave his subordinates a look, and they shuffled off in the other direction.

"It was foolish for you to try to escape," said the Captain. "But I admire your courage."

"Why am I in here?"

"For murdering one of Lord Pahalin's guards, of course."

"I didn't murder anybody!" Tim argued.

"You were one of the murdering party," said the captain. "Anyway, you haven't been formally charged with anything as of yet."

"Oh," said Tim in a tone of unexpected relief. "What does that mean?"

"It means you'll stay here indefinitely until the Lord decides what to do with you. Probably not longer than a day."

"What happens after that?" The relief had abandoned his tone.

"Either your friends will attempt some sort of rescue mission... unlikely, or they won't," he mused. "If the actual murderer can stand trial and execution, then you may be spared. If not, you'll likely do well enough for a scapegoat." He started to walk away.

Tim grabbed two of the bars and shook the door. "A scapegoat?" he shouted after the captain. "You seriously think that anyone will believe I chopped a guy's head off? Look at me! I'm only three feet tall!"

"What I think is inconsequential," said the captain. He turned away, walked out, and closed the door behind him.

"You won't get away with this!" Tim shouted, knowing there was every chance in the world that Captain Righteous would get away with it. He had to shout something.

"There there, little feller," came a voice from the cell across from Tim's. Tim hadn't noticed anyone in there before. The initial scan that Tim's eyes had made of his surroundings had probably just passed this guy off as a tarped over pile of moss-covered garbage and ignored him. Now that he focused on it, he recognized the shape as a human squatting in the corner. Well, he supposed he couldn't be sure it was human, but it was something like it. He was bald on top but had a long white beard. He looked to have been made out of tent parts. "Save yer breath," he said. "Ain't n'good gonner come from yellin'."

Tim said nothing. He stared at the old man until he realized two

things, suddenly and simultaneously. One was that being put to
death quickly might be a blessing compared to spending any
amount of time in here. The other was that he had been correct in
his guess as to what the hole in the floor was for. He turned his
head away as quickly as it would go, and shut his eyes as tight as
he could, but the image had already been seared into his brain.

"Pah!" said the man. "Ain't nothin' but nature runnin' her
course." He grunted, coughed, and then held his breath. The
following silence was broken by a sound that was going to haunt
him along with that image for the rest of his life. The old man
exhaled. "She's runnin' it pretty freely today."

Tim dropped down to his knees and hid his head under his arms.
He wanted to throw up, or cry, or both. But nothing came out.

The old man, having finished his business in the corner, stood
up and walked up to the bars of his cell. "There now, little guy," he
said. "What's got yer down?"

Tim stood back up, clutched a bar in each hand, and looked up
at the man. "What's got me down?" he said. "Did you really just
ask me that? Look around at where we are. I'm in a tiny cell in a
fucking dungeon, and I just watched an old guy take a shit. Sorry if
I'm spoiling your fun."

"What's yer name, lad?"

"Tim," said Tim distractedly.

"My name's Greely. Been in here fourteen years next week."

"What for?"

"A bunch of us got drunk one night and thought'd be a laugh to
go steal Lady Pahalin's laundry while it was drying in the garden.
Ye know how kids are."

"How'd you get caught?"

"Musta passed out," said Greely. "Next thing I knew it was the
middle of the day, and I was lyin' in the garden wearin' naught but
a sun dress an' lookin' up at four guards and the Lady herself.
Never could hold me liquor."

"And you got fourteen years for that?"

"Hmph," Greely muttered. "Got life for it."

"Life?"

"Course, I don't think they ever expected I'd make it this long.
Not ideal living conditions down here. You're right about that. Not
everybody makes it very long, but it can be done."

"Why bother?"

"How do ye mean?"

"I mean," said Tim. "What's the point of keeping yourself alive down here so long if there's no chance of you ever getting out?"

"I'm a lover of life," said Greely cheerily. "And every now and again, ye meet some interestin' folks down here. Take Gorp, fer instance."

"Who's Gorp?"

"He's the guy whose cell yer in, lad. He died a few months back. Dwarf, he was. Big stocky fella. I think there might still be part of his leg back there if ye look." Greely pointed to the back of Tim's cell. Tim followed his finger and saw something white poking out from behind his bed. "He only made it a couple of months. Wish he'd held out a bit longer. He knew some dirty jokes."

Tim was taking in only fragments of what Greely was saying at this point. The bulk of his attention was focused on a dwarven femur. "Where's the rest of him?"

"Rats took him away, piece at a time."

"Rats?" There was a hint of panic in Tim's voice.

"Oh sure," said Greely. "This place is crawling with them if you know where to look. And that's one of the secrets to makin' it down here. But he wouldn't have any of it. Too proud to eat a rat. Have ye ever heard of such nonsense. I'll tell you what, they weren't too proud to eat him when they got the chance."

"I think I'm going to be sick."

"Well do it over in the corner," suggested Greely. "It attracts the rats, and they're easier to catch if they're in the corner."

"I don't want to catch any rats, and I'm certainly not going to eat them," said Tim.

"Pah!" said Greely. "Another one." He shook his head. "We'll see how you feel about rat after you have to choose between it and the slop that Shorty brings you."

"Who's Shorty?"

"He's the jailor. You met him. Nice enough guy, for a goblin. But I think he only knows how to cook one dish. It looks like snot, garnished with bug parts. Tastes worse. Hold off on dismissing rat until you've tried that."

"I'm not going to be around that long," said Tim. "I'm getting the fuck out of here."

Greely smiled. "Is that so?"

"Fuckin' A that's so," said Tim.

"And how do ye propose to do that?"

"I'll use my skills," said Tim. "I'm just locked in a dungeon, for fuck's sake. I've been locked in dungeons hundreds of times."

"Really?" asked Greely. "Because when ye first got here ye were whimperin' about it like a little bitch, if ye don't mind me sayin'."

Tim ignored him. "The CM always provides a way out if you use your head."

"This must be a new record," said Greely. "I don't think I've yet seen a man lose his mind this quickly before, and I've seen plenty of men lose their minds."

"This lock is a piece of shit. It should be easy enough to pick."

Greely wheezed and laughed. "What're ye gonna pick it with? Yer willy?"

"There's bound to be something in here that I can use as improvised lock picks," said Tim, scanning the tiny cell. "I just have to look everywhere." He started to move the bed. It felt heavier than it looked.

"I wouldn't do that if I were ye," said Greely. The laughter had gone from his voice.

"Why not?" asked Tim, heaving as hard as he could against the bed, but moving it only a couple of inches. "Why is this bed so fucking heavy?"

"It's attached to a lead brick that covers a hole in the wall."

Tim rested, panted, and smiled. "There's a fucking hole in the wall?" He shook his head and laughed. "Let me guess. It's probably just wide enough for me to crawl through."

Greely shrugged. "Yeah," he said. "I suppose that it's about that big. But it won't–"

"Un-fucking-believeable," said Tim. "That's about the lamest setup for an escape that I've ever encountered." He set his feet firmly, and leaned hard against the frame of the bed. It started to shift. "Only Mordred would be so unimaginative as to– what's that noise?"

There was a loud scratching sound coming from behind the bed, presumably where the hole was supposed to be. Greely lowered his hands on the bars and frowned. "Rats," he said.

"Ew," said Tim. He considered grabbing the former dwarf's femur to hit the rats with, but then thought that touching a dead body was still more gross than trying to jump on a rat. He jumped up onto the bed, and waited for one of them to scurry past. He looked over to the side against the wall. "Oh my fuck!" he shouted.

What looked back at him was not what he expected at all. It was a rat all right, but it was about the size of a Rottweiler. It might have been bigger than him. And it looked pissed off. Two red eyes glared at him from behind a mouth full of needle-like teeth and saliva-clumped spikes of hair. Two claws scraped furiously against the mortar of the hole it was trying to squeeze itself through. He jumped off of the bed as though it were on fire, grabbed the femur like it was made out of second chances, and backed up against the corner of the cell with the shit hole.

The bone was a little less than half his height, but it was thick and solid. He gripped it with two hands, one at the top of the shaft, and the other around the ball joint. The knee end was thicker, and he imagined it would hurt quite a bit to be hit with.

He could still hear the mad scraping of claws, and guessed that the huge rat might be stuck in the hole. Part of his mind told him that he might have a better chance if he went back and pushed the bed back against the wall. He might push the rat back, or even hurt it. The majority of his mind, however, told him that he didn't want to be any closer to that thing than he had to be, and that cowering in the corner holding a bone was his best bet.

The scraping became rhythmic, and then started to get fainter. "Be on yer guard," said Greely. "Here comes the first one."

"The first one?" Tim shouted back at him. "How many are there?"

"Hard to say. There's a nest of them." He craned his neck and raised an eyebrow. "I'd say somewhere in the neighborhood of–"

"Aaaahhhh!"

Out in the open, the rat was even more horrifying. It barely had enough hair on it to qualify as a mammal. Its sides and back were scraped from squeezing through the hole in the wall, and tiny streams of blood trickled around filthy and sparse patches of fur. It took a second to eye him, and then lunged forward. Tim swung the bone like the bases were loaded, and missed the rat completely.

The rat didn't fare much better. Tim was small, but he was finding out just how nimble he was. He jumped up, kicked off the wall, and landed on his feet on the rat's tail. The rat shrieked, and Tim shuddered. The noise was so horrible that for a moment Tim lost control of his hand, and the bone clattered onto the stone floor.

The rat nipped at him again, and once again Tim jumped out of the way. He was more agile than this thing, and he might be able to dodge a few more bites, but he wouldn't be able to keep this up for long. He put his arms out to make himself look bigger. He wasn't sure if that worked or not, but he was able to initiate a slow clockwise face off with the rat. He hoped it would buy him enough time to grab the bone again. They didn't quite make it that far. Sensing that the rat was about to make its move, Tim dove for the bone, and the rat caught him by the foot. Tim screamed as the top and bottom of his foot was invaded by what felt like thousands of hypodermic needles, probably injecting entire civilizations' worth of bacteria in the saliva.

Tim ripped his foot away. It tore into ribbons as it raked across rat teeth. Tim swung the bone as hard as he could, and finally connected with the rat's face. It was an awkward angle, and it accomplished little more than buying him some time to stand up again.

With its face covered in Tim's blood, the rat managed to look even more terrifying than it had before. It jumped up at him and bit a small chunk of skin from his calf on the same leg with the injured foot. Tim held back his scream and tried to channel that energy into his swing. Too much energy. He swung wide again, and hit nothing but air. The room spun around, but he managed to duck out of the way of another rat bite. Tim held the rat at bay with the end of the bone. It stared back into his eyes, drooling his blood, whisking its leathery tongue around its lips, looking for another opportunity to strike. Tim saw that he had actually managed to do some damage to it when he hit it before. Blood flowed from a gash in its nose.

"Better hurry it along, lad," said Greely. "You're about to have some more company."

"Shit," said Tim, and did the only thing he could do. He took one more swing. He missed. "Fuck!"

The rat closed in for the kill, and Tim knew that one more bite would probably do it. He blocked the bite with the bone, and then tore it out of its mouth. The rat hissed at him, and Tim swung the bone around one more time. He connected squarely with the side of the rat's head. It fell over sideways, and Tim beat it a couple more times for good measure.

"Um," interrupted Greely. "Mr. Tim?"

Tim looked up, and then over toward the bed. There was the familiar sound of frantic scraping. Claws against brick and mortar. "Oh yeah," he said. "Shit." He crawled over to the bed, and tried to push it back against the wall. With only one good foot left to push with, the bed wasn't budging.

"He's nearly out," said Greely. "Get ready."

"Fuck fuck fuck fuck fuck," Tim muttered to himself. He examined the bone. It had a fracture running down it, and wasn't going to take a lot more abuse before it split in two. An idea occurred to him, and he deliberately smashed the bone into the floor, breaking off the weakened part. What he was left with resemmbled a sword more than a club. It would do nicely. He waved it around until he got a good feel for it, thrust it forward a couple of times, and then crouched down on the side of the bed. He'd only have one chance at this, but if he pulled it off, this rat should go down much faster than the previous one.

The scraping calmed, and stopped. Tim resisted the urge to run back into the corner. Claws clattered against the stone floor, and a second rat scurried toward its fallen mate, completely oblivious to any threats to itself. As soon as its head was in view, Tim thrust his weapon forward, straight into its neck. It didn't even have a chance to shriek. It just gurgled as its blood poured down the length of Gorp's former leg. The rat fell, and Tim wasted no time making another attempt to move the bed back against the wall.

"Ye got a third one comin' through," Greely warned Tim.

Tim winced in pain as he pushed with both feet to move the bed. It gave about an inch, and the scraping on the other side became more frantic. Tim braced himself for the pain, pushed with every ounce of strength he could muster, and succeeded in moving the bed back up against the wall. It didn't connect with the solid thud he had been expecting, but instead with a crunch and a screech. The screech kept on going. He'd caught at least part of the third rat with the bed. Maybe a front paw or its nose.

"Oh," said Greely. "Ye seem to have neutralized the third rat."

"He doesn't sound neutralized to me," Tim said over the screeching. He was sitting on the floor, thankful for what he was sure would only be a brief opportunity to rest. He put his mind to work on what he should do next. His escape tunnel was looking like less of an option now.

"What's on the other side of that wall?" he asked Greely, pointing to the wall behind him.

"Another cell," said Greely.

"That's it?" asked Tim. "Why didn't you tell me that before?"

"I tried to, but ye–"

"Fuck," Tim cut him off. "I'm back at square one," he said to himself. "Except now I'm nearly dead and I have two giant rat corpses for company."

He considered his current inventory.

1 broken bone. Not entirely useless as a weapon.

1 bed complete with lead brick. No immediate uses came to mind except for the one in which it was currently employed.

2 giant rat corpses. Food? He supposed they'd have to do if it came to that. They must have some kind of nutritional value if they've been keeping Greely going for so long. It was a shame that he couldn't give one to Greely. He couldn't think of anyone who would be more excited by the gift of a big dead rat. He hadn't had any time to really form any sense of affection towards Greely. In fact, if he had to make the choice right then, he probably would have judged him as an idiot and someone who he didn't like on the whole. But when you've got something you don't want, and there's someone else not fifteen feet away from you who you know would really want it, well that situation doesn't– an idea hit him. Rat bones. If he could get some of the longer, thinner bones out of one of these bastards, he'd be able to pick that lock with no problem.

Tim grabbed the shorter shard of bone that he had broken off from his makeshift weapon. He could probably use it to scrape some flesh away, dig down to some bone. Moving with only his hands, still in a sitting position, he made his way to the second rat. He poked at it with the longer part of the bone. It did not respond. He ran the bone sword through the hole in its neck through which he had killed it, and tried to leverage the body forward a little.

"Maybe ye should cut that guy loose," suggested Greely. Tim

hardly noticed the third rat's screams anymore. It was just part of the background noise to him. "Listen to him. He's suffering, he is."

Tim leaned forward, and then slammed his back as hard as he could into the bed. The rat gave a new shriek of pain, and then maintained its former screaming. "Fuck him," said Tim. "Did you see my foot? I might never walk right again."

Tim grabbed the rat next to him by the ear, and shoved it forward as far as he could. This meant that his back was pushing hard into the bed, and the third rat once again voiced his objection. He managed to get the front paw exposed from the side of the bed, and tried to cut away as close to the body as he could, but his bone weapons seemed less ideal for precision cutting than they had been with panicked stabbing. Once he removed the arm from the bulk of the body, he'd be able to whittle the flesh from the bone with greater care. Right now, he only seemed to be succeeding at mangling a corpse. With the help of his good leg and both arms, he finally ripped the leg off of the creature, and fell backwards.

"Change of heart?" asked Greely.

"What are you talking about?"

"Ye gonner eat that?"

"No, I'm not going to fucking eat that," said Tim.

"Mind tossin' it here, then?"

"No," said Tim. "Why would I go to all the bother to cut this thing's leg off just to toss it to you so you can eat it?"

"Dunno."

"I'm getting the fuck out of here. If I've got time, I might be able to get you out too. Or you can stay here and eat all the rat you like. Makes no difference to me."

"Well whatever yer doin', ye'd better get a move on it. Shorty should be making his rounds sometime soon."

Tim scraped furiously at the flesh on the rat's former forearm, trying to remove the skin without breaking the bones underneath. Digging down, he finally found the bones. He was able to remove one without breaking it, but the other one snapped. The bone he successfully recovered was slender, but strong. It would probably do. He would still need one more. He was getting the hang of flesh removal now, and he separated the bone of the rat's upper arm from the flesh around it without much effort. It was thicker, but not by much. It might do.

He pulled himself up to his feet, and hobbled over to the barred door, keeping as much of his weight as possible on his good leg. He put his ear to the lock, and felt around the inside of it with the rat bones. About ten seconds later he heard a click. He pushed. The door swung feely on its hinges.

"Well I'll be damned," said Greely. "Not a bad show, lad. Not at all."

Tim closed the door again. "Do you want to get out of here?" he asked Greely.

"Yar," said Greely. "I think I'd like to see the sky again."

"Are you willing to fight? I mean, if it comes to that?"

"If we get caught outside of these cells," said Greely, "ye can be damn well certain it's gonner come to that. I'll fight. If ye can kill two dire rats with naught but poor Gorp's leg, I'll manage te find somethin'."

Tim opened the door as carefully and silently as he could, and then went to work on Greely's door. "You really eat those things?"

"Nah," said Greely. "Not those bigguns. They can't get inte me cage. I just eat the normal rats that come in every now and again, when I can catch them. Shorty raises the bigguns fer himself. Takes away about one a week. I normally get a taste of it round the Great Harvest."

The lock clicked. Greely pushed on the door. Tim pushed back. "Not yet."

"Why not?"

"You said Shorty's due to come around soon, right?"

"Yar," said Greely. "So it's probably best we get our arses a movin', dontcha think?"

"No," said Tim. "He's pretty small. If we can catch him by surprise, we can take him out of the equation."

"Ye don't mean—"

"No," said Tim. "But we can at least lock him in one of these cells. We don't know what we're going to face out there, and we don't need any surprises from the rear."

"Well aren't ye a smart little guy?"

"You know, that's really condescending."

"Sorry."

"Listen. When he comes in here, he's going to head immediately over here and ask me what the fuck's going on with all these giant rats. You're going to open your door and grab him from behind. I'll get out of the way, and you can keep on shoving him into here."

"Right."

Tim spent a full five minutes wondering if they made the right choice to wait in their cells before Shorty finally showed himself. He walked into the hallway with a concerned look on his face, and nodded to Greely. Greely nodded back as if nothing was out of the ordinary. Shorty turned his attention to Tim's cell. His yellow eyes grew round and his jaw dropped open.

"My rats!" croaked the old goblin. "What've you done, boy?"

"Oh, I'm fine," said Tim. "Don't worry about me."

"Get back, you stupid, murdering half-wit." He raked his giant brass key ring across the bars of Tim's cell, and Tim instinctively stepped back from the noise. "What the devil?" said Shorty, as the cell door nudged back a bit. He looked up at Tim, who smiled and shrugged.

The next thing Tim knew, the goblin was engulfed in something that looked like a hairy broken box kite, and being pushed into his cell. Tim relieved him of his keys, and picked up his bone sword from behind the rat where he had hidden it. Greely stood up, and Tim pointed the blood-soaked broken bone down at the surprised looking goblin.

Shorty looked up at Greely. "What do you think you're doing, man?" It wasn't said in anger, or from any perceived position of authority. To Tim, it actually sounded like concern.

"It looks like I'm checkin' out early," said Greely.

"You'll never get past the guards outside," said Shorty.

"This here's a smart lad," said Greely, gesturing to Tim. "I'm sure he's got a plan fer that."

Shorty looked up at Tim. His face was a question mark.

"I'm... uh... still working out the finer details," Tim lied.

Shorty started to get up.

"Uh uh," said Tim, brandishing his bone.

Shorty scooted back, but remained sitting. "Is that rat blood?" He grimaced.

"Most of it," said Tim.

"I'll do as you say," said Shorty. "Just keep that away from me. Those things carry disease, you know."

Tim looked down at his foot. "Yes. That thought had occurred to me." He looked over at Greely and jerked his head back toward the door. When Greely was out of the cell, Tim backed out as well, and locked the door behind him.

"Sorry bout this, Shorty," said Greely.

Shorty shrugged. "I'd have done the same thing."

"So," Greely addressed Tim. "What's the plan?"

"What's that way?" Tim asked, indicating the direction Shorty came from.

"Shorty's quarters, I expect. I don't get around much."

"Let's see if there's anything useful in there," Tim said, and led the way briskly.

"Ye got some pep back in yer step, I see," said Greely.

Tim stopped and looked down at his foot. It still looked pretty bad, but not as bad as it had looked a few moments ago. "You know, you're right. I feel better. Not one hundred percent, but there is a noticeable difference. I wonder..." He bit his lower lip for a moment, and then shook the thought away. "We can think about that later. Let's keep going."

Greely followed Tim down the hall to a small wooden door which stood ajar a little way down the hall. Firelight glowed inside. Tim nudged the door with his bone, and revealed a cozy little room, complete with a bed, a rocking chair, a dresser, and a shelf full of books. On top of the dresser were a few items that Tim recognized immediately. His bow was here, as was his belt, with his dagger and rapier still sheathed in it. He walked in to grab it, and was bombarded with absolute silence.

The silence was so sudden and so complete that he assumed he'd just been struck unconscious, and wondered how he was able to continue seeing. No more screaming rats. No more footsteps. No more of the general white noise that he never even knew was there until it was all gone. He turned around to look at Greely. Greely put his hands out, palms up, and mouthed the word "What?"

"I can't hear anything," Tim mouthed back, completely unnerved that there was no sound coming out of his mouth.

Greely's face scrunched up, and he cupped a hand over one ear. "What?" he mouthed again.

Tim decided that this was just something he was going to have to figure out later. Time was too precious a commodity right now. He grabbed his stuff and walked back out. Upon crossing the threshold of the door, he got slammed in the ears with the sounds of screaming rats and a rush of white noise. He dropped his belongings and put his hands over his ears.

"Are ye all right, Mr. Tim?" asked Greely.

"Huh?," said Tim. He slowly removed his hands from his ears. "Yeah. Just a headache. You know, it's completely silent in there."

"Ye don't say," said Greely, and poked his head in. He prodded one ear with a finger, and then removed and inspected it. Then he farted. Tim was at just the wrong height for that. Greely pulled his head back out. "Yar," he said. "Silent as the grave. How about that."

"How is that possible?" asked Tim.

"I expect it's some sort of silence spell," proposed Greely. "Makes sense for a jailor in a dungeon. Ye'd go mad, listenin' te all those people screamin' their heads off all the time."

Tim shrugged. That was good enough for him. He buckled his belt, and slung his bow around his back.

He led the way back past the cells, with Greely following behind.

"Hey!" shouted Shorty. "Those are my things, you lousy thief!"

"I prefer the term 'rogue'," said Tim. "'Thief' is so second edition."

"First you kill my rats, and now you steal my things." Shorty turned his head. Tim thought he might have actually seen his red goblin eyes start to water. "Thirty years of service, and it's the first thing they ever gave to me."

"Why did they give it to you?" asked Tim.

"They said it was too small for any of them to use."

"So you knew it all belonged to me."

"That's why I haven't been wearing it," explained Shorty. "I'd very much like to stroll up and down here like a proper jailor, with some weapons strapped to my sides. But at the same time, I didn't want to rub it in your face. I was planning to wait until after you were dead."

"That's very thoughtful."

Shorty wiped his sleeve across his eyes and turned back to face them. "Hey, listen," he said. "I've been thinking. Why don't you take me with you?"

Tim raised both eyebrows. "Ha," he said. "Nice try, buddy. I don't think so."

"Come on now," pleaded Shorty. "I'm a prisoner in here, same as you."

"You've only been in there for a minute!"

"I mean, as a jailor. Do you think I get free reign of the castle? I haven't been through that door since they threw me in here." He indicated the door up the steps which the captain and his guard had exited through. "Once they get wind of me letting you escape, I'm as good as dead!"

Tim looked at Greely.

Greely shrugged. "He has been a loyal friend all these years."

"A loyal friend?" asked Tim. "He's been your jailor."

"But he's been pretty good about it, as jailors go. He's been the only consistent friend I've had to talk to for any significant length of time."

"I can't believe I'm considering this," said Tim.

Shorty looked at Tim without trying to hide the tears he was willing to well up in his eyes. "I've got sons out there, somewhere," he said. "I'd like to see them again."

"Oh for fuck's sake, all right." He grabbed the key ring and inserted a key. "I'm warning you, though. If you betray us, I will fucking end you on the spot. I'll put that before defending my own life even. Do we understand each other?"

"Absolutely, sir."

"Just call me Tim."

He started walking to the door.

"Would you mind, Mr. Tim," asked Shorty as humbly as he could manage, "telling us the plan?" Greely stood next to Shorty in solidarity.

Tim's shoulders slumped down. "I don't actually have a plan. I figured we'd just do our best to be sneaky and try to find the quickest way out."

"I beg your pardon, sir," said Shorty, "but that doesn't sound like much of a plan."

Greely nodded in agreement, but tried to look apologetic about it.

"Well what the fuck do you expect from me?"

"You had a pretty good plan to catch me," said Shorty. "I know Greely didn't come up with that."

Greely nodded enthusiastically. "That's right. That was all him."

"But there's only one of you, and you aren't any bigger than me," said Tim. "And we outnumbered you two to one. If they come back in here like they did when they brought me here, we'll be outnumbered, barely armed, tired, and underfed."

"I've got some leftover rat in my room," offered Shorty.

"No thank you."

"I'm not saying we ought to use the same trick twice," said Shorty. "But running out there without any sort of plan amounts to the same as suicide."

Tim looked around. "Okay, I might have something."

"See," said Shorty. "That wasn't so hard."

"I didn't say it was something good, and it depends on a lot of contingencies."

"What's a contingency?" asked Greely.

"Shit that could go wrong."

"Yer plan depends on a lot of shit going wrong?" asked Greely. "I like them odds."

"I have something for you," said Shorty, and ran off towards his room.

"But don't you want–" said Tim.

"It's for your leg," the goblin shouted back excitedly.

Tim let him go. His leg felt better than before, but he really wouldn't mind having it sorted out completely if Shorty had something that could help.

Shorty came back with a stoppered vial of a dirty brownish yellow fluid. "Drink this."

Tim looked at the vial doubtfully, took it and unstoppered it. His nose was immediately assaulted. "Blegh!" he said. "This smells like piss."

"Some of it is," said Shorty.

"I'm not drinking this."

"It's a healing potion," said Shorty. "It will heal your leg. There are more lives at stake than your own. Drink it."

"Is urine really one of the components of a healing potion?"

"Not exactly. I have limited resources down here. Sometimes I just have to make due. Come on now. One gulp. Don't even think about it."

Tim held his nose and downed the potion. It burned its way

down his throat like a shot of cheap whiskey. It exploded into his stomach like a fireball. His face held a wince that he dared not let go of. He was resisting the urge to vomit, not because he had any suspicion that this toxic waste was going to do his body any good, but rather because he knew his esophagus wasn't going to be able to handle a second pass. When the urge subsided, he allowed his face to relax enough to wheeze in a drawn out lungful of air. "Oh my god!" he said as soon as he was able to speak. "It's worse than piss."

He grabbed his right thigh with both hands as the sensation of burning hard liquor flowed from his stomach straight through to his leg. A tingling feeling, like the pins and needles one feels after the blood rushes back into a limb which had fallen asleep, coursed down the length of his leg. When the tingle reached the bite in his calf, the wound seared like it had been dunked in a vat of lemon juice, and Tim collapsed to the floor. Clutching his leg did him no good, and so he chose instead to writhe around on the floor, clenching his teeth and waiting in terrified anticipation for the effect to reach his foot.

Greely took a step toward him, but Shorty put up a hand to stop him.

"Ye didn't... er–" started Greely.

"He'll be fine," Shorty assured him.

"Ahahaha!" Tim screamed as the potion found his foot. He started pounding on the stone floor with his fists.

"Grab his arm," demanded Shorty, as he went to grab the other one. Greely hesitated, so Shorty continued. "His healthy foot isn't going to do us any good if he smashes his hands up!"

That made sense enough to Greely, who grabbed Tim's arm as tight as he could. Neither Shorty nor Greely was strong enough to keep Tim from flailing his arms any which way he liked, but they were providing enough resistance to keep him from hurting himself.

Tim's foot felt like it was roasting in a fire for a few seconds longer, and then the sensation left him altogether. His body went limp. Shorty and Greely relaxed their hold on him, and watched his chest heave up and down as he lay panting on the floor.

When he had enough breath in him to do so, he propped himself up on his elbows, raised his head, and looked down at his foot. It was still filthy with drying blood, but it was whole. He wiggled his toes. They seemed to be waving at him. He smiled at them. He wiped the sweat from his forehead and looked up at Shorty.

"It worked," said Tim, smiling.

"Of course it worked," said Shorty indignantly. "What kind of goblin do you take me for?"

"The kind that keeps an innocent man in prison awaiting his execution," said Tim.

Shorty rolled his red eyes. "I suppose I'm never going to live that down, eh?"

Tim hopped up to his feet. He kicked one leg out, and then switched to the other. He stomped the bare soles of his feet on the cold stone floor.

"Erm..." Greely cautiously interjected. "Ye said ye had some kind of a plan, did ye?"

Chapter 8

Julian was still scratching multiplication tables into the dirt with a stick, which Cooper was still failing to comprehend at all, when Dave returned from his prayers.

"Um... guys?" said Dave, approaching cautiously with his hands behind his back.

"What's wrong?" asked Cooper.

"Did you heal your arm?" asked Julian.

"Yeah," said Dave tentatively.

"Well done," said Cooper. "How many healing spells did you use up?"

"It just took one."

"Nice roll."

"Thanks."

"What's going on, Dave?" asked Julian. "What's wrong?"

"I... um..."

"For fuck's sake," said Cooper. "Spit it out."

Dave lowered his head and held out his right arm.

For a moment, the three of them stood there in silence. Then Cooper broke into laughter. He laughed so hard that he started coughing. He horked up a big gob of phlegm, spit it on the ground, and laughed some more.

Julian still didn't see what the problem was. And then it hit him. "Holy shit," he said, barely above a whisper.

The leopard skin armband that Cooper had stretched over Dave's wounds wasn't an armband anymore. It was now a part of Dave's arm.

"How did..." Julian said. "What did..." He reached out to touch Dave's furry forearm.

"Hey," said Dave, jerking his arm away. "Knock it off."

"What happened?"

"My best guess is that the healing magic didn't differentiate between my skin and the leopard skin. Like Cooper said, 'It's skin, ain't it?'"

"How does it feel?" asked Julian.

"Furry."

"That's too fucking awesome," said Cooper.

"But you're okay?" asked Julian.

"I guess so. How's Tim?"

Cooper stopped laughing. "It's hard to tell. He was down quite a few hit points about half an hour ago."

"You think the guards roughed him up again?"

"No. He lost real hit points this time." A look of panic overtook Dave's face. Cooper raised a hand to calm him. "Don't worry. Whatever happened, he came through in the end. The little fucker leveled up."

"Seriously?" Dave grinned.

"Yeah," said Cooper. I figure he had a scrap with one of the other guys in the prison yard or something."

"Prison yard?" said Dave. "Did you see the size of that town? I don't think he's in San Quentin."

"Whatever," said Cooper.

"Hey guys," said Julian excitedly. Dave and Cooper turned around to look at him. He was holding a character sheet. "Tim's back up to a full fifteen hit points."

"What the hell is he doing in there?" asked Dave.

"Maybe his cellmate is a Cleric," offered Cooper, "and Tim's been doing him favors." In case anyone missed the implication, he rolled his fingers into a tube and made an in-and-out gesture near his mouth.

Dave and Julian looked at him disapprovingly.

"We'd better get going," said Dave. "It's still early enough so that there shouldn't be too much traffic on the road. We might get lucky and find an isolated wagon. Is everybody still cool with that plan?"

"It's the only reasonable one that's been proposed," said Julian. They both looked at Cooper.

"I'm still convinced there's a solid strategy to be made involving burning the shit out of the town, but as I currently lack the mental resources to formulate such a plan, I will accept yours as a lesser alternative."

"That's very big of you," said Dave.

Julian let out a loud whistle and shouted "Ravenus!"

"Oh," moaned Cooper. "Don't call that thing back here."

"I'm going to send him out to scout for a good target."

Cooper grimaced, but Dave nodded approvingly. "Good idea," he said.

After only a few seconds, Ravenus flapped through the trees and onto Julian's shoulder.

"You called, sir?"

Julian removed the bird from his shoulder and set him down on a low hanging branch of a nearby tree. "Anything to report?"

"There's a troll about a hundred yards that way," he jerked his head to the side to indicate a direction deeper into the forest. "Shouldn't be much bother to you guys if you don't go near him. He's eating a deer."

"What's your new friend saying?" asked Cooper in a mocking tone.

"There's a troll a hundred yards that way eating a deer."

"I wish we had encountered the deer rather than the leopard," said Dave.

"At least we didn't encounter the troll," said Cooper.

"Maybe we should," said Julian.

"Why would we want to do that?" asked Cooper. "A troll would rip us to pieces."

"What if we took it by surprise," pressed Julian. "We would probably all be better off at level two when we try to rescue Tim. It's just one little troll against the three of us."

Cooper looked at Julian with a puzzled expression. "What, exactly, do you think a troll is?"

"I don't know," Julian admitted. "I mean, I guess it's not like one of those toys you put on the back of your pencil. You know the ones, with the crazy colorful hair?"

"Yeah," said Cooper. "I know the ones. And yeah, they aren't anything like that."

"What about the one in 'Three Billy Goats Gruff?'"

"The one that got killed by a goat?"

"That's the one!"

"No," said Cooper. "The thing over there would have nothing to fear from a goat."

"But if-"

"Not even a really big one."

"Oh."

"It's bigger than any of us, it could rip us limb from fucking limb, and it will regenerate hit points faster than we can dish them out."

"It must have some kind of weakness," said Julian.

"Fire," said Cooper. "Maybe electricity. I don't remember. Listen, I'll be happy to discuss all the reasons why we should leave here right now while we are leaving."

"Fine," said Julian. He turned to his familiar. "Ravenus. See if you can spot a good target for ambush on the road."

"Um..." said Ravenus, lowering his head.

Julian sensed the moral quandary in his friend's voice. "We're not going to hurt anyone," he said. "We just need a means of transportation through the city gates without being seen."

Ravenus's beady black eyes lit up. "Ah," he said with an air of relief. "In that case, I'll get right on it."

"Should we leave our camp set up here?" Julian asked Cooper.

"Not if you want to keep any of it," said Cooper, already taking down his poor excuse for a shelter. "If there are trolls around here, they'll rip all of this to pieces."

As they were finishing up the last of their packing, Ravenus flew down into the camp. "I've spotted a worthy target, master Julian, but you'll have to hurry. He's coming just up the bend now."

"Ravenus says there's a wagon coming, but we'll have to hurry to catch it."

"Sure he does," said Cooper.

"What if it's true?" asked Julian. "Will you believe me if there really is a wagon out there?"

Dave laughed. "That's supposed to be proof enough for us to believe your stupid bird can talk to you? He successfully predicted that we would find a wagon traveling on a road?"

"Screw you guys," Julian said, and then stomped off after Ravenus.

"When are you going to tell him that you believe him?" Dave asked Cooper.

"Give it some time," Cooper said. "This is more fun."

"Why can't we understand him?"

"Dunno. Maybe only a wizard can understand his familiar."

"I can totally hear you guys," Julian called back at them.

"Shit!" said Dave.

"Goddamn elf ears," said Cooper.

Ravenus led the party to a part of the forest that nearly reached the road. A small, four-wheeled cart trudged up the road toward Algor, led by a mule. Whatever cargo it carried was concealed by a dirty, ragged cloth. The driver was a stout man wearing a sombrero. He stared blankly at the road ahead, letting puffs of white smoke trail behind him, like the world's smallest steam engine.

"Check it out," Cooper whispered from his hiding place, crouched behind a tree.

"He's smoking."

"So what?" asked Dave.

"So that means that cigarettes are available somewhere around here."

"Oh, right."

Julian scratched his head. "He doesn't look too worried about the fact that he's traveling alone."

"So?" asked Dave again.

"So why is that? Is it because he's so much of a badass that he's confident that he can handle any threat that comes his way?"

"Good point," said Dave. "He doesn't look like much of a badass."

"Fuck it," said Cooper. "I'll go ask him." He jumped up out of his hiding place, roared a battle roar, and brandished his greataxe above his head.

"Shit," said Dave. He and Julian looked at one another, shrugged, and ran out after Cooper, roaring significantly weaker battle cries.

"Holy fucking shit!" said the cart's driver. He fumbled around in his belt until he found a small bag. He hurriedly tossed it at Cooper, hitting him in the face.

Cooper screamed. His eyes boiled with fury as he swung his axe around his head, preparing to bring it down and add another head to his collection.

"Cooper! Stop!" Julian and Dave were both shouting.

"Huh?" said Cooper. He lowered his axe. The driver swallowed hard.

"What are you thinking? We aren't supposed to kill the driver."

"He attacked me."

Dave picked up the bag that had hit Cooper in the face. Inside, he found about three dozen copper coins. "He attacked you?"

"Why don't I throw a sack of coins at your face and see if it hurts?"

"Don't be such a baby."

"Fuck you."

Dave looked at Julian and jerked his head back towards the driver. "You're on, dude."

The driver was petrified with fear, but still looked happy to be alive. He continued to stare in terror when Julian flashed a smile at him.

"We're really very sorry," said Julian. He took the money pouch out of Dave's hand, and held it up to the driver. "I think you dropped this."

Slowly, he reached out his hand to accept what was being handed to him. "If you don't want my money," he said shakily, "and you don't want to kill me, then why do you attack me?"

Julian held up an arm and Ravenus flew down to rest on it. The driver looked mildly impressed. More importantly, he looked a little calmer. Julian was finding he really had a knack for this diplomacy thing. "It's neither you nor your money we're after," he said. "We need to borrow your cart."

"Why do you want to borrow my cart?" asked the driver. His voice was steady and curious. "It is a piece of shit."

"What is the cargo that you seek to bring into Algor?"

"More shit," said the driver simply.

"I'm sorry?"

"See for yourself." The driver pulled back the cloth and revealed the cart to be full of manure, right up to the top.

Dave, Cooper, and Julian looked back and forth at one another, each waiting for the others to come up with a reasonable alternative to burying themselves in shit. Julian spoke first. "You'll probably want to grab some of that bamboo," he said, pointing over to a patch of bamboo growing nearby, "if you want to breathe."

Dave looked from Julian to Cooper. "You can't really expect us to-"

"Tim's in trouble," Cooper said. "Wherever they've got him locked up, he's having to fight. He's made it up til now, but who knows how much of that was blind luck. He won't hold out forever in there." He trudged over to the bamboo patch and tore off three straws, each about a foot in length.

"What's your name?" Julian asked the driver.

"Miguel."

"What do you say, Miguel? If you want your cart back when we're done, you're welcome to come along."

"If it's all the same to you, good people," said Miguel, "I think I'll just catch up with you on foot. Algor is not a big place. I'm sure I will find my cart."

"No way," growled Cooper. "The little guy comes with us. We can't have him alerting the authorities to our presence before we're ready to make our move."

"That's right," said Dave. "Anyway, my misery could use a little more company."

Miguel looked to Julian for a way out.

"Uh..." said Julian. "Maybe I should wear your hat and... what's that thing called?"

"It's a serape."

"And your serape until this is done. It'll be nice to have something clean to wear."

"Thank you, sir," said Miguel, handing over the hat and serape.

Dave nudged Cooper and whispered. "Did that guy just thank Julian for stealing his clothes and making him bury himself in shit?"

Cooper shrugged. "Good Diplomacy check."

"What do you think?" asked Julian, after donning the hat and serape. He held his hands out as if he had a pistol in each one.

"Not bad," said Dave.

"It's a good look for you," said Cooper.

"How much do you want for this?" Julian asked Miguel.

"I'm sorry?"

"I like how this looks on me," Julian explained. "I'd like to buy it from you."

"You want to buy my clothes?"

"That's right. Name your price."

"One piece of silver would be sufficient," said Miguel.

"Fuck that," said Julian.

"I humbly beg your pardon, sir. I didn't mean-"

"How much money do we have?" Julian asked Dave, who was holding the party's money.

Dave looked in the money pouch. "About six gold pieces. We've got some silver too."

"Give this guy a gold piece. He's really being a good sport about all of this."

Dave looked at Cooper.

Cooper shrugged. "It's C&C," he said. "How hard is gold to come by?"

Dave flicked a gold coin to Julian, who flicked it to Miguel.

Miguel caught the coin with both of his hands and looked at it. His eyes went wide, and a little bit watery. "May the gods smile down upon you, sir!" he said, attempting to remove his hat, and then remembering he was no longer wearing one. "This will feed my family for a-"

"Don't sweat it, dude." said Julian. "Do you know where the prison is in there?"

"Prison?"

"Jail? Correctional facility? Penitentiary? Place where they put the bad people?"

"Dungeon?"

"Sure."

"There is a small dungeon under the Lord's mansion," said Miguel.

"Hey guys," said Julian. "I think I'm going to have Miguel ride up here with me. He seems to know his way around."

Cooper just snorted his disapproval. Dave spoke his. "I don't think that's a good-"

"If it's all the same to you, sir," Miguel spoke up. "I think I'll ride in the shit."

Julian gave him a dejected look.

"I don't know what you've got planned," explained Miguel. "And I don't want to know. But after all is said and done, I'd like to ride away with my mule and cart full of shit without anyone knowing that I was a part of it."

Julian shrugged. "That's fair enough." He would have really

liked to have someone up there with him when he spoke to the guards at the gate though. In truth, he kind of envied his friends who would be hiding safely in a cart, buried in shit.

Cooper passed out the lengths of bamboo, and was the first to climb into the cart. The manure was dry and crumbly on top, but grew wetter, squishier, and warmer the further in he burrowed. "Not so bad once you're in," he said, grinning. He put his own bamboo straw into his mouth, closed his eyes, and ducked his head under.

"Not so bad for him," said Dave. "He's used to smelling like shit." He turned to Miguel. "After you."

Miguel shrugged. He tucked his gold coin into a pocket, put the bamboo in his mouth, and burrowed in next to Cooper.

Dave looked at Julian. "Good luck, dude. This should be a piece of piss for you. If you run into any trouble, just pull out our straws." He buried himself on the other side of Miguel.

Julian climbed up to the head of the cart, and covered the contents as best he could, leaving a little room on his end for the three straws to poke out. Ravenus perched on the edge of the cart next to him. He tugged on the reins.

"Uh... Go, mule," he said. The mule didn't move.

He turned to Ravenus. "I don't suppose you know anything about mules, do you?"

Ravenus shook his head and raised his wings in a shrug.

"You mind going and giving him a peck on the ass?"

"Not at all," said Ravenus, and flew down to land on the mule. The mule made an ineffective swipe at him with his tail, and Ravenus turned around and looked up at Julian. Julian nodded. Ravenus bent over and pecked the mule as hard as his beak would peck. The mule let out a whinny and started to walk.

It was a twenty minute trek back to the town gates. Julian could make out one guard leaning against the wall as he approached. "Well," he said out of the corner of his mouth to Ravenus. "Here goes."

"I have every confidence in you, sir."

The mule clopped along steadily to the entrance.

"Good morning," said Julian enthusiastically.

The guard, who had barely bothered to glance at him up til now, offered back a narrow-eyed sneer, as if to say that this morning was anything but good from his point of view. From the look of his bloodshot eyes, the previous night had been much better, at this morning's expense.

The mule continued through the gate to no one's objection, which was for the best, as Julian wasn't sure how to make it stop. The town looked much smaller from the inside, and Julian could see all of it. If there was anything that was going to pass for a "Lord's mansion," it was the building directly in front of him. To his right were a saloon, a general store, a blacksmith's shop, and a stable. To his left were a cluster of buildings which were not immediately identifiable.

Julian guessed that they had arrived during the window of time in the day not far after all the previous night's drinking had been done, but just before the current day's drinking had begun. The streets were empty, except for one guard standing outside of what Julian had guessed to be the Lord's mansion. He steered the cart around the side of the saloon and then behind it, hoping that this was not a conspicuous place to steer a cart full of shit, or, failing that, that the guard idly watching him was too hungover to give a damn.

Having made it behind the saloon, out of sight, as far as he could tell, from any eyes, he steered the mule directly toward the back of the building, trusting it to have the presence of mind to stop before ramming the wall with its head. He plucked out the bamboo straws. Six arms floundered up through the surface of shit like a stop motion film of plants sprouting out of the earth. They each dug frantically at their own faces.

Cooper reached his face first and sucked in a breath of air. His subsequent exhalation carried the words "You fucking asshole" toward Julian. He stood up, grabbed one of Miguel's arms, lifted him out, and set him down on the ground. Then he grabbed both of Dave's arms and pulled him upright. "You could have just knocked on the side or something."

"Sorry," said Julian. "I wanted to see what your reaction time would have been in a real emergency. Not very impressive, really."

Dave tumbled over the side of the cart and hit the ground hard. He lay on the ground panting. Miguel picked bits of shit off of himself and threw them back into the cart.

Cooper spent a couple of seconds getting his breathing under control. "Anyway. Good job getting us through."

"Thanks," said Julian, a little uneasily. "I feel different somehow. I don't know. It's hard to explain."

Dave sat up and caught his breath. "You're probably just relieved at having made it through a difficult, and potentially dangerous, situation. Give your heart a minute to calm down. You'll be all right."

"No," said Julian. "It's not that. This doesn't feel like when Melissa missed her period for a month. This is something else. It's a good feeling, I think."

"Holy shit," said Cooper. "I think I know what this is. Take a look at your character sheet."

Julian pulled the tube out of his bag, and unrolled his sheet. He raised his eyebrows, and looked at Dave and Cooper. "One thousand points, on the nose."

"So what are you now?" asked Dave. "A second level wizard, or did you take a level in sorcerer?"

Julian looked at the other side of his sheet. "Level 1 Wizard, Level 1 Sorcerer," he said.

"Sweet," said Cooper. "I don't think you're going to regret that."

"So I've got some more spells now, right? I can actually be of some use when we go in there."

"Nah," said Cooper. "You'll still be useless today. You've still got to study your spells for an hour."

"Study them from what?" asked Julian. "You said Sorcerers don't use a book."

"I don't know," said Cooper. "Study them from your head or whatever."

"Actually," said Dave. "I played a sorcerer last summer. He only needs to spend fifteen minutes concentrating on his spells."

"Oh yeah?" asked Cooper. "We could probably put off this rescue another fifteen minutes. Start concentrating."

"On what?"

"I don't know. Look at your character sheet. What spells do you have?"

"In my spellbook?"

"No," said Cooper. "Those are wizard spells. Look for a list of sorcerer spells."

"Okay," said Julian. "I found it, but it's blank." Holding the page in his hand, his thumb slipped, and he realized he was holding two sheets of paper. The second one had two lists of spells on it. One list was labeled 0-level, and the other was labeled 1st-level. "Hey look at this," said Julian without looking up. "It looks like I get to choose what I want. What do you think I should-" Looking up, he saw that everything around him was still. Cooper was staring at him, but at the same time not staring at him at all. It was more like he was staring through him. He got up to move, but Cooper's eyes didn't follow him.

He looked over at Dave, who was frozen in conversation with Miguel. Even Ravenus was frozen in midair chasing after a dragonfly. Leaves hung in the air in mid-fall from their trees. Julian reached out to touch a single white fluff of dandelion. It was solid and immovable.

Miguel's mule turned its head toward him. "Not this time, buddy," it said. "You choose your own spells."

"Mordred!" Julian said accusingly.

"That's right."

"Why are you talking through the mule. Why not the head?"

"It's stuck in Cooper's bag. This way is easier."

"So what do I have to do now?"

"Choose your spells," said the mule. "You get four 0-level spells and two first-level spells. Choose wisely."

Julian looked at the 0-level spell list. "Most of these 0-level spells seem to suck."

"That's why they're 0-level spells. If you use your imagination, some of them can be quite useful."

"Is Detect Magic a good spell?"

"Maybe."

"It's good enough. I'll take it. What about Read Magic?"

"You already know that one by heart because of your wizard level."

"This is so fucking confusing. Light looks useful. I'll take that."

"Okay," said the mule. "Two more."

"Ooh...," said Julian. "Mage Hand looks cool. That's like telekinesis, isn't it?"

"A very limited form, yes."

"I could see that being useful in a number of different circumstances."

"Now you're getting the hang of it."

"I should take one offensive spell. It's a choice between Acid Splash, Ray of Frost, and Disrupt Undead." He read the descriptions of all three. "The first two are weaker, but the third is limited in its potential targets."

"A conundrum," said the mule.

"I'll take Disrupt Undead. I'll grab some more badass all-purpose spells later on."

"Okay," said the mule. "That's 0-level taken care of. What would you like for your two first-level spells?"

"I want that Magic Missile spell again."

"Are you sure? You've already got it as a wizard."

"But I can only cast it once per day, right?"

"That's right."

"That sucks."

"Yes," said the mule. "I suppose it does. Okay, Magic Missile it is, then. What would you like for your other one?"

Julian looked over the list. "We'll probably need to make a speedy exit. The spell Mount, it summons a horse, right?"

"That's right."

"If I used it more than once, could I summon horses for my friends?"

"The description of the spell says the horse serves you."

"It would serve me well by carrying my friends."

"A reasonable argument. Sure."

"Then I'm done."

Time started up again. Leaves completed their journeys to the ground. Ravenus caught the dragonfly and perched on a post. The dandelion fluff blew away on the breeze.

"What the fuck?" said Cooper. "Julian?"

"Oh, hey," said Julian. "Sorry, I'm over here."

"Did you just cast a Blink spell?"

"No," said Julian. "I didn't see it on the list."

"That's because it's a third-level spell," said Cooper. "What just happened?"

"Mordred happened," said Julian. "He stopped time so you guys couldn't help me choose my spells."

"What an asshole," said Cooper. "So what did you choose?"

Julian showed him the list.

"Mount? As in what I did to your mom last night?"

"It summons a horse," said Julian. "I thought it might come in handy if we find Tim and need to get our asses out of here in a hurry. I can summon four horses if I don't use any other first-level spells."

"Hmm..." said Cooper. "Good thinking. That might come in handy after all."

Chapter 9

Mordred sat alone at a table in the dining area of the Chicken Hut, sucking the last bit of meat off of a chicken wing bone. He tossed the bone onto a pile of its peers, licked his fingers, and wiped them on his jeans. He was slurping down the remaining contents of a Coca-Cola can when the front door bells jingled. He covered his mouth with his hands to avoid spraying Coke all over the books and dice. What soda he didn't choke on exploded into his hands and ran down his beard and T-shirt.

"Oh shit!" he said between chokes.

"Sorry," said Katherine. "Didn't mean to disrupt your little nerd party. I forgot my... hey, where is everybody?"

Mordred doubled over, trying to hack the Coke out of his lungs. "They uh..." he stammered, "went out for more beer." That sounded reasonable enough.

"All of them?"

"Ah well, you know how boys are." He wiped sweat, coke, and chicken grease from his beard with the back of his hand.

Katherine narrowed her eyes at Mordred for a moment, and then broke off the stare and walked back into the kitchen.

It will all be over soon. She's a pretty girl on a Friday night. She's got no reason to suspect that anything is wrong with her bro–

A Super Mario Bros. ringtone rang out from the players' table. Shit. Mordred clutched his dice bag.

"Time to talk, Stuffed Crust," said Katherine, stomping back in from the kitchen. She pressed a button on her phone and the ringing stopped. "Where the hell is my brother?"

"I... I told you!" Mordred tugged at his beard. "They all went out for more beer."

"The shops around here are all closed," said Katherine. The pitch of her voice was rising. She was beginning to panic. "There are three full cases of beer in the walk-in freezer. Don't bullshit me, fat boy. You tell me where my brother is, or I call the cops!"

Mordred fumbled with the draw string of his pouch. "Look, I'm sorry." His mind raced to find words as he spoke them. "Your brother and his friends told me that they were going out for beer. It was just a few minutes ago." He grabbed a black die from the bag. "It's likely that they are just playing a trick on me. I'm sure they'll be back any second now."

"He wouldn't have gone out without his phone," said Katherine. Her voice trembled slightly. "Look," she pointed at the players' table. "Cooper, Dave, and that other guy. They just decided to leave their phones behind as well?"

"I assure you, they'll be back in just a minute. Why don't you join us?" He tossed the black die in Katherine's direction.

Katherine snatched the die out of the air and let out an exasperated shriek. "What the fuck is wrong with you?" She raised a hand threateningly. "I am going to tear your fat, hairy throat out!" Each of her fingers ended in long, painted nails that lent credence to her threat. She threw the die, missing his face only by an inch or two. It bounced off of a wall. She lunged at Mordred.

The die bounced off of a table before hitting the floor. Mordred raised his forearms to protect his neck, but Katherine vanished just before she could take some of his skin with her.

Mordred exhaled. "Great," he muttered. "Now I'll have to roll up a character for her."

He bent over to pick up the die, and the front door's bell jingled again. His heart nearly exploded.

"Take it easy, princess," said a man who must have outweighed Mordred by a good twenty pounds, but without an ounce of fat. The fluorescent lights shone off the top of his shaved head like it was made from metal. His black T-shirt didn't necessarily look like it had been painted on, but rather that it might have fit snugly when he started wearing it at the age of twelve, well before he had started working out. It looked less like something he wore to cover his torso, and more like something he wore to contain all of the boulders of which it was composed. Massive tattooed biceps ballooned out of the sleeves, leading down to forearms as thick as tree trunks, and then down to hands ending in fingers that looked like sausages carved out of wood. "Hey faggot, up here."

Mordred, suddenly realizing his eyes were scanning down the length of a man's body, jerked his head up to meet a pair of eyes that seemed to have been chiseled from chunks of ice. "Um..." he said weakly.

"Where's Kat?" said the giant. "I thought I heard somebody shouting."

"Um..." Mordred said again.

"Hey dipshit, speak up."

"Here," said Mordred, and tossed the black die to the animated pile of muscles in front of him. "Hold this."

"What the fuck?" he responded, catching the die. He held it up to his face, and his expression changed from contempt to happy recognition. "Sweet!" he said, following a swiftly retreating Mordred back to the gaming table. "You guys playing C&C?" he asked, excitedly. "Fuckin A," he said when he saw the setup on the table. He tossed the die down onto the table. "I used to play this shit when I was-"

Mordred rushed to the front door of the shop and locked it. He took in a deep breath, and the word "shit" escaped with his exhalation.

Chapter 10

"We'd better get some sleep," said Tim.

"But it's still early afternoon," Shorty protested.

"Do you know what time they're going to come get me in the morning?"

"Uh... no."

"Well then we have two choices," said Tim. "We can stay up all night, or we can get whatever sleep we can get now, and be ready for them when they get here."

"Erm..." Greely interjected. "If ye meant fer us to go to sleep, then why did ye make us put those dead rats in our beds?"

"One less thing to do when we wake up," said Tim. "It's not like that bed is really all that more comfortable than the floor, is it?"

"A man likes to sleep in his own bed."

"Don't be such a baby," said Tim. "If things go our way in the morning, you'll be kissing that bed goodbye for good."

"The same likely holds true if things don't go our way," said Shorty glumly.

"Good point. Now go to sleep."

Tim had no trouble getting to sleep. The screeching of the rat with part of its body stuck between the lead weight and the stone wall had become nothing but background noise to him. After what they'd done to him, the sound of one of them in agony soothed him like a lullaby. He wouldn't have said that he trusted Greely or Shorty, but he wasn't going to let that stop him from getting his rest. If they were going to kill him, so be it. He would have to put his faith in them for now. The alternative was staying up through the night and trying to outwit and outrun his captors without having had any sleep.

Greely and Shorty shared Greely's cell. Shorty had a nice, comfortable bed that they both might have slept in, but Tim had insisted that nobody enter Shorty's magically soundproof room in case there was some sort of emergency in the night.

As far as Tim could tell when he woke up, the afternoon, evening, and early part of the night during which they slept were uneventful, with the one exception that the stuck rat finally gave up its screeching and died. No light shone through the tiny window at the top of his cell. He looked into the other cell. Greely and Shorty were still sleeping. He put the threadbare blanket over the dead rat in his bed.

He let himself out of his own cell and into Greely's.

"Wake up," he whispered, nudging Greely with his foot.

Greely's eyes opened wide immediately. "Goddess of my heart's desire! We dance as silhouettes against the autumn moon!" Tim cleared his throat. Greely shook the sleep out of his head and looked up at him. "Oh, it's ye. Time to wake up, is it?"

He stood up, and Shorty turned over, pulling more of Greely's blanket onto himself. Tim shook Shorty's shoulder.

Shorty's red eyes opened and he hissed. He bared his rotten teeth at Tim. It was more frightening than the rats had been. Tim jumped back and yelped, which startled Shorty in turn. He shook his head, rubbed his eyes, and remembered where he was.

"Sorry about that," said Shorty. "I was having a dream."

"What the fuck about?" said Tim, backed up against the wall and still panting.

Shorty frowned. "Dunno," he said. "Don't remember. Ducks, maybe?"

Tim got his heart back under control and then positioned the rat on Greely's bed as best he could to resemble Greely. It wouldn't pass more than a rudimentary inspection, but if they were still there by the time inspections were taking place, then they would have already failed.

"This will have to do," said Tim, after he finished covering the rat's face with the blanket. "Ready for some waiting?"

Greely and Shorty shrugged. Tim walked up to the stairs leading to the exit door. The doorway itself was about six feet up. The steps leading up to it were only as thick as the door, leaving a space on either side between themselves and the wall.

"Greely," said Tim, "Come here." Greely came forward, and Tim led him into the space on the right side of the steps. "Crouch down a little. Yes, like that. Very good." He turned back to Shorty. "What do you think?"

"About what?" asked Shorty.

"Can you see him?"

"Of course I can see him," said Shorty. "He's right there."

"Oh," said Tim. He bit his lower lip. "Try crouching down a bit more," he ordered Greely.

"Like this?"

Tim turned to Shorty. "How about now?"

"What about now?"

Tim sighed. "Can you see Greely now?"

Shorty stared dumbly at Tim for a moment. He scratched his head until the light of recognition shone in his eyes. He gave an embarrassed cough. "Perhaps I should have mentioned my darkvision."

"What?"

"I can see in the dark."

Tim rolled his eyes. "Oh for fuck's sake," he said. "Greely, come on out of there. Shorty, you go in there."

Shorty stood in the shadowy space between the steps and the wall.

"What do you think, Greely?" asked Tim. "Can you see him?"

"Nar," said Greely. "He's pretty well hidden in there, I'd say."

Tim ran the plan through in his mind. "Okay, good."

"So that's the plan, is it?" asked Shorty. "We just duck back in the shadows, hope they all walk in without seeing us, and then try to duck out while they're not looking?"

"Just about," said Tim.

"Oh..." said Shorty. He swallowed. "Okay."

Tim closed his eyes and offered a smug grin. "There is one more little thing I haven't mentioned yet."

"What's that?" asked Shorty.

"It's nothing unless you've got some string," said Tim.

"I think I can come up with something," said Shorty. He scurried down the hall to his room and emerged a few minutes later with a spool of thread. "Will this do?"

"Perfect!" said Tim. He went back to his cell, found the bones he had used to pick the lock, and started working on the door of the cell where the giant rats were being raised.

"I've got a key, you know," said Shorty.

"Oh yeah," said Tim. "Right. Good idea." He unlocked the cell door, careful not to move it in or out, lest the rats know it was open. A couple of them snarled at him, but most of them barely noticed he was there. He carefully tied one end of thread around a bone, and wedged it into the lock.

"Hmmm..." said Tim, rubbing his chin. "Not bad." He looked at Shorty. "I don't guess you have a paintbrush down here."

"No."

"Not a problem," said Tim, walking back to his cell. He lay down on the floor and reached under the bed until he fished out what remained of the arm he had removed from the rat in his bed. He stood up, removed the blanket from the rat corpse, and stabbed a new hole in it with his dagger.

"I think he's dead," offered Greely.

"Thanks," said Tim. The blood was thick and dark, but still liquid. He cut an opening large enough to dip the severed limb into. Nice and sticky. He took it back to the rat cage, and pasted the thread along the cell's cross bar all the way back to the edge of the wall.

"All right," said Shorty. "Kind of gross, but it should get the job done."

Tim nodded, satisfied with his work.

"One question though," Shorty continued. "Why wasn't this part of yesterday's preparatory work?"

"Because I only thought of it just now," answered Tim.

"So," Shorty paused and scratched his head. "When I asked you before if your entire plan consisted of us hiding out in the shadows and hoping all the guards would walk by without noticing us?"

"Yeah?"

"Up until a few minutes ago, that was your entire plan?"

"That's right."

"And you thought that was a good enough plan to gamble all our lives on, did you?"

"Is being dead any worse than being stuck in here?"

"I've only ever explored one of those two options," said Shorty, "and I'm not in any hurry to explore the other one."

"I think we've got a good shot at this. If we all do-"

Tim was interrupted by the sound of voices on the other side of the door, and then what he guessed was the sound of the crossbar being lifted out of the way.

"Shit," he whispered. "They're coming. Greely! Get over here. Shorty, go to the other side." Each of them did what they were instructed to do without hesitation.

Tim and Greely crouched back into the darkness as deeply as they could. Tim ran his thumb and forefinger together to confirm the feel of the thread between them. The door creaked open.

"Prisoners! Stand and be counted!" shouted Captain Righteous. Having received no response at all, the captain stomped down the stairs. Two of his subordinates followed him halfway down.

"Shorty!" he bellowed.

Shorty cowered even deeper into the shadows but made no sound.

"Damn him and his stupid soundproof room," muttered the captain as he stomped toward the other end of the hall, six of his men following behind. Tim recognized one of them as Diego. The other five were all likely named Level One Guard.

Greely looked down at Tim. Tim shook his head. Not yet.

"If he wants to be deaf, I'll rip those giant ears off his ugly head." The captain marched swiftly down the corridor without so much as a glance into any of the cells.

Diego followed behind more slowly, raking a small metal club across the bars of the cells. "Wake up, you lazy little shits. Don't want to sleep through your last couple of hours in this world, do you?"

By the time Captain Righteous had made it into Shorty's room, the rest of his men had come to the prisoners' cells.

"Has Greely put on weight?" one of them asked.

"What's that sticking out of the little guy's bed?" asked another. "It looks like a tail."

"-round, you fools! They're getting away!"

The soldiers all turned toward Shorty's room. Their captain was just coming out of it, shouting and looking past them.

"Turn around, you fools!" he repeated. The men turned back toward Tim. Greely and Shory hurried up the stairs. Tim paused just long enough to give them the finger.

"What do you suppose that means?" The rearmost guard asked.

The others didn't bother to contemplate Tim's gesture. They drew weapons and charged, but were intercepted by a horde of dire rats swarming out of their cage.

Tim bolted up the stairs as fast as he could. Greely and Shorty closed the massive wooden door behind him. It took the combined strength of the three of them to lift the crossbar back into place, blocking the door shut. There was a brass plaque on the front of the crossbar. It read "Dungeon. Authorized Personnel Only."

"Now what do we do?" asked Greely.

Tim looked around. There was only one way to go, and that was up a full flight of stairs, ending at another wooden door. He raced to the top of the stairs, hoping that the door wouldn't be locked. To his amazement, it wasn't.

He had expected giant stone walls hung with tapestries, and suits of armor standing decoratively at the entrances to corridors. Instead, this place kind of reminded him of his grandmother's house. He was in a small room with white painted walls. There was a rocking chair in the corner, and a table with an oil lamp.

Oil lamp.

"We could burn the place down," suggested Tim.

Greely and Shorty looked at one another, and then back at Tim.

"What for?" asked Shorty.

Tim thought. "I don't know," he admitted. "That's just something we could do if we were so inclined."

"Maybe we should focus on getting out of here," suggested Shorty.

"Good idea," said Tim. "Let's go."

There was only one door out of the room, and it opened into a short hallway. Opposite the door was a bedroom, and just down the hall there looked to be a- Tim stopped, sniffed the air, and turned around. "Kitchen," he said.

"Huh?" said Greely.

"I'm fucking starving," said Tim. He tiptoed down the hall, following his nose to what smelled like freshly baked bread. He drew his sword silently from its scabbard and peeked around the corner. A man in a robe was standing at the counter, looking out the window and drinking a cup of coffee. The first thing Tim noticed about the man was his long, shiny clean hair. It looked like it should be the star of a woman's shampoo commercial. His neatly trimmed beard was also shiny clean, complete with a thick mustache, waxed to points sticking out at each end. He didn't seem to notice Tim.

"Ahem," said Tim.

"Ahooo!" screamed the man with the shiny long hair. He jumped, and a great deal of coffee sloshed over the sides of his cup.

"Shut your mouth or I'll cut your dick off," said Tim, pointing his sword. He was just the right size for a fully grown human man to take such a threat very seriously. "Who are you?"

The man looked bewildered at the question. "Why I am Pahalin, Lord of this manor!" he said. "And you, you must be the butcher I was told about who sliced the head off of one of my men."

"Yes," Tim sighed. "I cut your man's head off. He was kind enough to let me climb up his body, and then stand there patiently while I worked away at his neck with a hand saw."

"I... you... never mind that," said Lord Pahalin. "How did you escape my dungeon?"

Tim looked around the corner where he had emerged into the kitchen from. Greely and Shorty both looked hesitant to show themselves. Tim raised his eyebrows inquisitively at them. They looked at each other, shrugged, and stepped out into the open.

"Wretched traitors!" Pahalin hissed at them.

"How can they be traitors?" asked Tim. "Weren't they prisoners?"

Pahalin stopped to consider this. "Well they've been with us for so long," he said. "They felt like family almost."

"Well," said Tim. "As long as we're on the lam, we're going to steal a bunch of your shit." He brandished his sword at Pahalin, and without taking his eyes off him, groped around on a nearby table until his hand found an apple. He bit off a huge chunk of it, chewed it up, and savored the feeling of it going down to his eager stomach. "Greely! Shorty! Take whatever you can find. Food, weapons, money, whatever. Hurry up!"

Greely and Shorty collected a few loaves of bread, some dried meat, a basket full of apples, and a large bread knife.

"Let's go," said Shorty, waving the bread knife toward the door.

"Shouldn't we tie him up first?" asked Tim.

"With what?"

"Oh... yeah, all right." Tim followed Shorty and Greely out of the kitchen door and into the morning air outside.

ROBERT BEVAN

Chapter 11

Julian looked up at the white moon – just the one – fading into the lavender sky. "The sun will be coming up soon," he said to whoever was listening.

"You'd better run along now," Dave said to Miguel. "It's probably best that you leave town altogether, and try to sell your shit somewhere else."

"Right," said Miguel. "Good luck with..." he stopped to think. "Well, with whatever it is that you're doing." He climbed up to his place at the head of his cart and took hold of the reins. Dave, Julian, and Cooper offered a friendly wave as he rode out of sight around the corner of the saloon.

"Should we have just let him go like that?" asked Julian.

"What difference does it make?" asked Cooper.

"He could tell the guards about us or something."

"They're about to find out about us anyway."

"That's true," said Julian. He tipped up the wide brim of his new hat. "As far as I could see when we came in, there was only one guard at the entrance to the Lord's manor." He risked a peek around the corner, just in time to see the guard in question suddenly jerk his head up in attention, and run back toward the front door of the house. "He's going inside," he said. "Now's our best chance."

The three of them ran as quietly as they could, which wasn't very, toward the entrance of the big house. Inside they could hear shouting.

"Best to rush in there while their guard is down," suggested Cooper.

Julian looked to Dave. Dave shrugged.

They made a tiptoeing dash toward the front door. Dave made a grab at the handle, but Cooper caught him by the wrist.

"Stop," said Cooper.

Dave looked up at him. "Why?"

"I need to rage."

"What?" asked Julian.

Cooper shut his eyes tight and balled up his fists.

"What is he doing?" Julian asked Dave.

"Barbarians have a special rage feature to their class," Dave explained. "Once per day, he can go into a rage, and he gets a boost to his Strength and Constitution scores."

Cooper whispered a mantra to himself. "I'm very angry. I'm very angry."

Julian looked at Dave dubiously. "He doesn't look very enraged to me," he observed.

Dave smiled and shuddered at the same time. After a hard swallow, he nodded back at Cooper. "Look again."

There was no hint of white left in Cooper's eyes. The few gaps that weren't crawling with blood vessels were tinted pink. Snot ran freely from both nostrils, and drool from either corner of his mouth, and it was abundantly clear that he didn't give a fuck about any of that.

Cooper punched a hole in the door, which seemed to piss him off even more. He tore at the hole he had made with both hands, ripping large jagged chunks out of it. Julian and Dave stood back to avoid the flying debris. Cooper entered the house with a roar that might have either been triumphant or a reaction to getting a spear shoved in his eye.

Julian ducked inside with Ravenus flapping in behind him. Cooper stood on one side of a puddle of coffee and what looked to be the remains of a broken mug. On the other side of the puddle stood two terrified men. One was the guard from outside. The other was a man with shiny black hair, a fancy mustache, and a bathrobe. The latter was momentarily distracted from his terror when Julian walked into view.

"Where did you get that serape?" he asked.

Cooper raised his axe in the air and screamed again. Both men raised their hands in petrified surrender. He looked like he might bring it down on one or both of them. Julian didn't dare try to stop him.

Dave dared. "Cooper!" he shouted. "Stop! Don't kill anyone! We need to ask- Oh hello."

The man in the bathrobe stepped back behind his guard when

Dave waddled in with his giant mace in hand. Both of their gazes followed the head of the mace down to Dave's furry, leopard-patterned forearm. Dave took the mace in his left hand, and hid his right hand behind his back.

For a moment the only sounds in the room were Cooper's hard, snot-bubbled breathing, and the light flapping of wings as Ravenus kept his balance perched on the back of a chair.

"Could you tell us where the prisoners are kept?" asked Julian.

Neither the man in the bathrobe nor his guard dared lower their hands. They each pointed one finger toward the hallway.

"Just..." His voice shook with each word. "Just... down... the... hall."

"Second door on the right," offered the guard.

"Thank you," said Julian. He held up his arm and Ravenus perched on it, facing him. "You stay here and keep an eye on these two," he said. "If either of them move, you come and get me. We'll be right back as soon as we find our friend."

"Very good, sir."

"Thank you," said Dave with a small, awkward bow.

"Yeah, thanks a lot," said Cooper.

Julian looked at him. His eyes were back to normal. He wiped the drool off the corners of his mouth with his forearm. "Feeling better?"

"Yeah," said Cooper. "I'm cool. Let's go get Tim."

They found the door without any problem. A plaque on the crossbar holding it shut read "Dungeon. Authorized Personnel Only."

"I can hear something inside," said Julian, putting his ear to the door. "Sounds like a fight."

"Shit," said Cooper.

"What's wrong?" asked Julian.

"I just blew my rage."

"What are you talking about?"

"Barbarian rage," he explained dispiritedly. "I only get to use it once per day, and it's finished at the end of the encounter. I thought we were heading into the big battle back there, but it was just some random guard and a dude with shiny hair."

"So what are you saying?" asked Julian. "You can't fight?"

"Oh, I can fight," said Cooper. "It's just that my heart's not in it.

I can't get good and riled up beforehand."

"There are men in there who may be trying to kill your friend!" argued Julian. "That doesn't get your heart pumping?"

Cooper shrugged. "I'm as cool as a cucumber," he said. "Want to feel my pulse?" He offered his wrist.

"No thanks," said Julian. "Could you just move the bar off of the door please?"

"All right," said Cooper. With one hand, he lifted the thick wooden beam out of its supports and tossed it to the side.

Julian paused and turned to Dave. "Maybe it's best if-"

"Get out of the way," said Cooper. "I'll go in first." He opened the door.

The scene beyond the open door was absolute bedlam. Men in armor fighting giant rats. Limbs and swords were flailing around wildly. Five rats lay dead on the stone floor, and at least one of the soldiers was down. If he wasn't dead, he was close. The only thing keeping the remaining rats from finishing him off was the distraction of other men who were trying to kill them.

"It's them!" shouted a man who Julian took to be the leader. "You will pay dearly for your crimes!"

"I don't see Tim," Cooper said. "Should we go?"

"What have you done with our friend?" Julian shouted.

The man stabbed a rat, tried to move forward, but was caught in the calf by another one. He roared in pain and kicked it away. "You'd do better to concern yourself with what I'm going to do with you rather than what I'm going to do with that little shit when I catch up to him again."

Julian stood with Dave in front of Cooper, looking down the stone steps into the battle taking place in the corridor below. He was uncomfortably unaware of what he was supposed to do at a time like this.

"Come on," said Dave. "He's not in here. Let's just go."

"Hang on," said Julian. "Let's give Diplomacy a shot. He might know where Tim went." He shouted back to the man in charge. "I noticed you and your men seem to be in a pickle," he said. "Would you like some help?"

One of the other guards caught a rat in the throat with a lucky jab of his sword, and the captain kicked another one so hard that it stopped moving.

"If you really want to help me," said the captain, "you can all slit your own throats while we finish off these gods damned rats."

"Listen," said Julian. "We aren't very comfortable with killing people, but we really need to find our friend, so-"

"Ha!" sneered the captain. "That mongrel beast behind you seemed comfortable enough with killing one of my men."

"That was sort of an accident."

"An accident?" The captain stopped attacking rats for a moment. His chin jutted out, and the corners of his mouth pulled down in a tight scowl, as if he were trying to look angry, but his eyes flickered a betrayal of confusion and disbelief. "He chopped his fucking head off!"

"Right," said Julian, lowering his head. "I know what it must look like to you." He paused to search for the right words. "But you see, we were just playing a game, and Cooper thought that would be funny."

Dave elbowed Julian sharply in the arm. "Dude, you call that Diplomacy?" he whispered. "They're going to fucking murder us!"

"Men!" shouted Captain Righteous. "Kill the monster and the dwarf. Leave the elf for me."

The soldiers abandoned the three rats who were still trying to bite through their armor and turned toward Julian, Dave, and Cooper, weapons raised.

Cooper and Dave also readied their weapons.

Julian reached into a small pouch on his belt and pulled out a pinch of white hair clippings. "Horse!" he shouted, waving one arm in the air, and blowing the hair clippings out of the palm of his other hand.

After a sound like a single clap of hands, accompanied by a small flash of light, the two opposing groups found themselves looking at opposite ends of a very surprised looking horse.

"What the f-" was all Dave had time to say before he flew backwards into Cooper, who caught him but was unable to keep his balance. They fell backwards into a cranny between the steps and the wall. Dave had a horseshoe-shaped dent in his breastplate.

The horse bucked and whinnied, the soldiers stepped back, and the rats retreated into Shorty's room.

Julian was trying to pull a bewildered Dave off of an equally bewildered Cooper when Ravenus flapped into the room.

"Julian!" said the raven with alarm in its voice. "They're coming! You need to get out of here right now."

"I can't leave my friends here," said Julian. "I'll try to get everyone out, but you need to go find Tim."

"Who's Tim?" asked Ravenus.

"He's the guy we came to rescue," said Julian. "He must have escaped before we got here."

"Where do you think he went?"

"I don't know," said Julian. "Go back to where I summoned you. Look for him there."

Ravenus flew out of the dungeon just before the man in the bathrobe reached the door.

Cooper squirmed under the weight of Dave, and Julian pulled on Dave's arm, but it was no good. They were jammed in that little space pretty good.

Ravenus flew toward the door, and the man in the bathrobe raised his arms to cover his face. The effort wasn't enough. Ravenus managed to rake a talon across his face on the way out. The man screamed and flailed his arms ineffectually at the bird.

"Nice one, Ravenus!" Julian shouted after him as he flew out of sight.

The man in the bathrobe glared down at Julian with fury in his eyes, and blood running down from three slashes in his cheek. Fury gave way to shocked confusion when he spotted the rear end of a horse for the first time.

He peered further into the ill-lit corridor, past the horse, at the guards. "Give us a knock when you've finished this… whatever this is," he commanded. He stepped out backwards, continuing to stare at the horse, and closed the great wooden door behind him.

Julian knew he didn't have the time to stop them from locking the door, so he didn't bother to try. His first priority was to get his friends upright again while the people that were trying to kill them were still distracted by the horse he'd summoned. As he pulled Dave to his feet, he heard the crossbar clunking into place on the other side of the door. They were trapped.

"I've fucking had it with this job!" shouted the leader. He shoved his sword into its scabbard, threw down his hands in disgust, and walked into one of the cells. A dead rat was in the bed. It was covered by a ratty old sheet and looked to be sleeping. He kicked it off the bed and sat down. "This isn't what I signed up for." He looked over at Julian, who had finally gotten the rest of his party to their feet. "Hey elf," he shouted. "You want a truce? You got one."

"Huh?" said Cooper, only just coming around to where he was.

"Huh?" said one of the subordinate guards.

The leader glared at the soldier who questioned him. "Do you think you get paid enough to be locked in a dungeon to fight like a dog in a pit?"

"But they killed Thaddeus," the guard argued, but didn't quite sound like his heart was in it.

"Thaddeus was a dick," replied the leader. "Can you honestly say that you miss him?"

"Well, no, but..." He gave up and leaned back against the cell bars.

The remaining guards removed another dead rat from the bed in the cell across from where the leader was sitting, and put their wounded comrade on it. He was bleeding profusely from the lower leg.

"Maybe you should go help him," Julian whispered to Dave, "as a token of goodwill."

"Maybe I would," Dave hissed back at him, "if you get that fucking horse out of my way."

"Oh yeah. Sorry about that." Julian waved his arm and repeated his command word. "Horse!" The horse disappeared back into a pinch of horse hair.

As soon as the horse disappeared, the rats charged out of Shorty's room. One of them locked eyes with Dave, who looked to be in no mood for it.

Dave grabbed his mace with both hands and readied himself. "Fucking animals," he muttered. "I am so fucking sick of fucking animals today." The rat lunged up at him, and he swung his mace with all the strength he could muster. Everyone in the dungeon winced as the sound of a crunch coincided with a giant rat body flipping up through the air and against the bars of a cell.

The other two rats were less bothered about their fallen brother, and one of them had its eyes set on Julian.

Julian had no more love for these creatures than Dave did, but what he did have was a lot more fear of them. He yelped and ran into the one cage that had been holding neither prisoners nor rats, and tried to close the door behind him. It required a key to lock, so he just held it closed as best he could with one hand, and started to wave the other one around in the air. The rat's snout was poking through two of the bars, and it caught the bottom of Julian's robe.

"Methylchloroisothiazolinone!" Julian shouted, and pointed his free hand down at the rat. A sparkling arrow sputtered out of his fingertip and burned into the rat's side. It shrieked and let go of Julian's robe as a charred hole in its flesh smoldered and smoked. Cooper finished it off with a good solid kick to the other side. Its body flew down the hall into the room at the far end of the hall where it landed strangely without a sound.

The last rat tried to bite Cooper but barely managed to scratch his boot. Cooper swung his axe down and chopped the creature in two.

"You all right?" Dave asked Cooper.

"Yeah, I'm fine. Go see if you can do anything for that guy."

Dave set his mace down on the ground, raised his hands up in a gesture of peace, and started making his way slowly and cautiously toward the cell with the injured guard. "I'm a cleric, and I can help your friend."

"Then what are you waiting for?" shouted the wounded guard. "Quit fucking around and come help me!"

"Oh," said Dave. "I was just... I didn't know if-"

"Come on!" shouted another guard.

"Okay," said Dave, hurrying into the cell. He laid one broad dwarven palm on the guard's sweating forehead. "It will feel better soon."

The guard nodded his head, breathing shallowly and quickly. "What... happened..." He winced in pain, then continued. "to... your... arm?"

"Shut up," said Dave, and slapped him in the forehead. "I heal thee."

"I heal thee?" one guard mouthed to another, who shrugged in response.

Even the recipient of the spell looked questioningly at Dave, but only briefly. His head fell back as the spell began to take effect. He moaned as the redness of razor-burn on his cheeks and neck disappeared and he grew a fresh layer of healthy smooth skin. "Oh, that's nice," he said between moans.

Julian knew exactly how he felt. He remembered when Dave had healed him. He'd felt brand new again.

The guard clenched his teeth and closed his eyes when the healing power reached his mangled lower leg. He let out a cry and a shudder as the torn skin, muscles, tendons, and blood vessels fused back into a properly functioning mass of living flesh again.

"Darren, are you okay?" asked the guard who had been supporting his head.

"By the gods," said Darren, his eyes still closed. "I think I just came."

Dave and the guard simultaneously removed their hands from his head, which fell back with a thud against the not overly-soft mat on the bed.

"Ow," said Darren.

Captain Righteous stood up but remained in his cell. "My uncle is a priest of Pelor," he said to Dave. "What god do you serve?"

"Me?" asked Dave. "Oh, I don't serve any gods. The book said I could just pick two domains."

"What the hell are you talking about?"

"I'm not really religious."

"You're a fucking cleric."

"Yeah, well..." Dave paused, looking for the right words. "The party needed a healer, and I happened to have a pretty high Wisdom, so-"

"Yes," said the captain. "Your wisdom is overshadowed only by your modesty." He sat back down on the edge of the bed. "This is what the world has come to," he muttered to himself. "Godless fucking clerics."

Chapter 12

"What happened?" asked Katherine, wincing and shutting her eyes against the sudden burst of sunshine. Birds chirped somewhere above her. That was odd. She felt around for something to support her, and was surprised to grab hold of what felt like a tree. She cautiously opened her eyes and saw that she was, in fact, holding onto a tree. "Where am I?" she whispered. She looked around and saw only more trees. She was in a forest. That explained the birds well enough. But why was she in a forest? How did she get here? Why was she holding a sickle? What was that panting sound? She looked down, screamed, and dropped her sickle. A large gray wolf stared back at her with its sloppy pink tongue hanging out.

She tried desperately to scramble up the trunk of the tree. She'd only made it about three feet up when her hand slipped. Her back collided with the soft earth below. She rolled over, grabbed her sickle, and held it threateningly at the wolf, which only continued to stare at her.

Katherine stood up and bolted into the woods. The wolf trotted along behind her. She ran until the thought of running any further was less appealing than the thought of getting ripped apart by a wolf. Finally, she stopped to catch her breath. The wolf stood patiently next to her, not looking the least bit winded for its effort. Her arm instinctively jerked away when it tried to lick her hand, but then she relaxed. If it was going to kill her, it would have done so by now. She scratched under its chin, and it tilted its head back, as if to offer her more chin to scratch.

"Do you know me?" she asked.

The last remnants of her fear evaporated entirely when she saw a man dressed in a comically oversized blue shirt, yellow and blue striped leggings, and a large, red, floppy hat, complete with a giant green feather sticking out of the top, materialize out of thin air about forty feet away from her. She took a protective stance in front of the wolf before she even considered why she was doing it. Her hand, she was surprised to find, was wrapped around the handle of her sickle. Were these the battle reflexes her dad claimed to have developed in Vietnam? How would she have acquired battle reflexes?

Whoever the man was, he didn't appear to have seen Katherine yet. He didn't appear to be able to see at all. He was stumbling around with his eyes closed. Katherine moved closer, keeping close to the trees. She wasn't exactly hiding behind them, but she was keeping the option open. When he finally opened his eyes, Katherine recognized the icy blue shine at once..

"Chaz?" she asked.

"Kat," answered her boyfriend. "Is that you?"

"Yeah."

"Where are we? Why are you dressed like Conan the Barbarian?"

"Huh?" said Katherine, and paused for the first time to look at what she was wearing. Her clothes were entirely made of leather. Not the shiny black leather you buy at the mall, but dull brown leather that gave you a crystal clear reminder of just where leather comes from. It was stitched together with what looked less like thread and more like rope. She shrugged. She'd worn worse. "Why are you dressed like you couldn't remember if the parade you were going to was for Mardi Gras or Gay Pride?"

Chaz looked down at his own clothes. "What the fuck?" Then he looked back up at Katherine. "What happened to –"

Katherine gasped. "Look at your arms! You're skinnier than me."

Chaz wrapped the fingers of his left hand around his right bicep. The tip of his middle finger nearly touched that of his thumb. "This can't be –"

The wolf peeked its head out from behind the tree Katherine was standing next to.

"What the fuck is that?" shouted Chaz.

The wolf growled and bared its teeth at Chaz. Katherine, who had momentarily forgotten it was there, was briefly startled again, but logic had time to interfere this time. If it meant to hurt her, it would have done so long before now.

"Stop it," she said to the wolf, and the wolf immediately

stopped growling and sat down. She knelt down and reached a tentative hand out to touch it.

"Kat," shouted Chaz. "Are you fucking nuts? That thing will rip your arm off!"

"He's friendly," said Katherine. She let the wolf sniff her hand, but she still had to resist jerking it back when it licked her fingers. She patted it on the head, and it closed its eyes with obvious gratitude. "I think..." she paused, not having a clue as to why she felt this way. "I think he's mine."

"You think he's yours?" asked Chaz. "Do you remember going to the pet store and buying a fucking wolf?"

"Do you remember going clothes shopping at the Ladies Big and Tall shop?"

"No," said Chaz, with more than a hint of panic in his voice. "And I don't remember walking into the woods, and I don't remember dating a girl who wore antlers on her head. What's going on here, Kat?"

Katherine stopped petting the wolf and felt the top of her head. Sure enough, there were antlers up there, worked into the leather hood. She lowered the hood, and in doing so her hands brushed against her ears, which she discovered were pointed at the tops. "What happened to my ears?" she shouted. "What's wrong with my ears?"

"They're pointed." He put his hands up to his own ears, which were normal enough. His hands went from his ears to his shiny golden hair. "When the fuck did I grow hair?"

"It has a very nice shine and bounce," said Katherine, still feeling the points on her ears. "I wouldn't have pegged you for a blond."

"I'm not," said Chaz. He paused to think. "At least I wasn't." He lifted up his shirt until he found the top of his pants. He pulled the front of his pants forward and looked down. "Holy shit! I guess I am now."

"What happened to us?" asked Katherine. "Where are we?"

"I don't know how it happened," said Chaz. "But don't you think it's pretty obvious where we are?"

"Obvious?" Katherine shouted back at him. "No, Chaz. I don't, as a matter of fact. I'm wearing antlers on my head, my ears are deformed, and I've got a pet wolf. No obvious explanation for any of that comes to mind."

"We're in the game."

"What game?"

"Caverns and Creatures," said Chaz. "The game your brother and his friends were playing."

"This is how you play?"

"Not conventionally, no."

"Then how do you know-"

"It's the only explanation as to why you're now an elf, and I'm a... what the fuck am I anyway?" He looked down at his clothes again, pivoting his waist around to get a fuller view.

"You've got something on your back," said Katherine.

"Huh?"

"A broken guitar or something."

Chaz found the leather strap around his front and pulled the object up over his head, knocking his floppy hat off. "It's a lute," he said curiously. Why would I be... oh no." He turned to the sky and shouted. "A fucking bard? Really?"

"Chaz!" Katherine hissed, "Keep your voice down. We don't really know what's going on here. What's the matter with you? What the hell is a bard?"

"A musician," Chaz whined back at her.

"What's wrong with that?" asked Katherine. "You're a musician anyway."

"You'll see what's wrong with it if we're attacked by ogres or something, and the best thing I can do is sing them a song."

"So you're a bard, and you play music," Katherine attempted to organize her thoughts. "And I'm an elf. What does an elf do?"

"Elf is a race."

"Hold on a second. I'm not white anymore?" Katherine looked at her hands. They looked longer and more slender than usual, but they were white enough. Hell, they were whiter than the hands she was used to.

"Not that kind of race."

"So what race are you then?"

"I'm human, as far as I can tell."

"So other races aren't human?" Katherine asked suspiciously. "Do people play this game in the north?"

Chaz closed his eyes in exasperation. "You're thinking about races the wrong way."

"I'm trying to think of them in a post Civil War way."

"I'm not talking about skin color," said Chaz. "There could be black elves or Chinese dwarves or Mexican gnomes or whatever."

That sounded more racist than anything she'd ever heard before, but she was willing to give Chaz the benefit of the doubt. He had a couple of black friends, after all, and she had to admit that there was a lot that she had no idea about right now.

"Okay, fine," she said. "So you're a human, but you're also a bard?"

"Like I said. Human is my race. Bard is my class," he explained. "Just like you might have a guy who's a Jew, but he's also an accountant, or a guy who's black, but he's also a janit-"

"Chaz!"

"Oh shit, sorry." Chaz said. "That came out wrong."

"For fuck's sake," said Katherine. "I get it. Just stop talking. So your class is like what? Your job?"

"Something like that."

"So what's my class?" she asked, looking at the sickle she was still holding. "Farmer?"

"My guess would either be ranger or druid."

"Why?"

"I'm trying to remember," said Chaz. "It's been a while since I've played." He thought. "You seem to be a woodsy type. Leather and antlers and all that shit. You're in tune with nature."

"But I hate nature," argued Katherine. "I got so pissed off at my dad that time he took us camping instead of to the beach on our vacation."

"Look deep inside yourself," said Chaz. "Right now, do you really hate nature?"

"Yes," said Katherine. "I do. It's dirty, and smelly, and full of bugs and spiders and shit."

"Okay," said Chaz. "If you hate nature so much, why don't you rip this little sapling out of the ground?"

"Why the hell would I do that?"

"It was a returgical question. I'm challenging you to rip this tree out of the ground right now."

"What's the point?" asked Katherine. "This is stupid."

"Fine," said Chaz. "Then I'll do it." He stepped toward the

sapling, and was met with the point of Katherine's sickle at his throat. "Jesus Christ!" he said, putting his hands up.

"Oh my god, I'm so sorry," she said. She lowered her sickle and Chaz backed away. She leaned against a tree, and her hand involuntarily caressed the bark. "I guess I really do love nature."

"Well," said Chaz. "That settles that. You're either a ranger or a druid."

"I don't know what either of those are."

"I think a ranger is just a fighter who likes to live in the woods or something," said Chaz. "I remember he has a favored enemy. Is there any sort of creature or race that you feel a particular hatred for?"

"Are you asking if I'm a racist?" asked Katherine. "Are you sure you're not a ranger?"

Chaz lowered his head. "I guess I walked right into that one." He thought some more, running a hand through his shiny golden hair. "If you're a druid, you should be able to use magic. Can you use magic?"

"Sure," she said. She grabbed the wooden medallion hanging from a chain around her neck. It had the image of a tree carved into it, the leaves composed of clusters of tiny emeralds. She pointed it at the ground and said "Canis Lupus!" A gray wolf suddenly came into being on the ground where she had pointed her medallion.

"Jesus!" said Chaz.

"Holy shit!" said Katherine. "How did I do that?"

"You're asking me?"

"I can do fucking magic!"

The wolf looked around, looked up at Katherine, briefly regarded the other wolf, and then vanished.

"Kind of disappointing really," said Katherine.

"What are you talking about?" asked Chaz. "That was fucking awesome. What else can you do?"

Katherine held her medallion in one hand. With the other, she reached into a small pouch on her belt and pulled out a bit of glowing moss. She held it up and looked at it for a moment, and then placed it at the top of her sickle. "Luminus!" she said, and a sphere of light glowed on top of the sickle.

Chaz shrugged. "That's pretty cool too."

They watched the light for a few seconds, waiting for it to

vanish like the wolf had, but it continued to glow. It wasn't particularly useful right now, in the middle of the day. In fact, if they weren't in the woods right now, but rather out in the open sunlight, it's likely they would barely be able to tell it was working at all. It would probably come in handy if they had to travel at night.

Katherine waved her sickle around. The light remained attached to the top of it. "Well, I guess this one's going to stick around for a while," she said. "So what can you do?"

"I can play this," said Chaz, holding up his lute. "And I guess I can sing."

"Okay," said Katherine. "Play me something."

Chaz took a couple of test strums on the instrument. Pretty soon, his fingers took over and plucked the strings more quickly and elegantly than Katherine thought possible. The song wasn't one that Katherine was familiar with, but she had to admit it moved her.

"I didn't know you were that talented," said Katherine.

"I'm not," said Chaz. He stopped playing and looked closely at his hands.

"What was that song?"

"I don't know. It just came to me."

"It was really good," said Katherine.

"Thanks."

"Seriously," she said. "It was amazing. I think if you wrote some lyrics for that, you could get a recording contract or something."

"You think so?"

"Excuse me," said a voice that made both Chaz and Katherine start and scream.

Katherine tightened the grasp on her sickle, and Chaz throttled the neck of his lute, brandishing it like a weapon. They both turned toward the direction the voice had come from and didn't see many likely candidates for a source. A large black bird stared back at them from a low branch of a nearby tree.

"I'm sorry," said the bird. "I didn't mean to startle you. I saw your light and heard your music. That was lovely, by the way."

"Thanks," said Chaz.

"I um..." said the bird. "I don't suppose that either of you are named Tim."

Katherine responded immediately, not caring in the least little bit that she was talking to a bird. "What do you know about Tim? Where is he?"

"I'm sorry," said the bird. "I don't understand a word you are saying."

"What do you mean you don't understand us?" Katherine shouted back at the bird. "We're speaking the same language!"

"Er..." said the bird. "What's the best way to put this?" He flapped his wings and shook his head. When he spoke again, his speech was slower, louder, and very carefully articulated. "I'm sorry. I don't speak your language."

"I think he's fucking with you," said Chaz.

Katherine was growing more and more frustrated. This was her only clear opportunity to find information about her missing brother, and to find out what the hell was going on. "Listen, you stupid fucking bird," she said, more slowly and deliberately than normal, but not to the extent of which the bird had spoken to her. She was, however, speaking much louder than he was. "We're both speaking English!"

"I'm sorry," said the bird. "I haven't had the ability to speak for very long, you see. I only know the elven language, so if either of you know that, I would be very grateful if you could-"

"Do you know elven?" Chaz asked Katherine, interrupting the bird.

"I don't think so," said Katherine. "What's elven?"

"The language of the elves."

"Why the fuck would I know the language of the elves?"

"Because you're an elf."

One of Katherine's hands involuntarily went back up to her ear, feeling the point on top. "Oh yeah," she said. "Maybe I do. I mean, I must if I can understand what it's saying, right?"

"Makes sense to me," said Chaz.

"Then how do I speak elven?"

"I don't know. Maybe try a British accent?"

"What difference would that make?"

"We're in a game world," said Chaz. "When people play these games, they aren't expected to actually learn all of the languages that their characters know. Sometimes they roleplay it by using different accents to represent different languages."

"Those people will die alone."

"Give it a try."

"Why don't you give it a try? You could understand it."

"It's not my brother we're looking for."

"You know what?" said Katherine. "You really are a piece of shit."

Chaz had no response to this accusation.

"Fine," said Katherine. I'll do my best." She looked at the bird. The bird was looking back expectantly and impatiently. "G'day, matey."

Chaz cringed. "That was more of a cross between Australian and pirate."

"Talk to that bird right now or you're going to be wearing that fucking lute."

"Fine," said Chaz. I'll have to warm up first." He looked at the bird. "I am Arthur, king of the Britons."

"King of the who?" asked the bird.

"The Bri- Wait, is that a serious question?"

"It worked!" said Katherine. "You're talking to it."

"I'm sorry to bother you, Your Majesty," said Ravenus to Chaz. "I was just looking for-"

"I'm not really a king."

"Well then that's a very odd way to start a conversation."

"I'm not really a king," Katherine repeated, trying to get a fix on the accent.

"I wouldn't have suspected so, Miss... Tim, is it?" the bird asked hopefully.

"No," said Katherine. "Tim is my brother."

The bird turned to Chaz. "I thought you said your name is Arthur."

"No, it's not. I was just-"

"So you're Tim then?"

"No. I'm Chaz."

"Then who the fuck is Tim?" The bird spread his wings and ruffled his feathers in frustration.

"Tim is my brother," said Katherine. "This is Chaz, who is not my brother."

"I'm her boyfriend," said Chaz.

"Let's not get carried away," said Katherine. "My name is Katherine. We're looking for Tim."

"I'm Ravenus."

"You know," said Chaz, "I wouldn't mind grabbing something to eat either."

"We'll get some food later. Right now we've got to find Tim."

"Right," said Ravenus. "I was told to look for him at the campsite. That's about a quarter of a mile that way."

"How do you know Tim?" asked Katherine.

"I don't," said Ravenus. "He's a friend of my master."

"Who's your master?"

"Julian."

"Who the hell is Julian?" Katherine murmured to herself. Then she remembered that there was a player in the Chicken Hut who she hadn't met before. A guy who had come with Cooper. "Does Julian hang around with a couple of other guys?"

"Yes," said Ravenus.

"Do you know what their names are?" she asked, not wanting the bird to just agree to information that she was feeding it.

"Hmm..." said Ravenus. "I don't recall exactly. Julian introduced them to me once, but they don't speak elven, and I wasn't paying much attention. I want to say Wiggles and Jing-Jing."

"Dave and Cooper?" Katherine suggested.

Ravenus brightened up. "Yes, that's them!"

"Why aren't they all together?"

"I don't know," said Ravenus. "I came in after Tim was gone. I don't know the whole story, but I think they went to rescue Tim from prison, but he had already escaped, and then they got caught in prison. So I'm supposed to find Tim, and get him to rescue them."

"They couldn't have been here more than a few hours, and they're all in prison already. I'll bet anything this is Cooper's fault. What a fucking moron."

"Is he the giant one with the tusks?"

"What?" asked Katherine. "I don't think so." Then she thought about her own pointed ears. "I don't know. Maybe."

"Farts a lot and shits himself sometimes?"

"Probably."

"Yeah, he strikes me as kind of dumb."

"It's starting to get kind of late in the afternoon," said Chaz. "If we're going to find Tim at this campsite, we should probably make our way there."

The trip didn't take long before Ravenus said "Well, this is the place."

Katherine was surprised to find that she didn't need to be told that. She spotted details that she didn't even realize she knew to look for. Flattened patches of grass. A couple of broken twigs. A mutilated leopard corpse. "What the fuck is that?"

Ravenus flew down to inspect the leopard more closely. He pecked at a bit of exposed flesh. "It's still fresh," he said. "I'd say it hasn't been dead more than a day."

"What happened to its leg?" asked Chaz.

"Dunno," said Ravenus. "I think Dave was wearing it."

"Wearing what?"

"The leg. He had a leopard skin armband on his forearm when I first met him."

"They've gone feral," said Katherine. "They haven't been here more than a couple of hours and they've gone all Lord of the Flies."

"Do you think leopard meat is okay to eat?" asked Chaz.

"What?" said Katherine.

"I mean, we need to eat something. The bird said the meat was fresh. I've mentioned I'm hungry, and he said he's ravenous."

"Ravenus," Ravenus corrected.

"That's what I said."

"No, you said ravenous."

"What did you say?"

"Ravenus."

"As in 'very hungry', right?"

"No. As in my name. It's a play on words. I'm a raven, you see. It's supposed to be a sort of latin sounding, but also fierce kind of thing."

"Oh, right," said Chaz. "I get it. Clever."

"Thank you," Ravenus said smugly.

"So does that mean you're not hungry?"

"I could eat."

"I'm not eating fucking leopard," shouted Katherine. "We need to look for my brother."

"Calm down," Chaz said. "We'll find him. The bird -I'm sorry-Ravenus said your brother is due to be coming back this way eventually. The best thing we can do is to wait here, build a fire, and wait for him. Then when he gets here we can have some leopard meat already cooked up for him. If he just broke out of prison, he'll be hungry."

"You're going to listen to a fucking bird?"

"I beg your pardon, Miss Katherine," said Ravenus. "I'm no ordinary bird."

"What makes you so special?"

"I talk."

"Hmm... that's true."

"Listen to him," said Chaz. "He speaks British English. That means he's smart, right? Like a librarian or some shit."

Katherine looked at Chaz through narrowed eyes, unable to respond. She opened her mouth to respond anyway, but Ravenus cut her off.

"Listen, Miss Katherine," he said. "I understand you're worried. But wandering around in the woods is only going to make matters worse. If it helps alleviate your anxiety, I'll fly around and scout the area while you two get a fire going."

"All right," said Katherine grudgingly. "Go ahead. I'll get the fire going."

Ravenus flew off, disappearing into the trees.

"I'll go get some firewood," said Katherine. "You stay here and see if you can find anything useful in our bags."

"Don't go off too far," said Chaz. "It could be dangerous out there."

"Don't worry about me," Katherine said, bending down on one knee to pet her wolf on the head. "I've got more to protect me than a banjo." She stood up and walked out of the clearing, with her wolf following loyally at her side. "We're going to have to think of a name for you."

Chapter 13

The few small patches of light that showed through the forest canopy were beginning to change from blue to purple, and Chaz began to feel uneasy about being left alone. One small comfort he found was that it felt really good to take the pack off of his back. He hadn't realized how heavy it was until he set it down.

The first thing he noticed was the hilt of a sword sticking out of the top. What kind of adventurer keeps his weapon in his bag? He looked down at his clothes. Oh yeah. A bard. He pulled the weapon out to find that it was long and very thin. A fencing sword. A rapist? Raper? Rapper? Rapier? That was it. Rapier. Not exactly badass, but it gave him a better sense of security than his lute did at present. Strapped to the side of the pack he found what at first appeared to be just an oddly bent piece of wood. A stick or something. Closer examination revealed it to be an unstrung shortbow. Inside the pack he found the string, a couple of daggers, and a bunch of arrows bundled together.

"I'm armed to the fucking teeth," he said to himself. With a moderate level of surprise at the fact that he had any idea what he was doing, he strung the bow and nocked an arrow. He set his eyes on a particular notch of a particular tree, and let the arrow fly. It found its target with ease.

Digging deeper into his pack, he found what he was looking for. He pulled a hexagonal steel box out of the bag. A flame was embossed on the lid. He opened it to find a collection of dried strands of plant fiber and twigs. It looked like a bird's nest. Also inside were a bar made out of some kind of rock, and one made out of steel with a rough edge to it.

Scraping the two bars together, Chaz produced an impressive spray of sparks. He tried again, aiming at the box, and some of the sparks were caught by the thinner fibers, producing a small flame. The flame grew, and Chaz knew it was going to burn itself out in a couple of seconds. He found a torch in his pack and held the business end of it over the flame. It caught instantly, and the fire in the tinderbox burned out.

"Now what?" said Chaz. He had to admit, though, it felt good to have a burning torch in his hand.

With his free hand he dug around some more in his pack, until he found a metal tube with a screw cap on one end. He shoved the bottom end of his torch into the ground, and unscrewed the cap of the tube.

"I'll be damned," he said, looking at his character sheet. "I kinda suck."

He rolled the paper up and inserted it back into the tube. He was suddenly overcome with curiosity at what Katherine's character sheet might reveal.

Instinctively, he looked around first. He was still alone. He scrambled over to Katherine's bag and fished around until he found what he was looking for. "Druid," he said. "I was right." He noticed, however, that he was wrong about her being an elf. She was only a half-elf.

"Well done," came a voice from behind him. Chaz nearly jumped out of his skin, and turned around. It was Katherine. She was carrying a bundle of sticks and fallen branches under each arm. Her wolf was standing by her side, panting happily. "I see you've got a fire started."

"It's just a torch," said Chaz. Best to put all the cards on the table. "I hope you don't mind, I had a look through your bag."

"Why would I mind?" asked Katherine. "Unless it's full of sexy underwear and dildos. I mean, it's not even really my bag, is it? Just like this isn't my body, and whatever the hell I'm standing on isn't my world. Find anything useful?"

"I found you."

"What are you talking about?"

Chaz held up the paper he was holding. "This is your character sheet. It shows your stats, your skills, the spells you can cast-"

"Let me see that," said Katherine. She set the wood she had gathered on top of the remains of the previous fire, and snatched the paper out of his hand.

"I was wrong about you being an elf," said Chaz. "You're only half elf."

"What's the other half?"

147

"Human." He set the torch to the pile of wood.

"So what does that mean?"

"It means that one of your parents was an elf, and the other was a human. You've probably got some emotional issues."

"About what?"

"About whether you identify more with your elven or human side, about how neither side completely accepts you as one of their own," Chaz paused, and then added solemnly "And there's the possibility that you are the product of rape."

Katherine looked at him incredulously. "Where are you getting this bullshit?"

"Back when I used to play these games, I read some of the novels that were written by-" He was interrupted by Katherine's laughter. "What's so funny?"

"The thought of you reading a book."

"I read a lot of-"

"That fire isn't going to last very long," Katherine said. "We're going to need some more wood. The wood around here is a little damp, but it might catch if we're lucky. See if you can get some of that going, and I'll go forage for some more dry wood."

"Okay, but-"

"We don't have much time. It's going to be dark soon." She stepped back out of the clearing, toward the direction she had come from.

"I read lots!" Chaz shouted after her.

He started to gather some smaller twigs. They were indeed damp, but he thought they might be small enough to burn anyway. He tested a few of them and found he was right. They burned pretty well, in fact, but crackled and popped loudly, and produced an enormous amount of white smoke. Still, a fire was a fire. That leopard wasn't going to cook itself. After he was confident that the fire could handle it, he upgraded from sticks to thicker branches, and then even to some rotted sections of tree trunk.

When the fire got large enough so that he was satisfied that it would continue to burn through most of the night, he stood back and admired his work. Then he walked over to the leopard corpse. This wasn't going to be an easy task. There was some exposed muscle on the leg where the skin had been removed. That would be as good a place as any to start. With some effort, he cut a chunk of flesh off with his dagger, and carefully poked the end of his rapier through it. He sat on a stone upwind from the billowing smoke. He put the end of his sword into the fire and watched the meat start to cook.

This was the first time Chaz was able to really let his mind relax and think about shit that didn't involve immediate survival. He thought about his motorcycle. The rain had let up when he parked it in front of the Chicken Hut, but the weather was fickle that night. He wondered how much time had passed, and if his bike had gotten rained on. A sudden breeze blew through the camp and temporarily flattened the plume of smoke, revealing a face staring back at him. It wasn't Katherine's. It wasn't even human, not even close.

Chaz didn't remember much from his gaming days, but he knew a troll when he saw one. The green skin, the hair like a crop of moss growing on the top of its head, the yellow eyes, all were vaguely familiar. But what really gave it away was the nose, hanging like a dick in the middle of its face past its toothy grin, and even down below its chin.

Chaz immediately stood up and raised his sword at the creature. Both of their gazes fixed on the smoking hunk of meat on the end of it.

The troll rose to its feet with considerably less urgency than Chaz had shown, looking as though it wasn't sure it was worth the bother. Grabbing its spear with both gnarled hands, it hoisted itself up to a hunched standing position.

Chaz had assumed the creature had been sitting on a rock or a stump just like he had been, as they were at even eye level to one another while sitting. It had, however, been sitting flat on the ground, and now that they were both standing, the troll stood a full disgusting head taller than him. If they got far closer than Chaz hoped they'd get, he could imagine the tip of the dick-nose brushing the top of his hair.

Chaz flicked his sword to the side, and the chunk of cooked leopard meat flew off and landed nearby on the ground. He made a mental note as to where it landed so that he could go back for it. The troll licked its lips. It was probably thinking the same thing. One of them would be going back to claim it once the fight was over.

"Hello," said Chaz. His voice was shaky. "Can you... um... talk?"

"Technically, I shouldn't be able to talk to you," said the troll. "I only speak Giant."

Chaz relaxed. For a giant monster with a dick for a nose, it seemed friendly enough. "So why is it you can speak to me?" he asked.

"I just wanted to tell you I'm sorry it had to come to this," said the troll. There was something familiar in its voice, but Chaz couldn't place it. "I have nothing against you, you see," the troll continued. "You didn't offend me like your girlfriend, or her brother and his friends. You were just in the wrong place at the wrong time."

"Who are you?" asked Chaz. The answer was hiding at the front of his mind.

"The thing is," said the troll. "Now that you're here, I can't let you go."

"Wait a second," said Chaz. "Are you that fat fuck from the Chicken Hut?"

"You've just made this a lot easier for me," said the troll. It put the stone tip of his spear into its mouth, grinning and toying with it suggestively with its long tongue as it made small thrusts in and out.

"Um..." was the best way that Chaz was able to express his discomfort. As little as he wanted to see this demonstration, he didn't take his eyes off the troll as he inched his way backwards to where his torch was still sticking out of the ground and burning.

The troll moved with him, inching forward as Chaz inched back. The spearhead was covered with a thick coating of saliva. As if not content with how disturbing it was, it then proceeded to lick and suck on each of its clawed fingers.

Chaz felt the heat of the burning torch on his backside, and swerved around it, hoping that he hadn't just inadvertently made some kind of hip thrust that might be mistaken for a sexually suggestive gesture. Backing behind the torch, he pulled it out of the ground with his free hand.

The spearhead, as well as all of the troll's fingers, were positively dripping with saliva now. Its eyes didn't look the same as they had when it was talking to him. They were savage and hungry. With a speed Chaz hadn't thought it capable of, it hurled its spear at Chaz, piercing him just below his ribcage.

Chaz didn't scream. He couldn't. The physical pain, the terror, and the determination he had to hold on to his wits and his torch kept him from it. Instead he took a long and steady lungful of air, and let it back out with a prolonged "Aaaaaaahhhhh" that didn't rise above normal indoor conversational volume. Sweat abandoned every pore of his body like rats from a burning ship. He dropped to his knees, let go of his sword, and pulled the spear out. The pain of doing so was negligible against the pain of having it in him.

Chaz hadn't ever been stabbed before, but he had a strong suspicion that the pain he was feeling was more than a simple stabbing would have accounted for. This pain was life draining. It probably had less to do with the spear tip and more to do with the thick coating of troll saliva. It hadn't been sexual innuendo after all... well maybe some of it had been. It's not possible to lick the head of a spear without putting images of blow jobs into someone's head, but this troll had really seemed to be going beyond the call of duty. There was obviously some kind of head game at work.

The troll sauntered toward Chaz, rubbing the clawed ends of his fingers together. The sound was like half a dozen pairs of scissors cutting simultaneously. The scissoring sound was fast and frantic, but the troll walked at an unhurried pace, clockwise around the fire.

Fire! That was the troll's weakness. He tossed away his sword in favor of the torch. With more than a little effort, he stayed up on his knees, with one hand bunching his tunic over his wound, trying to keep in as much blood as he could, and the other hand brandishing his torch. He wanted to throw it, do damage from a distance, but doing so would only leave him defenseless. He held it in front of him, hoping that maybe the fire would deter any further advancement.

It didn't. The troll continued to move forward like the second hand of a clock. It actually smiled at the feeble attempt Chaz was making with his torch. "You know," it said, "That isn't going to affect me like you think it is. I'm not a standard troll."

"Don't bullshit me, man," said Chaz. "I know a troll when I see one. That limp dick hanging off of your face is a dead giveaway."

"I didn't say I wasn't a troll," said the troll. "I said I wasn't a standard troll."

"Yeah yeah, I know," said Chaz. "So you can talk. Whoopty shit. You ain't talking your way out of this, buddy."

"I'm a forest troll."

"What is that?"

"It's in the third Monster Manual."

"Do you have every book they ever released?"

"Just about."

"Well what the fuck difference does it make? You're a troll, and you're about to burn. I don't give a fuck what your habitat is."

The troll had paused in both his walking, and the scraping of his claws, when mention had been made of Mordred's book collection. Now he resumed both. "Forest trolls are weaker than their mountain cousins."

"Good," said Chaz with a cough. Blood began to well up in his mouth. He spit out a mouthful. "Then you'll burn even faster." He waved the torch threateningly.

"No, I won't," said the troll. "You see, we may be weaker, but we don't have the same susceptibilities to fire."

"Bullshit," said Chaz. "They wouldn't have made a fire-resistant troll. That's just stupid."

"I'm not fire-resistant," the troll corrected him. "Fire affects me the same way it would affect you. With that little torch, the best you can hope to do against me is something like four hit points' worth of damage, and my fast healing ability gives me back five hit points every round of combat."

"But that doesn't apply to fire damage."

"That's where you're wrong," said the troll. "A standard troll's regeneration doesn't heal fire damage, but my fast healing ability heals fire damage just the same as it would any other type of damage."

"So it's better than regeneration?"

"No. I can't regrow or reattach lost appendages with fast healing like a troll can with regen- What the fu-"

Chaz saw a blur of grey fur leap past him from behind. He fell over, dropped his torch, curled up into a ball, and hoped for the best.

Just outside Chaz's sphere of imagined security, a wolf tore a large patch of skin from the troll's torso. Its intent had obviously been to tackle it right into the campfire, but the troll had been just a little too quick for that. Having failed at its primary objective, the wolf still managed to take a couple of souvenirs with it. One was about half the skin from the troll's chest, including a nipple. The other, unfortunately, was three deep gashes in the side and a good solid dose of troll saliva. They each let out cries of pain.

"Where are you, druid whore?" the troll shrieked into the darkness beyond the campfire's glow.

As Chaz watched, new skin grew over the wound the wolf had ripped in the troll's chest. For a split second, curiosity overtook fear. "Dude, where's your nipple?"

The troll looked down at the fresh patch of skin on its chest. "Hmph," it said. "How about that? I guess nipples count as appendages." It shouted into the darkness. "If you've got anything to say to your boyfriend or your stupid dog, now's the time!" It laughed and spit on the ground. "Neither of them are going to be alive for very much longer!" It paused, but Katherine failed to take it up on its invitation.

It peered into the darkness, but was soon distracted by the sound of a low growl. It turned its head to see the wolf hobbling toward it, bleeding from the claw wounds in its side, but still baring a mouthful of very functional teeth. The troll took a step backward.

"I'm warning you!" the troll shouted into the forest. "Call this dog off. It's not just some fucking pet, you know. This is your Animal Companion. If I kill it while you're hiding behind a tree, you'll never forgive yourself."

The wolf did not back down. It limped slowly toward the troll, lips pulled back, baring teeth which shone yellow in the firelight. The hair stood up on its back as it snarled, growled, and drooled.

The troll took one more step back, and then stopped. "Fine," it said. "I warned you. The despair you are about to feel is very real indeed."

The wolf leaped up for a final desperate attack, and the troll snatched it out of the air by the throat. With one arm, the troll throttled the wolf, digging its claws into the beast's throat until it was wearing a full gauntlet of wolf blood. Any final whine or howl that the wolf might have wanted to exit the world of the living with only came out as a red mist from its neck.

The troll grinned and tilted an ear toward the direction the wolf had come from. There was no gasp. No shriek. No sob. The troll looked disappointed and confused, but not half so much as it did a second later when the wolf's limp body popped out of existence right there in its hand. It stared at its empty clawed hand, grasping a fistful of air and still dripping saliva, but no longer dripping blood.

Understanding dawned on the troll's face, and it nodded a begrudging approval. "I suppose you think you're pretty clever right about now," it said to the dark trees on the perimeter of the camp. "Well guess what. Your boyfriend here isn't going to just vanish into the air when I kill him. He's going to scream and cry and beg for mercy. And what are you going to do? Hide in the trees? Spend the rest of your short life wondering if you might have been able to save him if you hadn't been such a – OW! MOTHERFUCKER!"

The back end of an arrow sprouted out of one of the troll's eyes, and it looked to be having a hell of a time trying to pull it out. Suddenly, another arrow stuck into the smooth, nipple-less flesh of the troll's chest.

Chaz threw up. He wasn't sure if it had been a reaction to seeing the troll with an arrow sticking out of his eye, or thinking about the word 'nipple-less', or the poison in his body. He suspected he might have a fever as well. He wanted to feel his forehead, but needed both arms to hold himself up if he was going to avoid falling face first into his own vomit. There was no excuse for him to be lying here. There would be time enough to throw up after this thing was dead. He pushed back from his vomit and sat up. He looked around for his rapier and spotted it a few feet away. He started crawling on hands and knees toward it when he was knocked over in another rush of gray fur.

The wolf leaped into the air and caught the troll's throat in its jaws. The troll gurgled out what might have been a swear and stumbled backward. Trying to keep its balance, it jerked out the arm holding the arrow in its eye, pulling the entire eye out with it, along with a slimy trail of optic nerve. The wolf tore out the section of throat it had a grip on and pushed itself off the troll, knocking it backward into the fire.

The troll's screams and howls were like daggers in Chaz's

brain. When he was able to pull his gaze away from it, he saw the wolf lying down on its belly, happily gnawing away at troll throat.

The troll made one last effort to crawl out of the fire, but the wolf was having none of it. It bit hard into a foot which was sticking out of the flames and dragged the troll deeper in.

Chaz sat up again just in time to see the troll's remaining eye melt and run down the side of its face. It looked like an egg. Chaz threw up again. The troll's howls eventually gave way to a series of coughs, a gurgle, and then even that was drowned out by the crackle of the fire. The wolf let go of the troll's foot, and it fell lifeless to the ground.

After a moment or two had passed and the wolf continued to stand, growling at the burning corpse, Chaz reckoned that this wolf was the genuine article and took some comfort in the fact that Katherine would be close by. He crawled to the nearest tree and used it to support himself as he stood up.

He looked around, but there was no sign of Katherine. It was too dark, and the light was growing dimmer still. He looked with alarm at the campfire. Troll, apparently, didn't burn like wood. As more skin burned away, more blood, as well as other bodily fluids, leaked out of the fire to challenge the flames.

"Shit," he muttered. He was in no shape to gather wood, so he fell to his knees and looked for anything that might burn in his immediate surroundings. There were pine cones. He cleaned the area immediately surrounding him, hoping that this would keep the fire from going completely out before Katherine brought more wood. Then he scooted over a bit, mindful to avoid his puddles of vomit, and cleared the area around there as well. His efforts didn't seem to be making a huge difference, except that the thick white smoke which carried with it the stench of burning troll also now carried with it a trace of pine. This was of little comfort to Chaz, whose sphere of visibility was growing smaller by the second.

"Butterbean!" came Katherine's voice from the woods.

Chaz wondered, as he lazily chucked another pine cone onto the fire, if he were given an infinite amount of time and paper, and were asked to continue writing what he thought the next word he was going to hear out of Katherine's mouth just a moment ago, how many centuries and libraries' worth of paper he would go through before he came up with the word "butterbean".

The wolf seemed to be less confused by the word. It stood at attention, its ears perked up.

"Butterbean, are you okay?"

The wolf, Butterbean apparently, barked twice in the direction Katherine's voice had come from. Katherine stepped into the fading circle of light a moment later, carrying a bunch of sticks. It just might be enough to keep the fire alive.

"Kat," Chaz panted. "Hurry up. Keep the fire going."

Katherine dumped her entire bundle on the top of the pile, making less effort to keep the fire alive, and more effort to cover the sight of the scorched troll body. She grimaced, looked over at Chaz, and grimaced again.

"Oh my god!" said Katherine. "What happened to you?"

"Do I look that bad?" asked Chaz, bending over to spit out a gob of congealing blood.

"You look like shit."

"I got speared in the chest. I think that troll had poisoned saliva or something."

"Did it lick you?"

"No," said Chaz, "But he sucked on the end of his spear before he put it in me."

"That's kind of-"

"Yeah, I know. I'd rather not think about it right now." He threw another pine cone onto the fire, which was slowly starting to come back to life again. "You'd better go get some more wood."

"Let me take a look at your chest first," said Katherine. "Lie down."

Chaz acquiesced. Something had shifted gears in his head. With the threat of the troll gone, and Katherine here to look after him, the desire for a nice long nap washed over him. His eyelids suddenly became very heavy.

He couldn't have been out for more than half a second when he felt his face being slapped.

"You knock that shit off right now," said Katherine. "We'll get you cleaned up, and when I'm convinced you've got a good shot at waking up again, then you can go to sleep."

"Just five more minutes, mom," Chaz groaned.

Another slap in the face.

"Stay with me, Chaz," said Katherine. "You're really starting to scare the shit out of me."

Chaz shook his head. "Kat?" He looked down at his chest. His shirt was unbuttoned and Katherine was smearing away a coating of half-dried blood, looking for his wound.

"Did you find any water in our bags?" she asked.

"Yeah," said Chaz. "There's a waterskin in each of our bags."

"What the hell is a waterskin?"

"It's like a canteen, but made out of a goat stomach or something."

"That's so gross," said Katherine. "I'm not drinking any water that's been in a fucking goat stomach."

Chaz rolled his eyes, not wanting this to be his last conversation on Earth, or wherever the fuck he was. "It's been cleaned and treated."

"How clean can it be after being in a goat stomach?"

"I'm not talking about the water. I'm talking about the goat stomach." His face wrenched in pain. "It's no more gross than a leather bag, and it's water tight."

"Fine," said Katherine. She scrambled over on hands and knees to their bags and returned a few seconds later with one of the waterskins. She unstoppered the bottle and poured some of the contents onto Chaz's chest. He writhed in agony.

Katherine grimaced. "I don't think that's water," she said. "It's pink."

Whatever it was, it got the job done. She was able to wipe away enough blood to find the small puncture wound in his chest. "Is this what all the fuss is about?" she asked. "It's just a tiny little hole. It's not even bleeding anymore. That's good, right?"

Chaz spoke between deep, concentrated breaths. "There... was... a... fucking... spear... sticking... out... of... me..." He relaxed and closed his eyes. "It may have punctured an internal organ or something."

Katherine sniffed the neck of the waterskin. "If you had an internal organ punctured, you'd know. And you certainly wouldn't be moving around or throwing pine cones." She poured a little more of the liquid on Chaz's wound, letting some of it drip onto her finger tips. Chaz, breathing in suddenly, did sort of a reverse scream. Katherine tentatively touched the tip of her tongue to the tips of her fingers. "You know what?" she said cheerily. "I think this is wine!"

Katherine put the waterskin to her mouth and took a small sip. "Thank fuck, it is! I'll tell you what, Chaz. If there was ever a day when I needed a fucking drink, it's today."

Katherine sat cross-legged on the ground, and rested Chaz's head in her lap. He stared up at her. She took a long pull from the waterskin.

"Aaaahhh…" she said. "That's the stuff."

"Kat?" said Chaz, barely above a whisper.

"Yeah?" Katherine wiped the sweat from his brow.

"Where's your bow?"

"What bow?" asked Katherine. "I don't have a bow. I carry around a fucking farming implement, remember?"

Chaz gave up his struggle to stay awake. His vision blurred then faded then winked out completely.

Chapter 14

Katherine checked Chaz's pulse and the breath coming out of his nose. Content that he had both, she sat back and took a long swig of wine. "Fucking moron," she muttered, and let out a deep sigh.

A moment later, Butterbean let out a low growl, and then a series of sharp barks.

"Fuck," said Katherine. "Now what?" She stoppered her flask, picked up her sickle, and stood up.

Butterbean was peering into the darkness of the forest, his constant growl punctuated here and there by sharp barks. Katherine stood next to him, trying to see anything that looked like it might be cause for alarm. There was, in fact, something... maybe even someone, out there. Yes. It was a person, and they were walking towards her. Was the person really far away? Or was it... yes, it was a child, walking very slowly and cautiously toward them, arms outstretched, holding a small sword unmenacingly in one hand, and a bow in the other.

Katherine narrowed her eyes, unstoppered her flask, and called out. "It's a little late in the night to be bringing a basket of goodies to Grandma's house, don't you think?" She took another swig from the flask.

The figure stopped. Its arms dropped to its sides. "Kat?"

Katherine spit out a mouthful of wine, spraying her forearm and the waterskin. "Shit," she grumbled. "Tim?" she called out. "Is that you?"

"Yeah!"

"Well what are you doing out there? Get over here! I've got booze!"

"Er..." Tim said. "I don't know if you've noticed, but there's a giant wolf standing next to you."

"Oh, right," said Katherine. "Butterbean, shut up!"

Butterbean lowered his head and lay on the ground.

Katherine knelt down next to him. "Oh, I'm sorry, Butterbean. I didn't mean it like that. It's just that he's my brother." She stroked the wolf under the chin, and the look on his face told her that all was forgiven. "Come on over. He won't hurt you."

Tim cautiously closed the gap between them. Butterbean's eyes never left him, and there was still the slight purr of a growl coming from within him.

Katherine gave the wolf a small tap on the head. "Hey," she warned him. "That's enough."

Butterbean whimpered and lowered his head again. The growling ceased.

"He'll warm up to you," Katherine said to Tim. "Now how about you tell me why you are a little kid."

"I'm not a little kid," said Tim. "This is my full adult height. I'm a halfling."

"Is that like a dwarf?"

"No," said Tim patiently. "It's like a halfling."

"Come on, Tim," Katherine pleaded. "Spare me the PC bullshit. I've had kind of a trying day."

"It's not PC bullshit. Halflings and dwarves are two different things. Dave is a dwarf."

"Seriously?" Katherine laughed. "That's awesome." She passed the waterskin to Tim, who gratefully accepted it.

Tim greedily drank down a few gulps of wine. "God I needed that," he said. "Listen, Kat. Can you keep your wolf at-"

"Butterbean."

"What?"

"His name is Butterbean."

"Why did you call your wolf Butterbean?"

"Remember when we were younger, and our parents wouldn't let us have a puppy?"

"Barely. I must have been like four or five years old."

"Butterbean was the name I wanted to call the puppy that we weren't allowed to have."

Tim shrugged. "Fair enough. Listen. Can you keep Butterbean at bay. I'm not alone."

"Oh good. Did you go back for the guys?"

"What? No. You mean you haven't found them yet?"

"Found them?" said Katherine. "We only just got here a little while ago."

"Who's we?"

"Me and Chaz."

"Who the fuck is Chaz?"

"He's my boyfr- He's a guy I've been on a couple of dates with."

"Where is he?"

"He's sleeping. He got hurt by that... what was it? A troll?"

"I think so. Is he okay?"

"He could use some medical attention, but I think he'll pull through."

"You don't sound too concerned."

"Well he's kind of an asshole," said Katherine. "Didn't you say something about not being alone?"

"Oh, right." Tim turned around and whistled. Something shuffled in the underbrush, and he turned back to face her. "And you said something about me going back for the guys. Does that mean you know where they are?"

"Yeah. I think they're in prison or something after trying to break you out."

"What?"

"I'm pretty sure I got that right."

"How the hell do you know all this?"

"A little birdie told me."

"Kat," Tim shouted. Butterbean growled. Tim lowered his voice. "This isn't the time to fuck with me."

"I'm not fucking with you. Okay, so it was an average sized bird... actually it was kind of big, but it talked in a British accent, and it could only understand me if I talked in a British accent. It told me about your friends, and said it was looking for you."

"Where is it now?"

"Who knows. It was kind of annoying. I sent it off to scout the area."

"What smells like troll shit?" asked a voice from behind Tim. Butterbean got quickly to his feet and growled.

A small humanoid creature with red eyes and a batlike face walked up behind Tim. Katherine put an arm around Butterbean, but didn't hold him down very securely.

"Hey hey!" said the creature, raising his arms. "Take it easy! I come in peace. I smell wine. I- Oooh, who's the lovely lady?"

"Tim," said Katherine, standing up, and still holding on to Butterbean very litghtly. "Who- What the fuck is that?"

"Shorty," said Tim. "This is my sister, Katherine. Katherine, Shorty."

"That's your sister?" said Shorty. "You've got a messed up family tree."

"It's a long story," said Tim.

"I'm keen to hear it."

"Now isn't the best time, Shorty."

Katherine, unsure as to whether the little creature was ogling her or the wine she was drinking, took a step back from him and took another drink. She stoppered the bottle to show him, in no uncertain terms, that she had no intention of sharing it with him. She was emboldened by the presence of Butterbean, as Shorty didn't appear to want to come anywhere close to him.

"You've got some nerve calling him Shorty," she said to Tim. "He's taller than you are. Not by much, but still."

"That's his name."

"Actually, it's not," said Shorty. "My real name is Sh'urr Ghareth Marg Sh'urr. Pahalin's guards just started calling me Shorty to make fun of me."

"I'm not sure that's the only reason," said Tim.

"So how did you two meet?" asked Katherine.

"Shorty- Can I still call you Shorty?"

Shorty shrugged.

"Shorty and I met in prison. He was my jailor."

"They've got some lax rules at that prison," said Katherine. "So what's this? A field trip?"

"We escaped together, with- Hey, where's Greely?"

"Oh shit," said Katherine. "What the fuck is Greely? Shorty's pet bear?"

"No. He's just some old dude. Another prisoner. Wait here. I'm going to go see what he's up to."

"Tim," Katherine cried out, but Tim was gone. "Don't leave me alone with-" She looked down at Shorty, who was looking up expectantly at her. "What?" she said.

"You were saying something?"

"Look, I'm sorry. Okay?" said Katherine. "It's just that I've never seen a... whatever you are... before."

"A jailor?" he suggested.

Katherine rolled her eyes. "No... You know..." She waved her hand vaguely in the air.

Shorty looked down at his clothes, and back up at her in alarm. "A vagabond? Because lady, I assure you. Once I find my clan and get cleaned up a bit, I-"

"No," she nearly screamed. "Come on, dude. Don't make me come out and say it."

"Say what?"

"I'm not a bad person. This is all just very new to me."

"My dear, I honestly have no idea what you're talking about."

"Your species."

"My what?"

"Your... you know. Elf, Dwarf, Halfling, Mermaid, Fairy, Leprechaun-"

"Goblin?"

"Okay, sure. Goblin, Gremlin, whatever."

"No," said Shorty. "That's my race. I'm a Goblin."

Katherine lowered her head in shame. "I'm really sorry. I was just telling my boyfr- my er... friend over there how he shouldn't be racist, and now I'm the one-"

"Hey," said Shorty. "Don't sweat it. We are a race who have grown quite accustomed to being despised by others."

"Like Jews?"

"Whose?"

"Oh my God, why did I even say that? I'm just going to shut up now."

"It's all right, dear," Shorty said to Katherine. "Nothing we can't get over after sharing a drink or two together." He licked his lips.

Katherine stopped feeling ashamed of herself, and started feeling disgusted with Shorty. And then she felt ashamed of herself again.

She felt the waterskin in her hand. It was still about three-quarters full. "Okay," she said, and handed it to him.

The goblin accepted the bottle with trembling hands, as if he were forcing himself not to just rip it out of her grasp. He quaffed down wine with noisy slurps and gulps.

Katherine watched in disgust. He seemed to be nothing more than a mass of teeth and lips and tongue attacking that poor goat's stomach. She went to Chaz's pack, opened it, and pulled out his waterskin... nice and full. Shorty stopped drinking and watched her. Seeing the second flask, he smiled and raised his own to her. She raised hers and smiled back, unstoppered it, took a drink, and spit it out.

"Blegh!" she said, trying to spit more out even though her mouth was empty. "What is this shit?"

Shorty raised his eyebrows and frowned curiously.

"This one's got water in it!" she said. "Fuck!"

Shorty pulled his own flask close to his chest protectively.

"Where did they get this water?" Katherine continued raving. "In a sewer? Ew! I can still feel grit in my mouth! I'll probably have tapeworms in me the size of dogs tomorrow!"

Shorty offered a nervous grin and held out the waterskin. Katherine grimaced and shivered. Then she reconsidered, walked over, and took it from him. She wiped the neck with her hand, and poured some wine into her mouth from several inches above it. She handed it back. "Where the fuck is Tim?"

"I'm here," said Tim, walking out into the clearing and doing his best to support an old man who was twice his height and maybe equal his weight.

"Where did you dig up that corpse?" asked Katherine.

"Seriously, Katherine," Tim scolded her. "Not cool."

"How do you do, m'lady?" asked the old man.

"Um... hi."

"My name is Greely," he said, offering a hand to shake. The hand was spotted, misshapen, and ended in the longest and dirtiest fingernails Katherine had ever seen. She briefly touched one finger with the tips of her own index finger and thumb.

"I'm Katherine. Pleasure to meet you."

"The pleasure is all mine."

"You're probably right there."

"Katherine," Tim hissed. "He was in prison with me. He'd been there for years. He's practically been starved to death. Do you have any food here?"

"I think there's a chunk of leopard meat on the ground here somewhere."

"Ooh!" exclaimed Greely. "I haven't eaten leopard in ages!" He fell to his knees and started scouring the ground with much more vitality than Katherine thought possible.

Katherine took the waterskin back from Shorty and had a drink.

"I'm pleased to see you two getting along so well," said Tim.

Katherine looked at Shorty uncomfortably.

"Your fire's dying," said Shorty.

"That's true," said Tim. "We'll want a big fire to ward off anything else that might consider attacking us in the night, and to burn away the rest of that troll. The three of us should be able to gather enough wood quickly enough."

"Three of us?" asked Katherine, looking down at Greely.

"Give him a break, Kat. He's had a hard time. Leave him to find his leopard meat."

Tim, Katherine, and Shorty maintained a tight clockwise spiral around the campsite while gathering wood, and before long, the fire was tall, hot, and strong. The troll's body proved more resistant to just burning into a pile of ash than Katherine had expected, but then she'd never had to dispose of a body before. Once the body had given up all of the liquid it was going to give, the stench cleared up pretty quickly, and the flesh burned away to leave a freakish charred skeleton staring out through the embers at them.

Chapter 15

Dave watched nervously as Cooper paced in his cell. He looked bored. Cooper was known to do some pretty stupid and dangerous things when bored, even in the real world as a human being. The form he was in now was certainly stronger in the physical sense, and quite possibly less wise. The potential for disaster was akin to the potential for getting wet by jumping into a lake.

Julian sat alone in the cell across the hall. He was as still as a statue, his hands clasped together around the sombrero on his lap. He appeared to be asleep even though his eyes were open. Must be an elf thing. It would probably be best to let him rest. He needed it, and the sooner he could re-memorize his spells, the better. Dave looked over at the cell Captain Righteous was sitting in, and could see from the look on the captain's face that he also saw trouble brewing within the bored half-orc. Dave's eyes met the captain's for an instant, and then they each went back to watching Cooper. Dave sauntered toward captain.

"Mind if I join you?" Dave asked.

"Don't get too friendly," said the captain. "The only reason you and your friends are still alive is that I refuse to be coerced into following orders by being locked up like a common criminal. That wasn't part of the contract. That said, I don't care where you sit."

Dave's short, stout legs weren't going to enjoy sitting on the stone floor, and his heavy armor was going to make it difficult for him to stand up again, but he was tired. He sat down and leaned against the wall.

"You know," said Dave, nodding in Cooper's direction. "Cooper isn't such a bad guy."

Captain righteous looked in the direction Dave was nodding. "The half-orc's name is Cooper?"

"Yeah, and I'm Dave."

"I don't care what your name is, dwarf. What kind of name is Cooper for a half-orc? Does he make barrels for a living?"

"Um... I don't think so. Why do you ask?"

The captain closed his eyes.

"Listen," said Dave. "Like I was saying, he's not a bad guy. He's-"

"He's a cold-blooded murderer. You all are."

"He's really not though. He's actually got a pretty big heart once you know him well enough to see through the rough exterior. He had kind of a hard time growing up. His parents split up when he was very young. But that's not-"

"His parents?" Captain Righteous gave Dave his full attention for the first time. "Split up? Surely that abomination is the product of a vicious rape. Or do you mean to tell me that his orc father and his human mother were lovers once, who shared a quiet little cottage with a nice garden out front?"

"The truth is actually less believable than that."

"I don't believe you."

"Ha," Dave smiled. "I see what you did there."

Captain Righteous did not smile. "I don't know why you bother trying to defend your beast friend over there. You're in as much trouble as he is. The lot of you are going to hang."

"Let's put all that aside for now," said Dave. "We have a more immediate concern on our hands." He looked over at Cooper.

The captain followed Dave's line of sight. "I'm listening."

"Cooper has always been impetuous, short-tempered, and kind of... well, stupid isn't exactly the right word... Never mind. You know what I'm getting at. But now he's also immensely strong."

The captain narrowed his eyes at Dave. "What do you mean by 'But now'?"

"He's getting restless. He's bored, and he's trapped, and I think he might pose a threat to the safety of himself and others if we don't do something about it."

The captain shrugged. "We're all trapped. What do you propose I do about it? Tell him a bedtime story?"

"That's not exactly what I had in mind."

"Well then?"

Dave leaned in and whispered. "I think we should try to lock him in his cell."

The captain snorted contemptuously. "A truer friend there never was. Fine. It's as good an idea as any."

"Okay. Here's what I was thinking. I'll go to the next cell over and call him over to talk. While I've got him distracted, you pull the cell door closed."

"All right. That sounds simple enough."

Dave walked over to the corner cell adjacent to the one Cooper was pacing in. He pretended to be interested in the bodies of several dead rats, prodding one here and there with his mace. When he reached the corner, he called out in a loud whisper. "Cooper. Get over here. Check this out."

Cooper, desperate for any kind of stimulus, took the bait without question. He walked over to the bars opposite of where Cooper was standing, and looked down at the section of floor Dave was looking at. "What am I supposed to be looking at?"

"You'll see soon enough," said Dave.

"I see a dead rat. What about it?" Cooper's cell door slammed shut. "Huh?" Cooper turned around to face the door. Captain Righteous was holding it shut.

"Shit!" exclaimed the captain. "Where's the damned key?" He was shouting at Dave.

Cooper turned around to look back at Dave, who offered an apologetic frown. Cooper's face, on the other hand, wore the simple expression of 'I'll deal with you later.' He turned his attention back to the captain and two of his men who had come to help hold the door shut. He took a step in their direction.

"I'll only warn you once," shouted the captain with more than a hint of desperation in his voice. "Just stay where you are. Do you hear me?" The three men continued to hold the door.

Cooper didn't halt his advance. When he arrived at the door, he looked down at his arms, and then at the cell door. He gripped the door with both hands by the bar closest to the hinges. His arms, legs, and back muscles all flexed simultaneously, and after a series of metallic pops, the captain and his men found themselves holding a cell door which was no longer connected to a cell. Cooper, without a word to anyone, lay down on the cot and closed his eyes.

Captain Righteous and his men carried the broken door away and leaned it against a wall.

Dave bent down on one knee and whispered to Cooper through the bars of the adjacent cell. "Hey, Coop?"

Cooper opened one eye, which Dave mistook for him being

willing to listen. Dave smiled. Cooper sent a fist through the bars right into Dave's nose. Pain exploded into Dave's face as if Cooper's fist had gone straight through it. He heard his nasal bones crunch from the inside of his head. Liquid salty warmth ran from his nose to his lips, thickening in his moustache and beard. He fell over backwards, and landed on the body of a dead rat. He shrieked and rolled off of it, trying to hop to his feet as quickly as he could. He slipped in a puddle of congealing rat blood, his feet went up in the air, and he landed backwards, almost entirely on his head. His helmet made the difference between a mere concussion and a severe skull fracture.

Cooper closed his eyes.

The guards laughed. Even Captain Righteous let slip a small grin as he closed his eyes and lowered his head. Through all of it, Julian didn't even stir. He just continued staring out at nothing.

Not ready to attempt standing again just yet, Dave scurried back over towards Cooper on his hands and knees, just beyond what he judged to be the range of Cooper's fist. "Okay," he said. "I deserved that. I just saw that you were bored, and I wanted to keep you from starting any shit and getting us all killed."

Cooper didn't respond. He didn't even open an eye.

"Fine," Dave went on. "Sit there and sulk. But I mean really, dude. You're massively strong now. Think about some of the stupid shit you've done when you were bored before, and think about if you did something similar now. You would totally be throwing cars around, and people would totally be getting hurt. Just look at what you did to that door, and you were barely-" He paused, and leaned in close enough to risk another punch in the face. He lowered his voice to a whisper. "Hey, if you could break open that cell door so easily, who's to say you couldn't just smash your way through the main door up there?"

Cooper opened an eye. "It's worth a shot," he said, and started to get up.

"No," said Dave, his whisper loud and urgent. He looked up to see if anyone was paying attention. Julian was still deep in some glassy-eyed coma. Captain Righteous supervised his men in the task of moving rat corpses and wiping up blood. The guard called Darren rested in a bed with his leg propped up. Dave's spell had stabilized his wounds, but came one or two hit points short of healing him entirely.

Dave softened his whisper as Cooper lay back down. "If we succeed, those guards are going to turn on us. We're only going to get one shot at it. The three of us need to be ready to haul ass out of this place as soon as the door falls. And it would probably be wise to wait until you can do your rage thing again to heighten the odds of success. Get some rest."

"No," said Cooper.

Dave was sure that this was the best plan, and Cooper was going to fuck it all up. "Listen," he pleaded, but Cooper cut him off.

"You get some rest," said Cooper. "We'll need your healing. I"ll keep watch."

"But your rage," objected Dave.

"You need rest to replenish your spells," said Cooper. "The book doesn't say anything about me needing rest to replenish my rage. It's just a straight up once per day thing."

"No," said Dave. "Wizards need rest. I just need to wait until dawn."

"Oh right," said Cooper. "Then fuck you. I'm going to sleep."

A few minutes later, Cooper was snoring. Dave started to feel sleepy as well. He looked around for something to keep his mind off of sleep. Julian was no help, still in his trance. He didn't reckon he'd get much conversation out of Captain Righteous or any of his men. His eyes were heavy. It wouldn't hurt to just rest them a bit. Just a bit.

He came to with a start. One of the soldiers was standing over him.

"Fitful sleep?" said the soldier.

Dave scrambled up to his feet. He still had his mace in hand. That was good. He looked around the guard to see that Cooper was still snoring. He turned toward Julian, who had come out of his trance and was flipping through a book spread out on his lap. "Julian," he said, and braced himself against the wall to keep from falling back down. He spit out a gob of bloody phlegm. His broken nose was throbbing. "Are you all right?"

Julian looked up. "Yeah." He went back to his book.

"Don't worry," said the soldier standing over Dave. His smile revealed a mouth full of mismatched teeth. Some were crowned in silver or gold. Even the natural ones were different shades of brown, yellow, and various shades of something that Dave would never describe as white. "The Captain has some sort of qualm 'bout killin' a man in his sleep. We was ordered not to harm yous. Myself, I got no such hang-ups, but what's a man gonna do, right?"

Dave circled cautiously past the soldier and edged toward the cell door, never turning his back on him until he was outside. He went to the cell Julian was sitting in. "Julian," he whispered.

Julian raised a finger. "Just a second," he said. He ran a finger on his other hand across the page he was reading. "I just want to finish this... er..." he looked around at the guards, and then up at Dave. "... chapter."

"Oh, right," said Dave.

The guard in Dave's cell slunk out of it and walked over to where his own men were.

When Julian's finger reached the bottom of the page, he looked up. "What's up?"

"How long was I out?" asked Dave.

"Dunno," said Julian. "I went into a trance again. I've only been aware for the last half hour or so."

"Was that enough time to get all of your... um... reading done?"

"Yeah. What happened to your face?"

"Cooper punched me."

"Why did he do that?"

"I kind of deserved it. Never mind that. Do you know what time it is?"

"No. How would I know that?"

"Do you think it's after midnight?"

"I honestly have no idea. Why? Do you have somewhere you need to be?"

"Yes," said Dave, attempting some innuendo with his eyebrows. No hint of understanding shone in Julian's eyes, so Dave spelled it out for him. "On the other side of that door. We may have a plan for getting out of here."

"What is it?"

"Cooper is going to punch through the door."

"I think 'plan' is kind of a generous word for that," said Julian.

171

"What's that got to do with the time?"

"Cooper will need his rage to maximize his chances of getting through the door. He can only use that once per day, so we have to wait until it's a new day before he can use it again. Midnight will be a new day."

"That's so fucking stupid."

"It is what it is," said Dave. "Can you think of any way we can figure out what time it is?"

"Why doesn't he just try to rage. If it works, we'll know it's after midnight. If it doesn't work, we can wait a little while and try again."

Dave was shocked that the same idea hadn't occurred to him. "Brilliant. Let's go get Cooper."

Dave and Julian did their best to look casual as they walked to Cooper's cell, but Dave could feel the eyes of the guard with the colorful set of teeth looking at him. He chanced a look over his shoulder, and found he was right. His wasn't the only set of eyes watching them. Every guard who was awake was staring at them.

"Wake the captain," said the guard with the mismatched teeth.

Dave shook Cooper, who immediately punched him in the face again.

"Ow!" said Dave, burying his face in his hands. "Fucking hell! I thought we were cool."

Cooper sat up. "What's going on?"

"It's time to go," said Julian. "It looks like they might be on to us. We're just going to have to hope it's after midnight."

Dave wiped some fresh blood onto his knees. "Just try to look casual." By the time they had taken two steps toward the entrance to the cell, the captain was awake and the tension was too thick to bear. "Fuck it," he said. "Run!"

"What's going on?" asked Captain Righteous. "Stop them!"

"Okay, Coop," said Dave. "Can you rage? How do you feel?"

Cooper closed his eyes. "I'm really angry," he muttered to himself. "I'm really angry. I'm really angry. I'm really..."

"Is it working?" Julian asked Dave.

"I don't kn—"

Dave was interrupted by a roar like that of a dragon who had just stepped into an enormous bear trap. The first two guards to step out of their cell had their hair blown back with the force of the roar. They cowered back into their cage.

"I think it worked," said Dave.

"Get them, you cowards!" shouted Captain Righteous, pushing past his guards and drawing his sword.

Cooper ran past Julian and Dave, bounding toward the steps leading up to the thick wooden door which blocked their escape.

Dave and Julian hurried to follow, but stopped at the bottom of the stairs. "We'll have to stall them," said Dave, holding up his mace.

"With what?" asked Julian.

Captain Righteous's men organized themselves into a battle formation. Two rows of three men, shields held tightly together and swords drawn. They marched forward.

"With anything that comes to mind," said Dave. "If you've got some magic to use, now would be a good time."

Julian waved his hands in the air. "Horse!" he shouted.

"What?" asked Dave. His answer came as a long, white face staring back at him. It whinnied.

"Stay," said Julian.

Above them, Cooper was slamming fist after fist into the door, but making little perceivable progress.

The soldiers stopped, looking confused by the sudden appearance of a horse's hindquarters in their path. The horse shit on the floor in front of them, and then kicked back a leg, leaving a solid dent in the armor of one guard, and knocking him into the man behind him.

"Enough of this!" shouted Captain Righteous, stepping over his fallen men. He brought his sword down and cut the horse's other hind leg down to the bone. It collapsed in whinnying agony.

"Nyeeaaahhh!" Julian and Dave shouted in unison. They turned their eyes away from the flailing horse. Captain Righteous ended the beast's misery with a swift slice down the neck. Blood poured out and pooled all over the floor. The horse stopped its crying and kicking almost immediately. As suddenly as it had come into being, the horse, the blood, all of it, vanished into a small puff of white hair.

The captain took a step toward Dave and Julian, who were backing away from him. "You know, I didn't want to do that. I'm actually quite fond of hors-"

He was interrupted by the sound of Cooper smashing a fist into the wooden door. The smashing sound was accompanied by a sharp crack. Dave wondered if that was from the door or the bones in Cooper's arm. Neither looked to be phased from his vantage point.

Julian summoned another horse, right in front of where the first one had just vanished.

"Oh come on man," said Dave. "That's seriously not cool. You're supposed to ride those, not use them as meat shields."

Captain Righteous and one of his men had to jump into cells on either side of the hallway to avoid getting slammed with wild hooves. The captain thrust his sword between the bars of the cell and into the horse's abdomen. The horse screamed and bucked loud and hard enough to throw off the other guard's aim. He had been trying to stab the horse from the other side, but he didn't have as good of an angle on it, and missed entirely.

Julian and Dave caught up to Cooper, who was still wailing away at the door in bloody-fisted fury. A strictly visual observation of the door would have revealed none of the progress that he was making, but with every pound of Cooper's fist, there came the creaking and moaning sounds of wood, iron, and stone rubbing against each other. Something was giving way. Dave hoped that Julian's doomed horse would hold out longer than this doomed door.

Dave turned around just in time to see Captain Righteous stab the horse again. It was a deep thrust, and one that Dave was sure the horse would never recover from, even if the fighting stopped now. The captain pulled out his sword, and a torrent of blood gushed out after it. The horse didn't have a whinny left in it. Left to its own devices, it would have been dead six seconds later. But it was the captain's last remaining man, the one with the colorful teeth, who finally connected with the beast and brought it down. The horse disappeared. He and his captain stepped out of their cells.

"Coop!" shouted Dave. "They're coming!"

"Should I summon one more horse?" Julian asked.

"No!" said Dave.

Cooper braced his body by taking hold of the arched stone roof above his head, and gave the door a good solid kick with his heel. There was a clank and a thud on the other side of the door, made all the more audible by the fact that the door was now slightly ajar.

"Did it work?" asked Julian, still not taking his eyes off of the two men who were stepping carefully over horse shit and urine, which had not, unfortunately, disappeared with the horses. "Did he really break that beam?"

"I don't think so," said Dave, pushing the door all the way open. "Fuck me," he took a moment to admire Cooper's handiwork. "It looks like he tore the beam supports right out of the wall."

Cooper let out another roar. The sound of barbaric victory reverberated throughout the entire manor. Captain Righteous and his man halted their advance in amazement at such a roar, but quickly resumed once Cooper had finished. The only other response Dave heard was the yelp of a small dog, and a muffled screech from upstairs. Dave, Julian, and Cooper headed in that direction, not because they were looking for anyone else to fight, but because upstairs was clearly the only way out of the dungeon level.

Halfway up the stairs, Dave heard the sound of a cabinet door slamming shut somewhere up ahead of them. "We'd best be on our guard."

Cooper led the way through the door at the top of the stairs, followed by Julian, and Dave closed the door behind him. It had a small lock that wouldn't keep their pursuers occupied for long.

They hurried out the door and down the hall, and found where it opened up to the living room on one side, and the kitchen on the other. Cooper ran through the living room toward the front entrance of the manor. Halfway through he slipped, flew backward through the air, and came down with a nasty crack of the skull.

Cooper rolled over onto his belly. He was lying in a yellowish stream which ran across the length of the living room floor, beginning as a trickle through the closed, trembling doors of a cabinet.

"Are you okay?" asked Dave.

"Yeah," said Cooper. "Just my head. Nothing to worry about."

"What is that?" asked Julian crouching down to help Cooper to his feet.

Cooper touched his tongue to the puddle on the floor. "Pretty sure that's piss."

"Maybe we should-" he was interrupted by the sound of a booted foot smashing through a door.

"Shit," said Dave. "They're coming. Let's go."

Neither Cooper nor Julian hesitated to run after Dave through the front door.

The sky was black and starry. There were no guards posted outside, but they didn't fancy their chances of outrunning the two that were chasing them, not with Dave's short legs and heavy armor in the party.

"Do you have any horses left?" Cooper asked Julian..

"I've got two," Julian answered. "That is, if I want to give up my Magic Missiles."

"Fuck your Magic Missiles," said Cooper. "We need to get out of here."

"Fine," said Julian. He pulled out a pinch of horse hair from a belt pouch. "Horse!" he shouted, and blew the hair from his palm. It materialized at once into a small horse."

"Okay," said Cooper. "You two get on that one, and I'll get on the next one."

Julian put his foot in the stirrup and hopped up quickly into the saddle.

"I can't get up there," said Dave.

"For fuck's sake," said Cooper. He bent down and cupped his hands together.

Dave stepped into Cooper's hands, and Cooper hoisted him up onto the horse, who gave a small groan.

"This is never going to work," said Dave in a panic. "I'm going to fall off."

"Just hold on to me," said Julian. "Hold on tight."

Dave didn't need to be asked twice. Julian mimicked the horse's groan.

The sound of boots stomping on wood directed their attention through the open front door of the manor. The captain and his man were coming up the stairs.

"There they are!" the captain's voice bellowed from the hallway past the living room. The two men started to run.

"Hurry the fuck up," said Cooper impatiently.

"I can't reach my pouches," said Julian. "Dave! Loosen up a bit, man."

Cooper readied himself and his axe. The captain and his man were moving too fast. Even if Julian was able to conjure up this horse right now, he still wouldn't have time to mount it before they got one attack in. If they killed the horse, a fight to the death would be inevitable.

Dave loosened his grip. "Come on, Julian," he muttered.

Captain Righteous charged at full speed through the living room, eyes locked on Cooper. So focused was his attention on Cooper that he completely failed to notice the growing yellowish puddle on the floor. His feet slipped out from under him, and he might have done a full back flip if his subordinate hadn't been right behind him to absorb most of his inertia. The two of them spent a moment, regaining their bearings and flailing around in a puddle of pee.

Julian found the pinch of horsehair he had been searching for. Dave felt himself starting to slip off the back of the horse and hugged Julian tightly, squeezing the breath out of him.

The horsehair blew out of Julian's hand as he croaked the word "horse."

It was enough. A second horse appeared, and Cooper mounted it with ease.

"Um..." said Julian. "Go, horses." The horses did as they were bid. Dave squeezed Julian even tighter. They were only able to get the horses up to a slight trot without Dave seriously being at a risk of falling off.

For now, that was enough. They just wanted to put as much distance between themselves and their pursuers as possible.

Chapter 16

Tim passed around what little food he had stolen from Pahalin's manor, putting a portion aside for Chaz for when he woke up. Greely and Shorty passed on their portions, as they were content with leopard meat.

Tim approached Katherine, who was standing over Chaz. "He doesn't look so good."

"It's that stupid costume," said Katherine. "He's actually pretty hot in real life."

Tim sighed. "I was talking about his health. If we don't get him some help, I don't know if he's going to make it. That spear wound looks pretty rough. The skin is getting dark around the edges of it."

Katherine bit her lip. "Can you think of anything we can do about it?"

Tim shook his head. "Not until we find Dave. He can probably heal him. For now it's probably best to just let him sleep. You should sleep too. I'll keep watch." He called out to Shorty and Greely, who were arguing about where the best meat was on a leopard. "You guys get some sleep too. We've got a big day tomorrow."

Shorty and Greely wasted no time taking Tim up on his offer.

Tim paced around with an arrow nocked in his bow, thinking about how much easier it was to keep watch when it was just a game. You just declare what watch you're going to take, and you're told whether or not anything happens during that time. Two or three hours of game time pass by in a second. But this was real time. Mind-numbingly, exhaustingly, life-sapping real time. He sat down against a tree.

He woke up an indeterminate amount of time later to the sound of a loud screech from above. If he hadn't known any better, he would have sworn the screech sounded like "Hey!" He jumped to his feet, tried to shake the sleep out of his head, and looked up just in time to see a giant black mass of feathers swooping down toward him. Instinctively, he fired an arrow at it.

The black feathered mass fell out of the air with a cry of pain cut short by hitting the ground.

"Son of a bitch!" it screamed, looking at the arrow sticking out of its wing.

There was no mistaking it this time. There was a giant black raven standing in front of Tim, glaring, and it had just sworn at him.

"Shit," Tim offered apologetically, remembering to speak in a British accent.

"Shit yourself!" the bird screamed back. "This hurts, you know."

"Look, I'm sorry, okay," said Tim testily. "But you really shouldn't just sneak up on people like that."

"Sneak?" said the bird incredulously. "Why do you think I shouted 'Hey!' before I came down here?"

"I must have dozed off," said Tim. "I thought you were-"

"Who gives a fuck what you thought?" asked the bird. "Are you Tim?"

"Yeah," said Tim. "And I guess you're Ravenous?"

"Ravenus," the bird corrected.

"That's what I said."

"No, you said ravenous."

"And what did you say?"

"Ravenus, as in 'raven' plus 'us'."

"It's kind of a silly name."

"Sillier than Tim?" Ravenus let out a caw that sounded like a mocking laugh. "How did your parents know you were gay right out of the womb?"

"Hey fuck you, bird," said Tim. "There's nothing wrong with my name."

Ravenus let out an unintelligible screech at Tim, and Tim responded with his middle finger.

"Dude, what's with the noi- aaaaauuuuuggggghhh!" said Chaz. He opened his eyes and looked over at the fire. "Fuck, we're still here?" He looked down at his wound. "Jesus fuck, what's happening to my skin?" The dark patch around the wound had grown.

Katherine walked bleary-eyed over to Tim. "What's going on?"

She yawned, rubbed her eyes, and looked down. "Oh my god! What happened to you?" she asked Ravenus.

"Timberly here shot me."

"It's Timothy," said Tim.

"It's Fuckhead," argued Ravenus.

"You shot Jonathan's pet?" Katherine asked her brother. "Why the hell did you do that?"

"My master's name is Julian, and I'm not his fucking pet," demanded Ravenus. "I'm his familiar."

"You're getting quite a mouth on you," said Katherine. "You've been hanging around Cooper too long." She turned to Tim. "Why did you shoot him?"

"It was an accident," said Tim.

"Yeah," said Ravenus. "His arrow just sort of fell out of his hand."

"He came out of nowhere," Tim defended himself. "I thought he was attacking me."

"Would somebody mind taking this arrow out of my wing?" asked Ravenus.

"Oh, right," said Katherine. "I'm sorry. I'll get it."

"I'd rather he do it," said Ravenus.

"What difference does it make?" asked Tim. "I'm sure she's going to be more gentle than I am. Look at my giant hands and stubby fingers."

"Yeah, but if it hurts coming out, I'm going to bite the shit out of you."

"Fine, you little cocksucker. Come here." Tim walked over to Ravenus, got down on one knee, and tried to figure out the best way to pull the arrow out while causing the least amount of pain. The head of the arrow was barbed, so it wouldn't do to pull it out the way it went in. The fletching was bound to the shaft pretty tightly, and would be hard to remove, and probably uncomfortable going through the wound.

Then an idea occurred to him. "Okay," he said. "Hold really still."

Ravenus held still, but Tim could still feel him quivering.

As carefully and deliberately as he could, Tim broke the tail off the arrow and pulled the shaft through. "There you go."

Ravenus exhaled. "That wasn't so bad." Then he quickly bit

Tim's arm. It drew a small bead of blood.

"Ow!" Tim screamed and pulled back his arm. "What was that for, you ungrateful little shit?"

"Because fuck you, that's why!" Ravenus let out a wild caw and tried to fly to the safety of a tree branch, but only got in two flaps off the ground before the pain in his wing reminded him that he wasn't going to be doing any flying anytime soon. He smacked head-first into the trunk of the tree and fell to the ground. Katherine suppressed a giggle. Tim didn't.

Ravenus looked as pissed off as any bird that isn't an eagle is able to look.

"Where have you been?" she asked. "You've been gone for hours."

Ravenus lowered his head and kicked an acorn with one of his talons. "I met a nice young female raven, and... well, she was impressed that I could speak elven."

"You mean to say you were fucking this whole time?"

Ravenus lifted his wings in a shrug, flinching slightly at the pain in his wounded wing. "I'll just say that my cloaca is at least as sore as my wing."

"Nice," said Tim.

"Ugh," said Katherine. "Well the good news is that I'm not hungry anymore." She stomped back toward the others. "Fucking men, all alike." Then she stopped in sudden recollection and turned around. "You were supposed to be scouting the area to warn us of any danger!"

Ravenus stood up tall and proud. "I have nothing to report. The area is secure."

"We were attacked by a fucking troll while you were away!"

"Oh," said Ravenus, lowering his head. "I'm sorry." He picked his head back up. "Well, at least no one was hurt."

"My boyfriend was hurt!" Katherine shouted back at him. "He was hurt badly."

"Wait a second," said Ravenus. "Are you talking about that guy with the silk pirate shirt?"

"Yes."

"That guy's your boyfriend?"

"We've been on a couple dates."

"I wouldn't have thought he swung that way," Ravenus mused.

"So he still has his junk?"

"What?"

"His... I don't know what they're called on humans. His baby makers?"

"Balls?" suggested Tim.

"If you like."

"I'm really not comfortable discussing this with you," Katherine said.

"I'm sorry," said Ravenus. "Just curious."

"Then you should ask him."

"Oh..." said Ravenus with a hint of embarrassment in his voice. "So you two haven't actually... um..." He bobbed his head forward twice.

Katherine gaped down at the bird. "I'm seriously not talking about this. In fact, I really would rather not talk to you at all for a while. The next time you talk to me, I want it to be after you apologize to Chaz for the hole in his chest that he got because you were too busy fucking some floozy crow."

"Raven."

Katherine made like she was going to kick Ravenus, and he closed his eyes and lifted his good wing in defense. Katherine stomped off toward Chaz.

"Sheesh," said Ravenus. "I mean, I get where she's coming from, but... well, a guy like you can probably understand."

Tim looked down at Ravenus curiously.

"Before tonight, I've never had a lot of luck with the ladies, if you catch my drift."

"And what makes you think that I..." Tim sighed. "Never mind. I catch your drift. I probably would have done the same thing."

"Your sister's kind of a bitch."

"Yeah."

"Nice tits, though, if you don't mind me saying so."

"Actually, I'd rather you not."

The two of them stood in awkward silence for a moment until Tim spoke up.

"So..." he said. "Julian, Cooper, and Dave are all locked in that prison?"

"Yeah," said Ravenus. "They went to rescue you," he added.

"I know," Tim snapped.

"They're probably due to be hanged at dawn".

"I know!" Tim was nearly shouting. Neither of them said anything for a few moments, and then Tim went to join the others. Ravenus hopped along behind him.

"Hey, listen guys," said Tim. Katherine turned around, and Chaz lifted his head slightly, wincing in pain. Shorty and Greely were sleeping again. Tim gave them each a series of small kicks until they were awake. "Since we're all awake,-"

"Asshole," said Shorty, rubbing his eyes.

"We should probably be heading back to Algor to rescue the guys."

"What, now?" asked Katherine. Chaz lowered his head.

"Yeah," said Tim, knowing the response wouldn't be a popular one.

"Look at him," Katherine said, pointing to Chaz. "He's in no condition to walk. He's barely alive as it is."

"Then we'll have to either split up or leave him here," said Tim. "Dave is a cleric. He's this guy's best chance of recovery."

"No," said Katherine. "I think the best thing we can do is to stay together and try to figure out a way to get back home. Once we get back to the Chicken Hut, we can beat the shit out of that fat fucker until he brings back the other guys."

Tim cocked an eyebrow in consideration. "That sounds good," he said. "But they don't have that kind of time. They're going to be hanged in the morning."

"For what?"

"Cooper chopped off some dude's head."

"What the fuck?"

"It was before we got here."

Katherine looked confused. "You mean back at the Chicken Hut?"

"Yeah."

Katherine continued to look confused. "Cooper murdered a guy at the Chicken Hut?"

"No," said Tim, exasperated. "We were playing the game, before shit got..." He waved his hands around gesturing at everything around him. "... real."

"Okay," said Katherine, uncertainty heavy in her voice.

"It's role playing," Tim said. "We were sitting around at the table in the Chicken Hut, pretending to be these characters, and Mordred was describing the scene. He played the character of everyone that wasn't us—"

"What a bunch of fucking losers—"

"We were denied entrance to a city, and Cooper took the reason as being racist. So he-"

Katherine perked up. "Is Cooper black now? I mean, his character."

"No," said Tim, as patiently as he could. "He's a half-orc."

Katherine pursed her lips in thought. "Which half?"

"What?"

"I mean, is he like a mermaid?"

"Fucking hell," said Tim. He closed his eyes and tried to get back under control. "He's the offspring of a human parent and an orc parent. Just like you are a half-elf."

"Who would want to fuck an orc?"

"It's a good bet his human mother was raped by an orc."

"Oh," said Katherine. She glanced down at Chaz. "There's a lot of rape in this game."

"Anyway," said Tim. "What with it being a game and all, relatively free of any real life consequences, and with Cooper being kind of an idiot, he decided that the best way to combat racism was cold-blooded murder. It seemed funny at the time."

"You guys are sick."

"I guess Mordred didn't find it too funny," Tim continued. "He and Cooper rubbed each other the wrong way from the get-go. Anyway, after that we ended up here, with the entire city guard chasing us."

"Look, Tim," said Katherine. "I'm really sorry about your friends. But we have to get back home. We can't go breaking into prisons and fighting guys with swords. We could really get hurt. Dead even."

"They're in there because they were trying to rescue me," said Tim. "I'm not going to let them die." He knew Katherine wasn't too bothered about letting his friends hang, so he tried to think of an argument she could relate to. "Besides, we don't know how to get back home, or if it's even possible. If we're going to be stuck here, we would be better off with those guys. It's dangerous around here. You know that much already. We need them. Cooper is as strong as all of us put together. Dave can heal us, and believe me, we'll need some healing. Julian is... well, he's still finding himself, but he's got a lot of potential... and a talking bird"

"So what do you propose we do then?" asked Katherine. "Just waltz in there and beat down anyone who gets in our way?"

"That's normally our default plan," said Tim. "It's a bit of a walk to get there though. Maybe we'll think of something better on the way."

"And what about Chaz?"

"Leave Butterball with him. He'll be okay."

"His name is Butterbean," Katherine snarled at him. "And he goes where I go."

Tim thought. "What about Shorty and Greely?"

"You want to leave Chaz in the protection of a decaying old man and a gremlin?"

"Goblin."

"Whatever."

"Finding Dave might be Chaz's only hope for survival."

"You keep saying that," said Katherine. "I don't understand. Did Dave go to med school here or something?"

"He's a cleric."

"Yeah, I've heard. What the fuck is a cleric?"

"It's sort of like a priest."

"In my experience, when a person is dying, and they call for a priest, it usually means the fucker's on the way out."

"A cleric can heal wounds with a prayer and a touch."

Katherine narrowed her eyes.

"As far as the game is concerned, it's just another sort of magic. Just like how you summoned a wolf out of thin air."

Katherine's expression changed. He'd finally given her something she could understand. "Okay, fine. Do you think they'll go for it?"

"I'm pretty sure they don't want to head back into town and risk winding up back in prison again. I got the feeling that Shorty was going to bolt off into the woods by himself as soon as we started packing up to leave. I can't blame him for that."

"If you can talk them into staying, I'll go with you."

"Deal."

Tim walked over to where Shorty and Greely had fallen asleep again, and nudged them with his foot until they woke up.

"What?" snapped Shorty. "I had more peace in prison!"

"Guys," said Tim. "I need to ask a favor of you."

Shorty sat up with a glum and serious look on his wide face. He blinked his eyes a couple of times, and looked up at Tim. "Listen," he said. "I was going to wait until the morning to tell you this. We're not going with you. I know you helped us escape, and I'm indebted to you for that, but not so much as to risk being put right back in there."

"I know," said Tim.

"Oh," said Shorty, caught off guard. "Then what is it?"

"My sister and I have to go back. I need you two to stay here and look after Chaz while we're gone."

Shorty looked over at Greely, who didn't seem to be paying any attention. He looked back at Tim. "And what if you don't come back?"

"Then do your best to take care of him until he gets better."

"What if he dies?"

"Fuck," said Tim. "I don't know. Bury him I guess."

Shorty pursed his lips and looked to the side. "Can we... um... eat him?"

"Fucking hell," said Tim, and looked back at Katherine. Her agreement to go with him was balancing atop a very narrow fence. His mind scrambled to find ways to diffuse the shitstorm that was about to erupt. But no shitstorm erupted.

"As long as you promise to wait until he actually dies," she said. "I don't want you killing him beforehand."

"Of course not!" said Shorty indignantly. "What kind of savages do you take us for?"

"Jesus, Kat," said Tim.

"What?" she asked innocently. "I told him not to kill him. But if he's dead, who gives a shit whether his remains are eaten by worms or goblins?"

Tim shrugged. "Fair enough, I guess." He looked up at the sky, or at least the little patches of it that were visible through the treetops. "We'd better get moving. We don't know how long we've got before morning."

Tim and Katherine gathered their bags. They didn't bother to wake Chaz. He needed his rest. In the off chance that they were successful and really lucky, they might be able to return before he woke up anyway. Butterbean walked alongside Katherine, and Ravenus, unable to fly, perched on Tim's shoulder. They walked to the edge of the woods and out into the grass until the road was visible.

"We'll travel faster on the road," said Tim.

"But won't that make us more exposed?"

"Exposed to who?"

"I don't know," said Katherine. "Monsters, bandits, the city guards?"

"We're at more risk in the forest for monsters. I don't think bandits would be operating this close to the town. And as for the city guards, well... if we're going to end up fighting them anyway, it's probably best that we take down a couple out here, so there won't be as many there."

"I don't know if I'm going to be able to kill a person."

"I don't know that either," admitted Tim. "We'll just have to do our best and hope it doesn't come to that."

They hadn't been walking up the road ten minutes when Butterbean started to growl. He was staring straight up the road into the darkness.

"What's wrong?" Katherine asked.

"Stop," said Tim. "Shut that dog up."

Katherine knelt down and put her hand on Butterbean's head. She stroked his fur, and he stopped growling. "What is it?"

"Shhh!" Tim listened. "Horses, coming this way."

"How many are there?" Katherine whispered.

"I'm not sure," said Tim. "More than one. Less than five. Probably a night patrol or a search party or something."

"Search party?" asked Katherine. "What would they be searching for?"

"Me."

Katherine's voice shook. "What do we do?"

"Don't worry," said Tim. "We took out a troll. We can handle a couple of first level guards on horseback. That's not our problem."

"What is our problem?"

"We want to have as much surprise on our side as possible when we get to the town," he said. "The last thing we need is for these guys to ride back and warn the others that we're coming."

He looked to one side of the road, and then to the other. They were well out of any cover the forest could provide, but there were still a few scattered trees growing close to the road.

"Come on," said Tim, grabbing her arm and pulling her off the right side of the road.

"What are we doing?" she asked. "Tell me you have a plan."

"I have a plan." He dragged her by the hand past one tree and behind another a little farther away.

"Is it a good plan?" she asked.

"It's the only plan I've got," he said. "Hindsight will judge its merit. Stay here. Try to keep out of view."

"Where are you going?"

"Not far," said Tim. "Just back to that tree we passed on the way here. You'll be able to see me."

"Shouldn't we be fighting with you?"

"No," said Tim abruptly. "Not at first anyway. I'm going to sneak attack one of their horses."

"That seems like a pretty shitty thing to do."

"If we take out their horses, they won't be able to ride back and warn the others."

"All right, fine," said Katherine, but her tone suggested that she was not at all fine with it.

"When I fire that first shot, I'll have given my position away. Feel free to jump in anytime after that."

"Okay."

"Remember," said Tim. "Take out the horses first. You might even get lucky and pin one of the guys under his horse."

Katherine didn't respond, but Tim couldn't afford to waste any more time. He placed Ravenus on the ground next to Katherine and crept back toward the other tree. It was about twenty feet away from the road. He was going to have to wait until the horsemen were almost on top of him before he would be able to use his sneak attack bonus. It would be worth it though.

Only two horses, by the sound of it. And while they were moving too fast to be searching for something, they didn't seem to be in a terribly urgent rush, either.

Tim sat back against his tree and took out his bow. He shoved the points of two arrows into the ground, so they would be readily available to fire from where he was, and felt behind his back to make sure he knew exactly where to reach for the arrows still left in his quiver. The first shot was going to make all the difference. The horses were getting closer with each passing second. He wiped his palms on his pants and crouched down behind his tree, facing away from the town in order to fire his arrow just after they passed rather than just before. He closed his eyes. He was in the Chicken Hut, playing a game with his friends. He was just rolling a plastic twenty-sided die. That was all. It was just a game. He opened his eyes, gripped his bow, nocked his arrow, and waited.

Chapter 17

"Come on guys," Dave whimpered. "Can't we slow down a bit now. I think we've got enough distance between us and them." He was hugging Julian more tightly than he needed to, in the hopes that if he squeezed enough air out of the elf, he might be more inclined to take a break.

"Stop whining," said Cooper. "Just keep your eyes open for that wrecked wagon. When we see that, we can stop riding and look for Tim. It shouldn't be too much further."

"But my balls are killing me," Dave groaned. The magically summoned horse had only come with one magically summoned saddle, which Julian was sitting in. Dave was riding bareback behind him, constantly in danger of slipping off the rear of the horse and getting a hoof in the face.

"Fuck your balls," said Cooper. "We'll be there soon."

They rode on in relative silence for a few minutes. Dave tried to concentrate on the rhythm of hooves on the road. So focused was he in his concentration that he was lying face down in the road on top of Julian before he was able to mentally register the fact that their horse had vanished from beneath them.

Cooper's horse ran another thirty yards before he managed to turn it around. "What the fuck? What happened to your – wha!" Cooper's horse blinked out of existence, and he fell to the ground.

"Get off of me," Julian groaned.

Dave rolled off of Julian and on to his back. Julian sucked in a great lungful of air. Dave was dazed, but otherwise not too badly injured. His armor had protected his arms pretty well, and Julian had done a good job of breaking his fall. He sat up and looked curiously at an arrow lying in the road. "That's odd," he muttered to himself. "What's that doing th- Holy Shit!"

A wolf bolted out of the darkness and tackled Dave. Dave grabbed it by the neck and struggled to hold back the mouthful of snapping teeth trying desperately to bite into his face.

"Fucking hell, Dave," said Cooper. "Is your fucking underwear made out of bacon?"

"Help me!" Dave screamed.

Cooper raised his greataxe into the air, catching a gleam of moonlight on the massive blade.

"Cooper!" a voice rang out from the side of the road. "Stop!"

Cooper turned to look. "Tim?" He lowered his axe.

"Dammit, Kat! Call off Buttercup!"

"What?" said a woman's voice. A vaguely familiar face peeked out from behind a tree. She saw Cooper and screamed. "Canis Lupus!" she cried, and Cooper suddenly had a wolf gnawing at his ankle.

"Ow!" he said, and kicked the wolf in the face. It let out a yelp, landed on its back, righted itself, and growled at him just before it vanished.

"Will someone please fucking help me?" Dave shouted. The wolf's teeth were dripping with blood, and Dave's forearms were torn to shit.

Julian had only just managed to sit up. "Methylchloroisothiazolinone!" he shouted, pointing a finger at the wolf. A glowing, sparkly arrow shot out of Julian's fingertip and struck the wolf in its upper hind leg. The arrow disappeared into a whiff of smoke and burnt fur.

The wolf let out a small yelp and looked angrily at Julian, baring its red fangs and drooling pink tinted saliva.

"Call him off, goddammit!" Tim shouted at his sister. "That's Cooper and Dave, and... Julius!"

"Julian!" Julian shouted.

The wolf poised to lunge at Julian.

"No, Butterbean! Stop!" shouted the female voice.

Butterbean did as he was commanded, but continued to growl at Julian. He backed away, keeping the three of them in his field of vision.

"Come here, boy!" the woman shouted.

The wolf hesitated, but finally started to step further back.

"It's okay," the woman said soothingly. "They're friends."

Dave took a good hard stare at her. She was wearing a leather cloak with an antlered hood. Aside from her long pointed ears and almond shaped eyes, she could almost pass for –

"Katherine?" said Cooper

"When I told you to go fuck an orc, you really went the extra mile."

"Is that your wolf?" asked Dave.

"This is Butterbean," said Katherine. There was a cold edge to her voice.

"Fucking animals," Dave grumbled, holding up his bleeding forearms for her to see.

"What's up with your arm?"

Dave looked down at his leopard-spotted furry arm, and quickly hid both arms behind his back.

"Welcome back, boys," said Tim. "We were just on our way to go find you. You look like shit."

"To be fair," said Dave. "I have been mauled by wild animals twice in as many days. More than that, actually, if you count being kicked by a magical horse."

"Ouch," said Tim.

Cooper snorted and a blob of green snot shot down onto his chest. Katherine winced in disgust.

"Sorry," said Cooper, wiping the snot off with his finger and trying unsuccessfully to flick it onto the ground. "I've got a Charisma deficiency."

"No shit."

"How did you get here?"

"Presumably the same way you did," she said. "That fat bastard you guys invited into our place of business sent us here.

"Mordred!" snarled Cooper. He pulled the head out of his bag.

Katherine screamed and clapped her hands to her face. Butterbean lunged forward and bit Cooper squarely between the legs.

Cooper dropped the head and his bag, and his body hit the ground soon after.

"Kat!" Tim yelled. "Katherine, please calm down. Call off the wolf. Please! I can explain."

"You can explain that?" she cried, pointing to the head. "You guys are fucking animals! Everything they said about this game is true. Oh my god, what am I doing here?" Tears streamed down her face.

"Get it off! Get it off!" Cooper screamed.

"Come on, Kat," Tim begged her. "Just hear me out."

Katherine stopped crying long enough to whistle, and Butterbean came back to her.

Cooper was crying now as well. "Fucking dog bit my dick off," he said, rolling around on the ground in agony. Blood seeped out from below his loincloth.

"I'll give you one minute," Katherine said to Tim angrily. "And if you can't provide me with a good enough explanation as to why you are totally cool with your friends carrying human heads around in their bags, then-"

"Then what?" asked Tim. Dave guessed it was meant to sound challenging, but it came out sounding hopeless. "What will you do? Leave? If you know how, then by all means lead the way. We all want to get out of here, Katherine. Just calm down and listen to me."

Katherine sat down and hugged Butterbean. She kissed him on the top of his head, extra praise for biting Cooper in the balls. "I'm listening."

"Remember when I told you about how we got in trouble because Cooper chopped that guy's head off?"

"Yeah."

"Well that's the head."

"I could have figured that much out by myself," she said. "It doesn't explain why you guys are carrying it around. What is it, a fucking trophy?"

"Don't be silly," said Tim. "We're not barbarians." Cooper groaned. "Okay, well technically, he is. But that's not why he's carrying it." Katherine's expression did not soften. "It's a conduit," he said.

"You had better start using words I can understand before I turn your tiny prick into wolf shit."

"Sometimes Mordred communicates with us through it."

"Mordred? You mean the guy back at the Chicken Hut?"

"Yes," said Tim. "The guy who sent us here."

Katherine wiped away her tears. "Show me," she said.

"Show you what?"

"The head. Turn it on or whatever. I want to talk to him."

"It's not a fucking walkie-talkie. You can't just turn it on at will."

"Then how does it work?"

"He chooses when he wants to talk to us," Tim explained. "I mean, you can try to talk to him. Ask him a question or something. But if he doesn't want to talk to you, it's not going to happen."

Katherine looked down at the head. It lay on the ground next to Cooper, facing away from her. As she approached, Cooper crawled backwards away from her on his elbows, looking as though he was making an extreme effort not to pass out from the pain.

"Dave!" he shouted. "Where the fuck are you?"

"I'm right here," said Dave. "What do you need?"

"What do I need?" he asked, as if he couldn't believe the question had been asked. "I need my fucking scrotum reattached!"

"Oh, right," said Dave. He placed his hand on Cooper's forehead. "I hea..."

"That's not where I was bitten," said Cooper between agonized gasps of breath.

"Dude, I'm not touching your balls. The spell will work." He refocused his mind. "I heal thee!"

Katherine laughed and shook her head. "I so don't belong here. I should be down at Bar Bones right now having scummy men buy me Mojitos. But no. I'm here, in some strange fucking woods with my little brother and his geeky friends, wearing antlers on my head, being attacked by giant monsters and passing around a booze-filled goat stomach with..." She stopped, her eyes and mouth frozen wide open.

A faint glow shone from the point where the palm of Dave's hand rested on Cooper's forehead. Cooper's eyes closed and his breathing became heavy. A small moan escaped his mouth. His shoulder and arm muscles began to twitch. His fists clenched shut, and a spasm of pain rippled through his face. His hands opened suddenly, and his mouth widened into a grin. He began to laugh. It was a shaky, but sincere laugh. The kind of laugh your heart makes after you bet money you don't have bluffing with a pair of fives and win. The skin on his knuckles, split open from pounding on the door of the jail, grew and fused back together. The wave of spasms continued down from his chest to his abdomen, and then below it.

Cooper let out a roar that shook the leaves on the trees. Katherine took a cautious step back, and even Butterbean cowered behind her. That was probably for the best, because Cooper evacuated his bowels in a spray that would have reached both of them otherwise. The spell coursed down his legs and sparked out at the tips of his big toenails.

The roar ended, and Cooper lay on the ground, panting, and cupping his freshly healed balls with his freshly healed hands.

"What did you do to him?" Katherine asked Dave.

Dave stood up. "I healed him." He touched each of his index fingers to the opposite forearm and whispered the words again. "I heal thee." The wolf bites melted away.

"Really?" Katherine kicked Cooper, who was still rolling around on the ground with his hands on his crotch. "Hey, Cooper. You okay?"

Cooper's eyes were still shut tight, and tears flowed back toward his ears. "Just let me savor the moment a little longer."

"You know, you shit yourself."

"Yeah," said Cooper, letting out a long exhalation. "I know."

"Chaz needs you, like right now," Katherine said to Dave.

Ravenus also addressed Dave, but Dave only received it as a series of ear-splitting squawks and caws.

"Oh great," said Dave. "Look who's back. Julian, can you shut your bird up, please?"

"He just wants you to heal him," said Katherine. "Tim shot him in the wing."

"Nice one, Tim," said Dave. "Next time aim for the beak." He stopped. "Wait a second, you guys can understand him too?"

"Sure," said Tim. "He's actually pretty cool when you get to know him. He's got quite a mouth on him when he's angry though."

"I'm glad you made a new friend," said Dave. "But let's get our priorities in order. We need to band together and stay alive until we can figure out a way to get back home, agreed?"

They all nodded.

"I'm limited in my capacity to heal," Dave continued. "I don't want to sound cold-hearted, but I think we need to put the needs of our human... well, I guess human isn't exactly the word... our companions that came from our world, the real world, before the needs of our avian friends."

Scowling, Julian picked up Ravenus and placed him on his shoulder.

"Listen Julian," Dave said, trying to sound sympathetic. "I know you care about the bird, but this Chaz guy is one more in the party that could help us survive a fight, and –"

"Actually," said Tim. "Ravenus is a pretty good scout. Also, Chaz is a bard."

"A bard?" said Dave as if he'd been punched in the gut. "Seriously?" He turned to Julian. "All right," he said. "Let me see the bird."

A couple of minutes later, Ravenus was flying around, cawing joyfully and darting through the treetops.

"Shit," said Julian, wincing and wiping bird shit out of the bleeding claw marks in his shoulder. "Next time Ravenus needs healing, remind me to put him on the ground first."

Cooper stood up and picked up the severed head. He looked at Katherine. "We can give this a try after we take care of your... um... friend."

"I'm sorry," said Katherine. "Could you please... how do I put this delicately?... go away?" She was visibly trying to hold back a gag. "It's just that the sight..." Tears welled up in her reddening eyes. "...and the smell of you makes me want to vomit."

"Yeah, sure," said Cooper, shoving the head into his bag and skulking away.

The group made their way back to camp. A starved old man and a little creature, no bigger than Tim, crouched over the prone figure of a man dressed in colorful silks. The little creature ran a long, thin finger through the man's shiny golden hair.

"Ahem," said Tim.

"Shit!" snapped the little creature, jerking its hand back. "That was... um... fast."

"How's he doing?"

The creature shrugged. "Same as before. You guys find your cleric friend?"

"Is that a goblin?" asked Dave.

"Oh," said Tim. "Yeah. Dave, Shorty. Shorty, Dave. And this is Greely."

"Are you the cleric?" asked Shorty.

"Um... yeah," said Dave, stepping into the light of the fire. "Stand back and let me take a look."

"He's all yours." Shorty and Greely went to sit down by a tree on the other side of the fire.

Dave knelt down next to the man in the colorful clothes. He was sleeping fitfully and sweating. Dave opened his shirt.

"Who are your friends?" Cooper whispered to Tim.

"A couple of guys I broke out of prison with."

"I can heal the wound," Dave announced to the group.

"Okay," said Katherine, hopefully. "Good."

"But," said Dave. "There appears to be more wrong with him than a simple puncture wound. What did you say did this to him?"

"A troll," said Tim.

"Bullshit," said Cooper. "There's no way a first level druid, a second level halfling rogue, and a fucking bard are going to take down a troll. What did he do? Lull it to sleep while you slapped it to death with your dick?"

"It wasn't a regular troll," said Tim. "It was a forest troll or something."

Dave looked up. "A forest troll?" He thought for a moment. "Are those the ones who have the poisonous saliva?"

"Oh Oh!" shouted Katherine excitedly. "He mentioned something about saliva before he fell asleep. Something about the troll going down on the spearhead before it stabbed him."

"Well," said Dave. "That's that, then. I think he took some Constitution damage. Quite a bit from the looks of it. The good news is that I can patch up the wound. I won't be able to do anything about the Constitution damage though. He's just going to have to rest for a couple of days and let it work its way out of his system." Dave placed his palm on Chaz's forehead and closed his eyes. "I heal thee."

Chaz's body shuddered briefly, though there seemed to be no pleasure running through it. His head fell to one side and he threw up. None of this interrupted his sleep.

"I've done what I can," said Dave. He lifted Chaz's shirt to show everyone that the wound had healed.

"Nice work," said Tim. "We might still have a couple of hours before the sun comes up. We should get some rest. I'll stay up and keep watch."

"Take a load off, little guy," said Cooper. "We all got enough rest tonight in the dungeon. We'll keep an eye on things."

"Thanks," said Tim. He walked over to his bag, collapsed to the ground, and fell asleep almost instantly.

Katherine walked over to where Cooper was sitting.

"Um, Cooper?"

Cooper turned around and looked up at her. He had one finger lodged up to the second knuckle in his nose. Seeing Katherine, he quickly removed his finger and sucked it clean. Katherine suppressed another gag, and Cooper ashamedly put both hands behind his back.

"Sorry about that," he said. "It's my Charisma score. I just can't help doing things that other people find extremely gross or offensive."

Katherine closed her eyes and steadied her breathing. "Well," she forced a shallow laugh. "You were always kind of gross and offensive."

"Is there something you wanted?"

"I want to talk to Mordred."

Cooper looked over at Dave and Julian.

Dave shrugged. "Why not?"

Cooper pulled the head out of his bag and placed it on the ground facing up at Katherine.

"Fire away," said Cooper.

"What?" asked Katherine. "I just talk to it?"

Cooper shrugged and nodded.

"I found it helped to have it at eye level," said Julian. He picked up the head and walked over to the tree he'd been standing near when he had summoned Ravenous. He wedged it into the forked branches. "There you go. Now just pretend it's alive and connected to a body."

Julian stepped back, and Katherine eyed him dubiously. She looked at Cooper and Dave, who were staring back at her expectantly. She turned back and faced the head.

"Hello?"

The head gave no response.

"Hello in there!" she shouted. "Anybody home?"

Still no response.

She turned around. "Are you guys fucking with me?"

They all shook their heads.

"Because if you are, I'll sic my wolf on you."

They all crossed their legs, but maintained that they were not, in fact, fucking with her.

Katherine approached the head, moving slowly and cautiously toward it. "Mordred! I want to talk to you." She moved in even closer. "I know you're in there, and I'm not going away until you talk to me." She moved closer still, searching for any sign of awareness in its cold, dead eyes.

Cooper lowered his head, anticipating what was going to happen next.

Katherine whispered. "Mordr-"

"Greetings, Shazanna!" said the head in the tree, eyes wide and grinning broadly.

Katherine screamed and jumped back. She took a moment to regain her composure, started to say something, and then stopped. "Who the fuck is Shazanna?"

"Why you are, of course!" said the head. "What do you think of your character? Were the antlers too much?"

"What is going on here?" she asked. "Why am I..." She waved her arms around, grasping for the right word. "...Shazanna?"

"It was a pregenerated character. I always keep a few on hand in case there are any surprises."

Katherine got right in its face and shouted as slowly and clearly as she could, like an idiot trying to communicate with a deaf person. "I don't know what the fuck you're talking about!"

"I'm sorry," said Mordred. "Did you need something explained?"

"Yes!" shouted Katherine. The head looked patiently at her. "Why did you send us here? What do you want from us?"

"Me? All I wanted was to play a game." The face wasn't smiling anymore. "Your brother and his friends are here because they'd rather act like clowns than play the game properly. You are here because you are a big bitch. Your boyfriend is-"

"He's not my boyfriend."

"Whatever," said the head. "It's regrettable that he got mixed up in this. He might have actually wanted to play the game rather than just get drunk and clown around."

"Wait a second," said Katherine. She actually started to laugh. "This is just about you being pissed off because some guys made fun of you?"

"What else would it be about?"

"I don't know," said Katherine. "I thought maybe you needed us to retrieve the Magical Ring of Social Adequacy from the Haunted Island of Skullfuck and bring it back to you or something."

The head in the tree seethed as she spoke, right up until the very end, when it smiled. "Back?" it said. "Whoever said anything about coming back? Nobody's coming back."

"What do you mean?" asked Julian. "What about when the game is over?"

The head's eyes looked at Julian. "You don't get it yet, do you? This game doesn't have an ending. It's not like checkers. You're in a different world, and you're going to be in it until you die. So make the best of it."

"What happens when you go to sleep or go home or whatever?" Julian went on. "Surely you aren't going to hang out at the Chicken Hut running the game until we all die, are you?"

"Whether I'm here or not, the world you're in will keep going. "I just control things when I'm around. You'll really want to be careful when I'm gone though."

"Why's that?"

"Because when I'm running the show, I like to keep things level appropriate. It makes the game more fun if neither side is guaranteed victory. You're all still very low level. There are creatures in these woods that you are being protected from right now. But when I leave, my protection goes with me."

The light of consciousness went out of the eyes.

Katherine confronted Dave, Julian, and Cooper. "What the fuck did you guys say to him?"

Cooper scratched his head. Dave bit the corners of his moustache.

Julian spoke up. "I think Cooper told him to suck his big black menhir."

Katherine looked at Cooper. "What the fuck does that even mean?"

Julian started to explain, but Katherine cut him off. "Never mind. I don't care. I think this is all bullshit. He's not going to let us die here over some childish insult. He's just trying to scare us, teach us a lesson. After he's had his fun, we'll be back in the Chicken Hut, and he'll be halfway across town."

200

"I don't know," said Dave. "I mean, if you're a guy who manages to acquire a set of real magical dice that can transport your perceived enemies to another world without any repercussions... I mean, that kind of power must go to your head."

"I don't buy it," said Katherine. "No one is that big of an asshole. He's just a fat loser who got his feelings hurt and wants an apology."

"I already apologized to him," said Cooper.

"Yeah," snapped Julian. "Right before you told him to suck your menhir."

"What the fuck is a menhir?" asked Katherine.

"It's a-"

"Shut up."

"Ahem," said Mordred. The group turned around to find the head alive again and looking down at them. "You'd do well to take me seriously."

"If you want to be taken seriously," said Cooper, "you'd do well to stop wearing a cape."

The others laughed.

Cooper doubled over in pain. A stream of shit ran down the inner parts of his legs, and he fell to the ground, clutching his stomach.

"What the hell is wrong with you?" Katherine shouted at the head in the tree. "Were you rejected by the girl in high school who slept with the chess team and the janitors?"

"No, Katherine," Cooper struggled to say between agonizing cramps. He breathed in and out a couple of times, and Katherine looked down at him with unmistakable compassion on her face. "Don't... blame... yourself..."

Julian and Dave started to laugh. Cooper might have been laughing as well, or he might have been having a seizure. It was hard to tell. Katherine walked over and kicked Cooper as hard as she could in the gut. He threw up. Katherine jumped out of the way of Cooper's vomit, and Cooper moaned as he lay sprawled out on the ground.

"You know," said the head in the tree. "You aren't the first group I've sent over there. If you don't yet realize the gravity of the situation you're in, you can ask them just how much of an asshole I can be. If you survive long enough, you're bound to run into some of them eventually."

Cooper continued to lie on the ground. Dave, Julian, and Katherine looked back at the head in silence. The head in the tree grinned wickedly. "That's right. Now you understand." He let it sink in some more, and then switched to a businesslike tone of voice. "No, you aren't the first I've sent over, but I think you might be my favorites. I'll tell you what I'm going to do. I'm going to grant you a full night's peaceful and uninterrupted sleep, and when you wake up, you'll have all of your spells and abilities refreshed and ready to go."

A tear rolled down the side of Katherine's face.

"Oh stop it, sweetie," the head mocked her. "You're going to make me cry. Not enough? Okay, I'll go one further, but this is really stretching the bounds of my generosity. All of you who haven't made it to second level yet, I'll just go ahead and give you the points you need. How's that? Feel better? Good. Sleep tight." Once again, the head lay dull and vacant in the tree.

Cooper stood up. "Hey, don't worry, Kat. We'll talk to the others about this in the morning. We'll figure something out."

Katherine looked up at the sympathetic face of the half-orc and broke into a convulsion of sobs. Maintaining the presence of mind to seek out a spot relatively free of filth, she buried her face in his chest.

Cooper did his best to avoid the uncomfortable antlers trying to poke him in the face and patted her head with a giant clawed hand. "Come on, guys," he said. "We should get some sleep while we can."

"We're supposed to be on watch," said Dave.

"Mordred said he was going to give us a pass for the night," said Julian.

"Do you trust him?"

"Good point," said Cooper. "He might just up and decide to kill us all in our sleep or something."

"If he wanted to outright murder us," argued Julian, "why wouldn't he just send a giant dragon down to eat us all right now?"

"That's a fair point," said Dave. "But I'm not going to give him the opportunity to catch us all asleep. You guys go sleep if you want to. I'm going to stay up."

Over the course of the next hour, after everyone else had fallen asleep, the previous night's restlessness began to take its toll on Dave. His eyelids grew heavy, and Julian's reasoning started to make a whole lot more sense.

He leaned his back against a tree and slid down. His ass had barely touched the ground when sleep washed over him. It was deep and dark and dreamless.

Chapter 18

The sun had been up for a few hours when the rest of the camp started to stir. Rays of sunlight beamed through the forest canopy as grunts, yawns, joint-crackings, and groans disturbed the tranquility of the morning. They had made it through the night unmolested. Whether that was due to blind luck or Mordred keeping true to his word, Julian didn't know. He knew that it wasn't due to Dave's diligence. For all of his talk, he hadn't even lasted four hours, which was how long it took before Julian came out of his nightly trance.

"What's cooking?" asked Cooper as he walked toward the still blazing fire, licking his lips and cracking his enormous knuckles.

"I did my best to salvage the rest of that leopard," said Julian, scraping a chunk of cooked meat onto a large piece of bark that had a couple more pieces already on it. "It smells pretty awful, but it's all I could come up with."

"Smells great to me," said Cooper. "I'm starving." He popped a piece of meat into his mouth and went to grab another.

"Uh uh," said Julian. "I was barely able to scrape enough meat off for everyone to have one piece. You've just finished your breakfast."

"How am I supposed to –"

"Blegh," said Chaz. "What's that smell?"

"Breakfast," said Julian. "Leopard meat."

"I'd rather starve."

Cooper looked at Julian hopefully. "Can I have his?"

"No," said Julian. "I was able to salvage a couple of large pieces of leopard skin. Why don't you go see if you can make something with those?"

"Like what?"

"I don't know. Towels or something."

"Does anyone have any wine left?" asked Katherine, staggering toward the fire. "My head is killing me. Oh, hey Chaz. Good morning. How are you feel- Fuck! What is that smell?"

"Leopard meat," Chaz responded. "That's our breakfast, apparently."

"I'm not eating that shit," said Katherine. "Butterbean!"

The wolf ran up to Katherine eagerly.

"Come on, boy. We're going to go catch us some real breakfast." She and Butterbean walked into the woods.

Tim yawned and rubbed his eyes as he woke. The he sniffed the air. "Jesus Christ, what's that-"

"Fuck you," said Julian. "It's breakfast. If you don't like it, don't eat it."

Tim caught a brief glance of his sister before she disappeared into the trees. "Where's she going?"

"Leopard meat isn't good enough for her," said Julian. "She thinks she's going to find something better."

"She's going alone?"

"She's got that wolf with her."

Tim shrugged. "Hey, Chaz. Good morning. How are you feeling?"

"Shitty."

"Shittier than yesterday?"

"No," said Chaz. "Better than yesterday. Fuck. Better by miles. But still kind of shitty."

"Hang in there," said Tim. "Dave said you took some Constitution damage."

Chaz looked up in alarm. "Shit!" he said. "I'm a bard. My hit points are low enough as it is."

Tim laughed. "Relax. He said it'll come back to normal after you get a couple days' rest. Did you see your spear wound?"

"Huh?" Chaz looked down at his chest. "Fuckin-A! Who healed me?"

"Dave."

"Where is that dude? I've got to thank him." He started to get up, but Tim put his hand on his shoulder and gently pushed him back down.

"You need rest," said Tim. "I'll get Dave." He stood up and turned to Julian. "Where's Dave?"

Julian shook his head and glanced at a nearby tree. Dave lay face down, fully dressed in his armor, on the other side of it.

Tim walked over and nudged him with his foot. "Hey Dave!"

Dave started to pick himself up. His face and beard were covered in dirt.

"Did you sleep like that?"

"Huh?"

"It doesn't look very comfortable."

Dave wiped some dirt from his eyes. "What's that smell?"

"Leopard."

Dave yawned. "It smells like Cooper's asshole."

Tim laughed. "Yeah, I know. Don't mention that to Julian."

"I'm right here, dickheads," said Julian.

Dave shook his head. "Dude, we've got to talk."

"What about?"

"No," said Dave. "Not just me and you. Everybody."

"Well Katherine went out to look for something else to eat."

"Thank fuck."

"What's this about?"

"We talked to Mordred last night."

Tim pursed his lips and nodded. "All right. Let's get everyone together."

"Greely!" shouted Tim to the old man he had brought to camp with him. "Would you mind pissing a little farther away from the camp? It's bad enough we've got Cooper shitting all over the place."

Julian glanced at Cooper. He didn't appear to have taken any offense, or even show any acknowledgement of what Tim had just said at all.

"Sorry!" the old man shouted back. "I'll be more—" He stopped and sniffed the air. His eyes darted around, and soon locked right on Julian's. "That's my leopard!" He tied the cord on his threadbare pants and stomped toward Julian with what might have been murder in his eyes.

"What?" asked Julian, taking a step back.

"None of you wanted it yesterday, and you said I could have it!"

"We've all got to eat," Julian said, trying to stay calm. "It's the only food we've got."

Ravenus flapped around over Greely's head. Julian sensed the bird was ready to attack if this confrontation turned physical. "What's going on?" he squawked.

"Holy shit!" shouted Dave.

Julian and Greely stopped arguing. Everyone turned to look at Dave. Even Shorty sat up, rubbing his temples.

"What's up?" Tim asked.

"I can understand the bird!" Dave shouted. A shiny-toothed grin shone through his dirt-matted beard.

"Who gives a shit?" said Shorty, and lay back down.

"Yeah," said Cooper. "I mean, that's cool and all, but I've got to agree with the little guy on this one."

Dave's excitement was not lessened in the slightest. He responded first to Cooper. "Don't you remember, you giant stupid fuck?"

"I'm sorry," said Cooper, twisting his pinky finger in his ear. "I didn't quite catch that. It sounded something like 'Please punch all of my fucking teeth out.' Was that right?"

"Last night!" Dave continued. "When we talked to Mordred."

"Yeah?" said Cooper, giving his knuckles another good crack. "What about it?"

"Don't you see?" said Dave. "That's why I can understand the bird. I got some extra skill points that I put toward learning elven. We leveled up!"

Cooper's face brightened. "Oh yeah, that's right!"

"Everybody check your character sheets!" shouted Dave, looking for his bag.

It wasn't long before everyone had pulled their sheets out of their scroll tubes, and were reacting to what they saw. Everyone, that is, except for Shorty and Greely. Greely took the opportunity to steal all of the leopard meat while the party was distracted.

Dave frowned. "Four lousy hit points?"

"Four isn't too bad for a cleric," said Cooper."

"I have a Constitution of 17," Dave complained. "That's a plus three bonus. That means I rolled a 1."

"Oh yeah," said Cooper. "That blows." Then he yelped with excitement, looking at his own character sheet. "Sweet! I got eleven more hit points. That puts me up to 26!"

"I didn't level up," said Tim.

"About that," said Dave, suddenly far less enthusiastic than he had been. "Mordred said he was bringing us all up to level 2. You were already there, so I guess you didn't get any charity points."

"What a shithead," said Tim. "I really can't wait until we get back." He pounded his fist into his open palm. "I am going to beat the shit out of him."

"Um... Tim," Dave said quietly. Tim looked up at him. "That's something else Mordred talked about last night. He said we're never coming back. And I um... I think he meant it."

"What do you mean never?" asked Tim. "You mean never never?"

"Yeah," said Dave. "He said we're going to die here."

"That's just tough talk," said Tim. "He's just trying to scare you."

"I don't think so," said Dave.

"Let's just wait until Katherine gets back, and we'll have a group discussion about it," said Tim.

"All right," said Dave. "I'm going to go and figure out what spells I should pray for today."

"I still don't get that," said Julian. "If you don't worship any particular god, then who do you pray to?"

Dave shrugged. "I just pray."

"You'd better go do whatever you've got to do to get your spells ready," Tim said to Julian.

Julian picked up his spellbook and found a relatively quiet spot where he could concentrate. The only spells he had to prepare in advance were his wizard spells. He picked Magic Missile again without even thinking about it. He liked that spell. The end result wasn't as awesome as he had hoped it would be when he read the description, but he liked the tingle in his fingertips and the crackle of magic running through his forearms just before the release. An extra Magic Missile might make a big difference, but he still resented the fact that he had to spend fifteen minutes memorizing the same gestures and incantations that he'd already memorized a number of times before. He didn't bother choosing any zero level wizard spells. That would have added another forty-five minutes to his prep time, and the payoff from those shitty spells wasn't worth the time. If he needed any zero level spells, he'd have enough as a sorcerer.

Sorcery was a lot easier than wizardry. In the same amount of time it took to memorize that one lousy Magic Missile spell, Julian could have his entire host of sorcerer spells, a total of five zero level spells and four first level spells, ready to go. The best part was that he didn't even have to choose which ones he wanted beforehand. No, the best part was not having to rely on that giant goddamned book.

And so a total of only thirty minutes had passed by the time Julian finished all of the preparation he intended to do. He walked back to find Chaz strumming lazily on his lute. Tim was chucking pine cones into the fire. Cooper was chucking pine cones at Ravenus, who was dodging them with ease.

"Knock it off, Cooper," said Julian. Cooper spat on the ground and threw another pine cone. Ravenus turned his head to watch it fly by a foot away from him.

Tim looked up. "Finished already? That was fast."

"Dave's not finished yet?"

"Nah. He's going to be at it for another half hour at least."

"Cooper was right," Julian admitted. "I should have been a sorcerer from the beginning. Wizardry kind of sucks."

"They both have their advantages and dis –"

"Help!" shouted Katherine.

Tim and Julian jumped up at once. Julian noted with some surprise that Cooper did not stop throwing pine cones at Ravenus, and Chaz didn't miss a single note on his lute. Then it came to him. They hadn't heard the scream. Their ears weren't as sensitive as his and... shit. Tim was gone.

"Cooper!" Julian shouted. Cooper threw a pine cone at him, and missed by a long shot. "Katherine's in trouble."

Cooper's face turned serious. His tusked underbite was even more pronounced than usual. "I'll get my axe."

Chaz put down his lute and propped himself up on one elbow.

"Stay here, Chaz," said Julian. "Get your rest. You're no good to anyone in your current state. We'll take care of this. Ravenus! Stay here and keep an eye on the camp. We should be back in just a few minutes. Come find me if there's any trouble."

Julian ran off in the direction that Tim had gone, with Cooper crashing through the forest behind him.

"Katherine!" Tim shouted. "Hang on! We're coming!"

Katherine screamed. As Julian got closer, he could hear the snarls and growls of a creature he sincerely hoped was her wolf.

"Help me!" cried Katherine.

Julian plunged through the underbrush and into a clearing. His jaw dropped open. On the other side of the clearing, about twenty yards away, Katherine and her wolf faced off against the biggest ant Julian had ever seen. It was at least as big as a horse.

Tim had obviously not been quite as overcome with the creature's awesomeness. He charged at the massive ant as fast as his little legs could carry him, and broadsided the beast with his sword. It was a solid hit. The blade of Tim's sword plunged into the ant's thorax, all the way to the hilt. He pulled the sword back out and swung around for a second strike, and then stopped. His arms dropped to his sides. Katherine was laughing.

"My hero!" Katherine shouted, clapping her hands and smiling.

It was only then that it occurred to Julian that the ant wasn't moving. It wasn't even standing up. It's body was flat on the ground with its legs sprawled out in different directions. A closer inspection of its face revealed the back of an arrow shaft poking out of each eye.

The wolf started snarling and growling, tugging at one end of a giant antenna. Katherine held the other end, yanking it left and right.

"There's a good boy. Who's afraid of a stupid big ant? No, not you."

"Why were you screaming?" asked Tim, panting and out of breath.

"I needed some help," Katherine said. "I can't carry this thing back to camp by myself.

"You are such a fucking bitch."

Cooper finally struggled his way out of the trees. "Jesus Fuck!" he shouted, and charged at the ant with his great axe.

"Cooper, no!" Tim shouted, but he hadn't even managed to finish before Cooper had sliced the ant's head off.

"Ha!" said Cooper. "How do you like that, you big fucking ant!"

"Okay fine," Tim admitted to his sister. "That's some pretty funny shit."

After Cooper realized what was going on, even he had a sense of humor about it.

"So you really took that big bastard down all by yourself?"

Cooper asked Katherine as they walked back to camp. Katherine led the way, the brambles and vines seeming to move aside to let her pass, but doing no such favors for the rest of them. Tim carried the ant's head in his arms. Cooper had the rest of the ant slung over his shoulder.

"Yeah," said Katherine. "The poor thing barely knew what hit him. I borrowed Chaz's bow. Did you know I could fire a bow, Tim?"

"No," said Tim, spitting out some bits of leaf and bark from a branch that had just slapped him in the face. "I didn't know that."

"I didn't know it either," said Katherine. "I'm really a good shot with it too. Thwack! Thwack! One in each eye."

"I'm proud of you, sis," said Tim. "I'm sure you'll-"

"Hey, you two. Shut up," said Cooper. "I've got an idea." He put the ant body on the ground.

"That's not really your strong suit," said Tim cautiously.

"Fuck you," said Cooper, grinning. "This is going to be awesome. Here, give me that head."

Before Tim had any time to object, Cooper grabbed the ant's head out of his hands and put one finger over his lips.

"Shhh..." he said. "Go into camp, and watch Dave. Don't say anything to him. Just watch."

Tim looked at Cooper doubtfully but said nothing. He looked at the ant head in Cooper's hands, and then up at Cooper's tusky grin. Some sort of recognition clicked inside of him, and he smiled. "Okay," he said. "Come on, Kat. We won't want to miss this."

"What about the ant?" asked Katherine.

"We'll come back for it."

Julian stayed behind with Cooper. He plucked the arrows out of the ant's eyes and scooped out as much goop as he could from inside the head. He put the ant's head over his own. It fit perfectly. He turned toward Julian.

"How do I look?" asked Cooper.

"Better," said Julian.

Cooper offered a clawed middle finger to a tree just to the right of Julian. "Only problem is I can't see." He took the head off.

Cooper circled around the outside of the camp's perimeter. Julian followed behind him, not worried about being sneaky, as he couldn't hope to make as much noise as Cooper was. After about ten minutes, Cooper stopped.

"There's Dave," he whispered.

Dave was about thirty yards away, on one knee with his arms raised in the air and his eyes closed. He was chanting quietly, but the words were unintelligible as far as Julian could make out.

"Okay," Cooper whispered. "I've just got to make it past that tree, and then the one over there. Then the way is clear." He put the ant head back on and stumbled toward the first tree, groping around at empty air until he found it. He repeated the routine toward the second tree, making enough noise to wake the dead. Dave was so deep in his meditation that he didn't even stir.

"Braaauuuuugggggghhhh!" Cooper shouted as he jumped out from behind his tree, waving his arms menacingly and looking slightly to the right of where Dave was kneeling.

Dave's eyes opened as wide as cue balls. He lost his balance and fell on his side.

Cooper jumped up and down, hopping from one foot to the other. "Braaauuugggghhh! Braauugghh! Braaaaaaaauuuuuuuugggggghhhhhhh!"

A few seconds more of this passed before Dave was able to summon the wits to scream. And then only a few more seconds before he realized what was going on and stopped screaming.

Cooper's shouting turned into laughing, and he slapped his big meaty thighs. Laughter sounded from the direction of the camp as well. Dave turned around to see everyone peeking out from behind trees at him, chuckling up a storm.

"Fuck all of you guys!" Dave shouted. He scrambled on the ground, trying to stand up. Before he succeeded, he found a nice fist-sized rock. "And fuck you too, Cooper!" He chucked the rock at Cooper. It bounced off of his ant mask.

"Ow," echoed Cooper's voice from inside. "What the fuck, man?"

"You think that was funny?"

"Yes," said Cooper. "I thought it was fucking hilarious."

"You couldn't have waited until I finished my prayers? I was almost done!"

"All right dude, calm down," said Cooper, tossing the ant head onto the ground. "Go ahead and finish up your prayers."

"I have to start from the beginning now," said Dave. "I need a full hour of uninterrupted concentration."

"Oh," said Cooper. "That blows. Well, you'd better get back to it then. By the time you're done, breakfast should be ready."

"Breakfast?" asked Dave. The anger had left his voice. He licked his lips. "What's for breakfast?"

Cooper gestured down at the head on the ground. "Ant," he said, grinning.

"Are you sure we can eat that?"

"They do it all the time on those survival shows," said Cooper. "They're arthropods. They probably taste like lobster."

"Your mom tastes like lobster."

"Nice one," said Cooper.

Dave raised his middle finger at the camp and got back down on one knee. He looked up at Julian and Cooper. "You mind?"

"Right," said Cooper. "Come on, Julian. Let's go get that ant."

"So," said Tim when Cooper and Julian returned. "Does anyone know the proper way to cook ant?"

"I say we just chuck it on the fire and let the meat boil in the juices," said Cooper. "The shell will just act like a pot."

After waiting for any objections and hearing none, Cooper went ahead and dropped the ant body onto the fire. After a few minutes, a tendril of steam rose out of the hole where Tim had punctured the thorax.

"How long should we wait?" asked Katherine.

"We don't want to take any chances," said Tim. "This is a big fucker, and we want to make sure the meat cooks through. Let's give it until Dave finishes his prayers."

"Who's he praying to anyway?" asked Katherine. "Jesus?"

"He's not praying to anyone," said Tim.

"I don't understand."

"He didn't choose a god when he made his character," Tim explained. "He chose two spell domains. Destruction and Healing. I guess he's praying to those."

"I don't see how-"

"You should be able to understand this better than anyone," said Tim. "His spells work the same way yours do. Did you choose a god?"

"I didn't choose anythi- wait a second... I have spells?"

"Of course you have spells," said Chaz, with some irritation in his voice. "Where the hell did you think those wolves were coming from that disappeared after a few seconds?"

"That was a spell? I thought it was just something I could do."

"Nope," said Tim. "It's a spell."

"But I didn't pray for it."

"Can you do it now?"

Katherine closed her eyes and steepled her fingers. She opened her eyes and put her hands down. "No," she said. "There were some words I said or something. I don't remember what they are now."

"Shit," said Tim. "Hurry up. Go and prepare your spells. Fuck, we're never going to get out of here."

"How do I prepare my spells?"

"Look at your character sheet," said Tim. "There should be a list of spells that you can cast. Pick which ones you think will be the most useful, and meditate on them."

"Okay," she said uncertainly.

"Hey bard," Tim called out to Chaz. "Did you get your spells ready yet?"

"Yeah," said Chaz. "Finished that up a while ago."

"Thank fuck," Tim muttered. He turned to Cooper. "If you don't mind, we should really get that fire going a little stronger. Can you go rip some dead branches off of some trees or something?"

"No problem," said Cooper. He ran off into the woods.

"Don't go far!" Tim shouted after him.

"Anything you'd like me to do?" asked Julian.

"Shut up," said Tim.

"Can do," Julian said bitterly.

"No, really," said Tim. "Shut up. I thought I heard something." Julian shut up and concentrated.

"Did you hear it?" Tim whispered.

"I hear quite a lot of crashing and thrashing about over there," said Julian.

"No," said Tim, peering off in another direction. "That's just Cooper tearing down trees. I thought I heard something over there."

Julian followed Tim's line of sight, but all he could see were trees.

"What did it sound like?"

"I don't know. It just sounded like something other than the normal sounds of the woods."

"Should I get the others?"

"No," said Tim. "It might have been nothing. Let them focus on their spells. God knows we'll need them."

"What about Cooper?"

"He's getting firewood. We need to get that fire going stronger if we're going to eat that ant meat." He stopped to think for a moment. "Still, tell Ravenus to be ready to go get him if anything jumps out of the trees to kill us."

Julian called Ravenus and relayed Tim's instructions.

"Are you expecting something to come out of the trees and kill us?" asked Ravenus.

"This is C and C world," said Tim. "I'm always expecting something to come out of the trees and kill us."

Ravenus nodded. "Shall I scout out the perimeter?" he offered.

"Fuck no," said Tim sharply. "The last thing we need is for you to be off fucking some floozy bird while we're getting ripped to pieces by a bunch of ogres or something. Stay where we can see you."

"I'll just wait up in the top of this tree here then, shall I?" suggested Ravenus. "Good view from up there."

"Fine," said Tim.

Julian nodded his agreement with Tim's decision, and Ravenus flew up into the higher branches of the tree.

Tim and Julian stood still and listened, neither of them hearing anything but the sound of branches being ripped off of trees off in the direction Cooper had gone. From the sound of it, Cooper was really enjoying the task. They continued listening, bows in hand, ready to fire.

Time passed. It might have been as few as fifteen minutes, or up to an hour. The uneasy feeling that there was something out there watching them, combined with the strain of continuous diligent listening, made it seem like much longer. They were only able to cap it at an hour because nobody had returned from their meditations yet. When the source of the sound finally gave itself away, it wasn't with the crack of a twig, but rather with a horrified and incensed outcry.

"In the name of all the gods!" an all too familiar voice shouted. "What is the meaning of-"

Julian nearly jumped out of his skin. "Ravenus, go!" he shouted. "Find Cooper!" Ravenus flew off.

Captain Righteous Justificus Blademaster stepped into view. He was dressed in polished silver armor with golden accents. It showed no signs of ever having seen combat, but it looked more than capable of holding its own in one. The same held true for the huge steel shield he carried in one hand, and the longsword he brandished in the other. This was not what he had been wearing when they met him a couple of days ago. This looked to be more like what Julian imagined a knight might wear to church or something.

"You!" Tim said.

"I thought I might find you boys here," said the captain. "Where are the rest of you?"

"They're gone," Tim lied."

"Like hell they are," Captain Righteous said, taking a step forward. Tim and Julian took a step backward in response, holding up their bows, but having little confidence in them being able to penetrate the captain's impressive suit of armor. "Give me the half-orc, and I'll let the rest of you live."

"Listen," said Julian, feeling about as menacing with his bow as a baby brandishing a soggy cookie. "You've got the wrong idea about Cooper. He's not a bad guy. And he didn't kill your man. I mean, not really."

The captain regarded him in stern disbelief, and then sheathed his sword. Julian breathed a sigh of relief and lowered his bow.

"Not a bad guy," the captain repeated to himself. "Didn't really kill my man."

Julian smiled. Captain Righteous did not.

"Then how do you come to be in possession of this?" he bellowed, reaching behind his shield with his free hand and producing the head of the slain guard. The head winked each of its eyes alternately and waggled its tongue at Tim and Julian, all out of view of the captain holding it.

"You need to put that shit away when you're done using it," said Tim.

The captain was dumbfounded for a second, which wasn't an expression they were used to seeing on his face. "What unspeakable acts of-"

"I'm sorry," said Tim. "That came out wrong."

The captain dropped the head to the ground, where it lay still. He drew his sword again and took another step forward, moving past a tree that had, up to that point, been obscuring his view of Chaz. He stopped. "Who the hell are you?" he demanded.

Chaz neither stood up nor answered the captain's question. He simply started strumming his lute, and began to sing. "Hush, little baby. Don't say a word. Papa's gonna buy you a-"

Tim collapsed to the ground in a heap and began to snore.

Julian glared at Chaz.

"Oops," said Chaz.

Captain Righteous shook his head. "Last chance," he said to Julian. "Save yourself. Tell me where the half-orc is."

Chapter 19

One by one, Tim's senses came back to him. As he lay in darkness, he could feel something prodding into his ribs. He wasn't exactly being kicked... more like nudged with a foot. A familiar smell invaded his nostrils. Boiled crawfish? No, not exactly. Something not unlike it though.

"Tim!" someone said from directly above him. "Tim, wake up!"

Sleep felt too good. He'd just pretend he couldn't hear... just for a few more minutes.

"Tim!" came the voice from above, more insistent than last time. Nudges turned into kicks.

Sleep wasn't going to be an option. Tim yawned, rubbed the sleep out of his eyes, and looked over to his right. Greely and Shorty were cowering behind a rock, gesturing at Tim to be quiet and not give away their presence.

What's going on?

He looked straight up and found Julian staring down back at him. Julian nodded forward. Tim followed Julian's nod to find a pair of shiny steel boots standing in front of him. Above the boots, Tim slowly raised his head. Shiny steel shield. Shiny steel breastplate. And finally, the shiny steel gaze of Captain Righteous Justificus Blademaster. Shit. The situation came back to him all at once. He pushed himself backward with his feet and elbows.

"Listen," Julian pleaded, taking a step back. "I know this looks bad, but we're really not the guys you want."

"That's right," said the Captain patiently. "I want the half-orc."

"No," said Julian. "You want our Cavern Master."

The captain paused. "Shorty?"

"What?" said Julian, his eyes flickered toward Shorty's direction and back again. Shorty grimaced, but remained hidden behind the rock.

"No!" said Julian.

Captain Righteous snorted a condescending laugh. "Cavern

218

Master? Did he tell you to call him that? Kind of a lofty title for that little imp. Don't worry. I'll take care of him after I take care of your lot."

"No," said Julian. "I wasn't talking about Shorty, I was-"

He was interrupted by what sounded like an elephant charging through a bamboo field. Cooper emerged from the trees with half a forest's worth of dead branches in his arms.

"Guys," said Cooper between pants, his face hidden behind the load he carried. "We have a problem."

"No shit," said Julian.

"Huh?" said Cooper, dropping the branches. "Shit," he said. "What's he doing here?"

"You!" shouted the Captain, turning to face Cooper. "At last, you will pay for your heinous crimes!"

"Dude," said Cooper. "Now is really not the-"

"Braaaauuuuggghhhh!" came the muffled sound from behind the captain. He turned to face the new threat. It appeared to be a short, stout, humanoid figure with the head of a giant ant... and a beard.

The captain stumbled back. "What the hell is-"

"Rock-a-bye baby, in the tree top," Chaz sang as he strummed his lute.

The captain paused and yawned. "In the tree top? Why would a baby-" His musing was interrupted by another yawn.

"When the wind blows, the cradle will rock."

"Surely it's a lot more practical-" yawn "-and a lot less dangerous to just keep the kid on the-"

"When the bough breaks, the cradle will fall."

"That's exactly the sort of thing-" yawn "-I'd be worried would happen-" He fell to his knees and dropped his sword on the ground.

"And down will come baby, cradle and all."

"What kind of parents-" yawn "-What kind of song-" The captain fell forward into the dirt.

Julian looked at Chaz. Cooper looked at Dave. "Nice work," they both said.

Dave took off the ant head. "Just a little something a big asshole taught me."

Chaz stopped playing his lute. "You know, he's right. I never thought about how fucked up that song is."

"Guys," said Cooper. "We're in some deep shit. Where's Katherine?"

Tim looked down at the captain. "If we tie him up, he won't be any threat. We might even be able to calm him down if we can get him to listen."

"It's not him I'm worried about," said Cooper. He pointed at Dave. "It's him."

"Me?" Dave asked.

"No," said Cooper. "The little guy whose head you're holding. I think his friends and family are coming to look for him."

"Shit," said Julian. "How many?"

"I don't know," said Cooper. "I saw maybe four or five."

"Hey boys!" shouted Katherine, running into the clearing with Butterbean following close behind. "We've got a problem." She stopped to catch her breath, and looked down at the captain. "Who's that?"

"Another problem," said Julian. "What's wrong?"

"More ants are coming," she said.

"Shit," said Julian. "How many did you see?"

"I don't know. A lot."

"That's too many," said Dave. "We have to get out of here."

"Where?" asked Cooper. "How?"

Tim spoke up to the crowd circled above him. "What about the cart?"

"What cart?"

"The one we were in when we arrived here."

"The one that got torn to shreds?" asked Julian impatiently.

"Sure," said Tim. "I mean, we ripped the cover off, but it's still got wheels, right?"

Julian thought for a moment. "Hell, there was plenty of grass around there. The horses might even still be okay."

Tim sat straight up. "Hurry up," he said. "Grab whatever shit you can carry. We have to get out of here now."

Cooper tore down the canvas from the bushes where he had attempted to make a shelter, and spread it out on the ground. "Throw all your shit on here," he said. While everyone did that, he went over to the ant on the fire, and ripped its legs off one by one. Each leg ended with a chunk of steamy white meat, and it didn't smell at all unpleasant.

A din of clicking, chattering, and buzzing penetrated the clearing.

"What the hell is that?" asked Julian.

"Ants," said Cooper and Katherine in unison.

"Shit, seriously?"

"What do we do with him?" asked Tim, looking down at the captain. Getting nothing in the way of response outside of uncomfortable silence and averted glances, he explained the options as he saw them. "If we leave him here, it amounts to the same as outright murdering him. We'll have to bring him with us."

"But won't he just try to kill us all as soon as he wakes up again?" asked Dave. "I mean, we've gotten lucky a couple of times. That luck is going to run out sooner or later if we keep this jerk alive."

"Are you comfortable leaving him here to be eaten by ants?" asked Tim.

Dave lowered his head. "No."

"He'll be less of a threat without his sword," said Julian. He picked it up and swung it around to get a feel for it. From the look on Julian's face, Tim guessed it felt pretty good. It was truly a beautiful piece of craftsmanship.

"Okay," said Dave, shrugging. "Should I wake him up?"

Tim took a second to think. The ant noises were growing louder. Treetops swayed just beyond the perimeter of the camp. "Cooper, do you think you could carry him?"

Cooper snorted. "Sure." He brought the four corners of the canvas together, and held them with one hand. With the other hand, he scooped up the sleeping captain and hefted him over his shoulder. "Wanna take another ride?"

"Okay," said Tim. He hopped up on top of the makeshift sack, made himself as comfortable as he could, and readied his bow. "Let's get out of here."

Julian and Dave led the way along the path Cooper had cleared on the way to the camp. Cooper took up the rear with the captain on his shoulder and a huge bag dragging behind him, with Tim riding on top of it.

The ants' heads started peeking into view as soon as the party had started moving. Tim fired an arrow at one, but it went wide and hit a tree. The ant he had fired at didn't even look distracted. Several of the ants gathered near the fire, their antennae moving wildly about in the presence of their fallen, charred, and now legless brother. Chaos turned to order as a different sort of ant came on to the scene. It was bigger than the others, and the carapace was thick and spiked on the front shoulders. It had mandibles like jagged scimitars. A few clicks and a whir from this ant, and the others got into formation and began marching behind heading straight for Tim.

Cooper ran as fast as he could, but was held back by the weight of the captain and the drag of the sack. The ants were gaining ground, and Tim's arrows seemed to have little to no effect at slowing their progression. Cooper hadn't taken more than a few strides when the captain woke up and demanded to know what was going on.

"Fucking hell!" Cooper shouted. "Take a look behind us!"

The captain picked his head up. "Oh shit," he said. "Put me down. We'll move faster if you aren't carrying me."

"Do you promise to behave yourself?"

"Yes, by the gods!" he shouted. "They're gaining on us."

"How do we know we can trust you?"

The captain sighed. "I swear by the sword that was passed down to me by- Hey, where's my sword?"

"We're keeping it safe for you," said Cooper in as motherly a tone of voice that his half-orc throat could muster. "You can have it back when you promise to stop trying to murder us with it."

"Cooper!" Tim shouted. "Put him down, goddammit! They're right on top of us!" He fired an arrow that finally connected with the soldier ant's eye. The ant let out a scream that sounded like a lion roaring through an electronic voice synthesizer.

Cooper set the captain down.

Captain Righteous stared into Cooper's eyes. "This isn't over."

"Fuck off," said Cooper. "Move along before we're all ant shit."

After a few more strides, he heard the captain shout again. "Hey, wizard!"

"Actually, I'm more of a sorcerer now," said Julian.

"Give me back my sword!"

"No." said Julian.

"Shit."

"Cooper!" Tim shouted. "Run faster!"

The soldier ant was nearly right on top of Tim. He scooted backwards on the sack, but there wasn't much further he could scoot. He fired another arrow, but it missed the eye and bounced off the ant's shoulder.

"Aaaauuuuggghhh!" Tim screamed as the ice tong-like mandibles caught hold of his foot. The ant immediately stopped running, trying to pull Tim off the sack. Tim dropped his bow and held on with both hands.

"Tim!" Cooper shouted.

"Keep running!" Tim shouted in response.

The ant not only stopped moving its legs, but also started curling its body around, as if it were trying to sit up.

The pain in Tim's foot was excruciating. It felt as though the creature might actually succeed in ripping it right off. All Tim wanted to do was to cry, puke, and pass out, but he forced himself to hang on.

The ant finished curling its body around, and now Tim could see why. The back of its abdomen ended in a giant stinger. A dark brown liquid oozed out from the end of it. Tim kicked frantically with his good foot, but that only ended up providing the ant with a suitable target. The stinger pierced the bottom of Tim's foot, and Tim felt the burning heat of the acidic venom flow inside him.

He was too agonized to scream. His eyes and his jaw clenched shut. With all of his strength, he kicked his legs as hard as he could. It was enough to shake the ant loose. The ant rolled over, briefly halting the progress of the worker ants behind him. This would be the perfect time to finish the fucker off if he still had his bow.

The soldier ant quickly got to its feet and resumed the chase.

"You okay back there," asked Cooper.

Tim looked down at the bleeding messes that used to be his feet. He choked back a sob. "Just keep running," he said. "Run like a motherfucker."

Adrenaline took charge over fear and pain for the moment, and Tim grabbed the shortsword from the scabbard at his side. He waited for the ant to come to him. Acid burned in his foot, and hatred for insects burned in his brain. He waited.

"Come on, you big mother fucker!" Tim shouted. "There's

plenty more of me left. Come and get it." That was a lie. This was the second time he'd had his feet mutilated by an oversized animal. There was not, in fact, much more of him left. He was probably down to a single hit point. He was barely holding on to consciousness.

The soldier ant moved in for the kill. Tim held onto the sack with one hand, and held his sword in the other. His vision blurred with tears and sweat.

Tim looked into the one huge remaining functional eye of his attacker. He saw neither pity nor malice. No cunning plan of attack, no sense of self preservation. Just a target, a mission, and a robot-like determination to carry it through. When it was close enough, it opened its mandibles wide. If it closed them again, Tim would be dead.

Tim also lacked any plan more complicated than 'kill ant'. His sense of self-preservation was bleeding out of his feet. He brought his shortsword down as hard as he could, and sliced the ant's face in half. Dark red blood, hot and sticky, spattered all over Tim's face.

The soldier ant's jaws let go of Tim, and it collapsed to the ground. The workers who had been following it huddled around, chittering confusedly for lack of clear orders.

Tim's adrenaline rush subsided, and the pain returned. He lost his hold on the sack, slid off onto the ground, and threw up. He tried to push himself up with his arms, but as soon as he put any pressure on his feet, he screamed and collapsed face first into his own puke.

"Shit!" said Cooper as he stopped running.

The next thing Tim knew, Cooper was kneeling over him. "Looks like you took one of those fuckers down," he said. "Good job." He picked up Tim's shortsword and carefully placed it back in its scabbard as if he were playing with a doll.

"Cooper," Tim wheezed. The pain in his right foot was excruciating, but the pain in his left foot, where he'd gotten stung, was worst of all. It had started to make its way up his leg. "You've got to get out of here. Take care of Katherine."

"Come on, big guy," said Cooper. "Dave will fix you right up, good as new." Cooper picked him up and tucked him under his arm like a football. The smell was so atrocious that it temporarily distracted Tim from the pain in his feet. Tim coughed up some more vomit. It ran down Cooper's arm and dripped off his elbow, but Cooper didn't even seem to notice.

The ants quieted down until only one of them could be heard. It might have been just Tim's imagination, but he had the distinct impression that the clicks and buzzes he as now hearing were new orders.

Cooper grabbed the corners of his sack and resumed his retreat.

Just as Tim had feared, the ants seemed to be getting organized again. They parted from the path, and another soldier ant stepped into the commanding position.

"Fuck," said Cooper, taking a peek behind as he ran. The trees were thinning out, and the path was getting grassier. They were nearly out of the woods, but only in the literal sense.

"I see the wagon!" Julian shouted, somewhere ahead of them.

After another few seconds, Tim could hear other familiar voices.

"Greely!" shouted Dave. "Go wait in the wagon."

Then came the Captain's voice, nearer than Dave's had been. "You have your magic," he said. "Don't make me go into battle with no weapon."

"No way," said Julian. "You're just going to have to sit this one out, cap'n. If you want to come with us, you can go wait in the wagon."

"But if you're going to fight all of those ants, you'll need my help."

"Fight them?" said Julian. "If we wanted to fight them, we would have stayed where we were. We're going to get the hell out of here."

"And how do you propose to do that?" the captain argued. "Bandits have made off with the hors-" He stopped, and then spoke up again. "Oh, right."

Now that the trees had thinned out, Cooper was making much better time. The ants were still a healthy distance away, but they were gaining ground just the same.

Tim heard his sister's voice. "Where's Tim?"

"He's with Cooper," Julian shouted back at her. "They ought to be coming out any time now."

And then Tim felt the light of the sun on his face. He looked up and saw that they had cleared the last remaining trees of the forest. He saw his friends up ahead. He saw his sister. He saw Shorty and Greely scrambling into the back of the horseless wagon.

Then he turned his head to look back in the direction they had come from. He saw ants. Dozens of them, maybe hundreds. They crawled out from between the trees all along the perimeter of the forest.

"Dave!" Cooper shouted.

"What?" Dave called back. Tim looked ahead. Dave's face was as gray as ash.

"Get over here! Tim's hurt! He's hurt bad!"

"Tim!" Katherine shouted, running towards Cooper.

Julian ran after her, and Dave followed in behind him. They reached Cooper a few seconds later. The soldier ant in the lead was already tearing a hole in the sack.

"Take Tim," Cooper shouted.

Before Tim had time to register what was happening, he was wrapped in one of Cooper's enormous hands. A second later, he was sailing through the air.

He thought of his feet. Landing is going to hurt.

Landing did hurt, though not half as bad as Tim had expected. Julian caught him, and placed him gently on the ground in front of Dave.

Katherine gasped. "What happened to his feet?"

"He'll be okay," said Julian, without much conviction in his voice. "Dave. Can you fix him?"

"I'll do what I can," said Dave.

"What about Cooper?" Tim asked.

Cooper was facing the approaching ants. He drew his great axe. Without the trees to limit the ants into a single line, they began to spread out. A worker ant crawled up next to the soldier ant nearest Cooper. The soldier ant climbed up onto the sack and looked down at him.

"I'm really angry!" Cooper declared, and swung his axe down at the soldier ant's head. The blade cleaved straight through the head and lodged into the head of the worker ant, killing the former, and severely wounding the latter.

The worker ant made a half-hearted attempt to bite Cooper, but failed. Katherine's wolf rushed up and finished the job by tearing a leg off.

"I heal thee!" Tim heard Dave shout above him, and felt the palm of a hand touch his forehead.

Tim opened his eyes wide, sucking in so much air that it seemed he should have expanded to twice his size. He looked down at his feet. They had stopped bleeding, but were still torn and misshapen. Tim moaned, half in ecstasy, and half still in pain.

"Are you okay?" asked Katherine.

"No," Tim groaned.

"Let me try again," said Dave.

"Hurry it up, guys," Cooper shouted, bringing his axe down on another ant. Tim looked back. The workers were starting to surround Cooper, and there looked to be no end of them coming out from the trees. He even spotted a few more soldiers, hurriedly making their way through the workers toward him.

"I heal thee!" Dave shouted, laying his hand on Tim's forehead again. Relief hit Tim like a wave smashing against a rocky shore.

"Ohmyfuckinggodthatfeelsgood!" Tim shouted. He jumped to his feet and stomped on the ground. "You know, it's worth having your feet gnawed off by ants just to be healed like that."

"You're about to get another chance!" said Cooper, backing up. "Is everyone okay now?"

"I'm good," said Tim.

"Let's get the fuck out of here!" said Cooper, holding two ants at bay with his axe.

Julian, Dave, Katherine and her wolf started running toward the wagon.

"Come on!" Tim shouted at Cooper.

Cooper swatted an ant off the top of the sack with the flat of his axe, grabbed the corners of the canvas, and shouted at Tim. "Run!"

Tim and Cooper raced toward the wagon with a swarm of giant ants in tow. Cooper soon overtook Tim and plucked him up off the ground with his legs still flailing in the air and slung him over one shoulder. Tim could hear the half-orc grunt as he ran. He wasn't dragging the sack behind him anymore. He was carrying it up off the ground in his right hand.

The rage, Tim thought. He's even stronger now. He looked up. Giant ants were still pouring out of the woods.

"Everybody in the wagon!" shouted Cooper when he got within

thirty yards of the wagon. His raging sprint had put some distance between them and the ants, but it wouldn't be long before the ants closed the gap.

"Can we all even fit in there?" asked Dave.

Cooper had reached the rest of the party by that point, and answered Dave's question by picking him up and throwing him into the wagon. He tossed the sack unceremoniously on top of Dave, and then set Tim gently down.

"I don't get it," Katherine said to Julian at the front of the wagon. "Where are we supposed to get horses?"

"Let me take care of that," said Julian. "Can you ride?"

"How the fuck would I know how to ride a… oh wait. Come to think of it, yes I can."

"Cool," said Julian. "Then you ride up front with me."

"Ride what?" asked Katherine.

"Horse!" Julian shouted at the empty air. A brown horse appeared in front of him, complete with bit, bridle, and saddle.

"Nice," said Katherine. "But won't it disappear after a few seconds? I mean, that's what happens when I magic up a wolf."

"Nah," said Julian. "This spell lasts a good two hours." He turned away from her. "Horse!" he said again.

A second horse appeared. This one was black, with patches of white spots here and there, but similarly equipped. The horses remained perfectly still while Julian hitched them to the wagon.

Tim stared in fascination. Horses, saddled and bridled, just appearing out of thin air like that. For such a mundane, often overlooked spell in the game, it was really something to witness firsthand. He watched Julian and Katherine mount their mounts, and then his enchantment was interrupted. Someone lifted him off of the floor.

"Sorry, little dude," said Chaz. "We're going to have to sit on each others' laps until we get clear of those ants."

Tim looked around. Shorty sat on Greely's lap across from him and Chaz. Dave sat alone next to Chaz, being too heavy to sit on anyone else's lap, and not having much in the way of a lap himself. Across from Dave sat Captain Righteous. Cooper stood behind the wagon, brandishing his axe at the first line of ants who were now only yards away. Tim wondered what was going to happen if he attempted to sit on the captain's lap.

"Julian!" Cooper shouted. "Please tell me you're ready to go!"

"We're all set," Julian shouted back. "Hop in."

Cooper swung his axe down and caught a soldier ant in the head with the flat of his axe on the upswing. Six feet of ant backflipped into the air, leaving the workers under its command without instruction.

Tim's worries about the captain's lap proved to be unfounded. Cooper chose to sit on the floor of the wagon, with his feet hanging off the back. "Go!" he shouted.

"Go, horse!" Julian commanded, and the wagon lurched forward.

Cooper turned his head toward Dave. He didn't even need to look up. He raised an empty clawed hand. "Crossbow."

Dave kicked around some of the spilled equipment from the canvas sack until he found two crossbows. He handed one to Cooper, and loaded a bolt into the one he kept for himself. No one objected when Captain Righteous grabbed a bow for himself, but Cooper paused long enough to give him a look with his enraged, swollen red eyes that expressed in no uncertain terms what the penalty would be for turning said bow on anyone inside the wagon. The three of them fended off the ants until the wagon got up to a speed that the ants were unable to keep up with.

"I'll be having that back now," said Cooper when they were safely far away enough from the ants. His rage had subsided, but Captain Righteous was still in no position to argue. He handed Cooper the crossbow. Cooper tossed it over his shoulder into the pile of miscellaneous equipment. It landed on something with a clank that made the captain turn his head. From beneath the canvas shone the corner of something large and flat.

"Is that my shield?" asked Captain Righteous.

"Huh?" said Cooper. He craned his neck around to look behind him. "Oh, yeah. I picked it up when you fell asleep."

The captain's face brightened for the first time since any of the party had met the man. "Thank the gods!"

"You can owe me one," said Cooper.

"What is that sticking out from under it? What sort of provisions do you people travel with?" asked Captain Righteous. He reached down, but Dave kicked at his hand.

"Hey," said Dave. "Mind your hands. No one gave you

permission to root around in our shit."

"What is that?"

"Ant leg," said Cooper, grabbing it for himself. "God, I'm starving." He took a bite. "Oh my god, it's fucking heavenly."

"Really?" asked Tim.

"Try it," said Cooper. He passed the leg back to Tim.

It was still warm. Tim took a bite from the fleshy end at the top, where the leg had once connected to the ant's body. The taste wasn't entirely unlike that of boiled crawfish, but the texture was off. Ant meat was a lot chewier. Though they hadn't prepared it with any seasoning, it had a natural spiciness to it. "Shit, he's right! Who knew ant tasted this good?"

Cooper grabbed a second ant leg, stood up and bit off another chunk of meat. He shouted out to the few remaining ants he could still see. "Thanks for the meal, fuckers!"

The rest of the group devoured the ant meat, and passed some of it along to Katherine and Julian. Tim wondered, if he ever got home and was able to bring some giant ants with him, if they could be farmed. This meat would bring in a whole lot more customers than the Chicken Hut was bringing in.

The only person who didn't seem to be enjoying the feast was Captain Righteous.

"You know, of course," said the captain, "that the ants who just attacked us were following the scent of their fallen comrade."

"No shit?" said Dave through a mouthful of ant. "That's good information to know for the future."

"Still," said Tim. "I think it was worth it for this meat."

Cooper let out a huge belch, directed at Captain Righteous.

"You, sir, are a truly disgusting creat-" The captain paused. His face became pale and gravely serious. Those of the group who had been laughing now stopped and followed his gaze down to the floor of the wagon, where a severed head looked back up at them.

"You are all animals," said the captain. "And when I take back my sword that you have stolen from me, I will slaughter you all like the rabid beasts that you are."

"Yes," said Tim in his most businesslike tone of voice. "But until then, do you think you'd be open to at least listening to an explanation?"

"Plead for your lives if you like, cowering worms. It will make no difference. I will personally make sure that each of your heads rolls around on the floor of some cart."

"Okay, good," said Tim. "Hey Chaz. You're a bard. You've probably got the highest Charisma score of any of us. Maybe you should take this one."

Chaz started. "Me? Take what?"

"Just explain about the head."

"That shit all happened before I got here," said Chaz. "I've got no more idea than him why you guys are traveling around with a dude's head in your bag."

"Oh yeah." Tim thought for a moment. He wasn't going to be able to sell this story. Not on this guy. Not unless Mordred started talking through the head in his presence, and there didn't seem much chance of Mordred being cooperative. He decided to go with an entirely different approach.

"We outnumber you eight to one," he continued. "We are armed. You are not. We've had many opportunities to kill you, and yet here you sit among us. We could kill you right now, but we don't. We aren't murderers."

"And yet my comrade's head rolls around on the floor of your stolen wagon."

"There's an explanation for that."

"Oh I'm sure it's a good one."

"It's a long story."

"It's a long ride to Cardinia," said the captain. "Please, feel free to pass the time entertaining me with your lies."

"Cardinia?" asked Tim. "Is that where we're going?"

The captain eyed Tim suspiciously. "Unless you know of a different city that this road leads to."

Dave spoke up. "What kind of place is Cardinia?"

"What?" asked the captain. He looked around as if waiting for a punchline, but everyone continued to stare back at him expectantly. "How is it that you don't know of Cardinia?"

"We're not from around here," said Tim.

"I was informed that you were traveling from that direction when you attacked-" he looked down at the head on the floor.

"Put that in a bag, would you Cooper?" said Tim.

"Oh, right," said Cooper. He put the head in his bag. "Sorry about that. Go on."

Captain Righteous stared at the half-orc in confused disgust.

"So it's a big city then, is it?" asked Tim, hoping to bring the captain's attention back to him.

"Huh?" said the captain, turning back to Tim. "Oh, yes. Is it a big city? It's only the second biggest city in the entire realm." He looked around in astonishment at all of the faces looking back at him, obviously thirsty for information that should be common knowledge. "How is it that none of you have heard of Cardinia? Her port serves as a trading hub for ships from all over Dalgar."

"And Dalgar," Tim continued. "I'm sorry. This is going to sound like a stupid question, but since you already don't have a very high opinion of us, what the hell. Is Dalgar the name of this realm? Or is it-"

"Dalgar is the name of the world!" exclaimed the captain. "Where are you people from?"

"Not from Dalgar," said Cooper.

"Our planet is called Earth," said Tim.

"Your planet?" said the captain. "There isn't a planet in the heavens called Earth. Do you mean to say you descended here from the stars? You're all mad!"

"Yeah," said Tim. "I figured you'd think that. So anyway, if this Cardinia is a world-wide trading port, it should be pretty big. Maybe we can find some information there."

"Information about what?" asked Chaz.

"About getting home."

"Mordred was pretty clear about that not being a possibility," said Dave. "But he said there are dozens of other people he sent here. We might run into some of them."

"I'll settle for finding some booze and smokes first," said Cooper. "This town ought to have some decent taverns."

"All you are going to find in Cardinia," said the captain, "is a swift end to your worthless lives."

There followed an uncomfortable silence.

Tim cleared his throat. "So, how long a ride is it to Cardinia?"

Captain Righteous sighed. "At this pace, we should be there before nightfall."

Chapter 20

Every second of the next hour and a half passed by at a snail's pace for Dave. The sun glared down on them, and without the protection of the canvas cover, most of the party succumbed to exhaustion. The relative safety of the moment made for a good time to take a nap. Even Katherine looked to be having trouble keeping her eyes open atop her horse. Julian may or may not have been in one of his elf trances. It was hard to tell from behind him, and while he was wearing that ridiculous sombrero.

Tim was sprawled out on the floor of the wagon just below Dave's feet. He looked peaceful. In fact, everyone seemed to either be dozing or well on their way to it. Everyone, that is, except for himself and Captain Righteous. Dave chanced a glance at him, and was met with the captain's steely stare. Dave turned away.

Whatever sense of peace and security everyone else was feeling, Dave didn't feel it at all. Sure, they were now well beyond the reach of the ants, and that was good. And yeah, Captain Righteous was unarmed and technically their prisoner, but that was of small comfort. Dave could see in the captain's eyes that he was forming a plan, waiting for an opportunity to present itself. And even if no such opportunity arose, then what? What were they going to do with him? Just send him on his way in this new city? He'd be rearmed and up their asses again in no time.

Every now and again, they would pass a cart or wagon headed in the opposite direction, presumably on its way to Algor. Upon seeing the state of the party's wagon, and the unlikely combination of races riding in it, most of them would give it a wide berth and hurry their horses along without so much as a friendly wave on the way past.

Dave leaned back and tried to formulate some sort of plan in his mind for what their next move should be. Most of all, he thought about how they were going to get back home. Mordred couldn't really be planning to keep them here indefinitely. And what about the police? Six people just went missing. Surely there would be an investigation. They'd find Mordred's tire tracks. DNA. Phone records. Dave slumped forward, cradling his bearded face in his meaty hands. No, they'll probably just walk into the Chicken Hut, see the role-playing books and dice, and write us all off as having made a suicide pact or something.

"What the f-" shouted Julian. Dave looked up, but saw only a sombrero floating down like a leaf where Julian should have been. "Gowrrgh- shit!" Julian continued, but his voice was coming from below the wagon this time.

"What?" Katherine said, trying to shake the sleepiness out of her head. "Who?" She looked over to see Julian missing. "Aaahhh!" she screamed, and then fell out of sight.

The wagon rolled to a stop, but not before rolling over both of them. Dave stood up and looked ahead. The horses were both gone, as if they'd never been there to begin with. He turned around. Julian lay face down on the ground about twenty yards back, and Katherine sat up and rubbed the back of her head.

Tim sat up. "What happened? Why have we stopped? What's going on?"

Dave had no satisfactory answers to these questions, so he kept his mouth shut.

Captain Righteous looked to be as surprised as anyone, but spent less time asking questions and more time seizing an opportunity. He hopped off the back of the wagon and reached Julian before anyone had time to react. He unsheathed his own sword from Julian's scabbard, and placed a boot firmly on Julian's back.

"Nobody move," said the captain, placing the tip of his sword against the back of Julian's neck. "Or you'll have another head to play with."

Tim punched Chaz in the shin until he woke up. When Chaz was able to fully appreciate the situation, he kicked Cooper in the back several times before he woke up as well. Katherine stood up and drew her sickle, but dared not move forward. Her wolf barked and growled, but Katherine ordered him to stay back. Greely and Shorty sat perfectly still, no doubt contemplating what the best means of escape would be.

Tim stood up with his hands raised.

"I'm warning you, halfling," shouted the captain, his foot heavy upon Julian's back. "Stay where you are."

"If you hurt him," Cooper shouted, "I'll rip your fucking-"

"Cooper!" hissed Tim. "Shut up."

"Don't tell me to shut up," Cooper said. "I've had it with this pacifist bullshit. That's my friend he's got over-"

"I've got an idea," Tim whispered.

Cooper checked his anger. "Is it a good one?"

"Nope."

"All right," said Cooper. "Run with it, dude."

Tim turned back to face the captain. "I'm coming out," he said. "Alone and unarmed."

"Stay where you are!" shouted the captain, but too late. Tim had already hopped off the back of the wagon.

"Katherine," said Tim.

Katherine refused to take her glare away from the captain's face. "What?" she barked back to her brother.

"Take Buttercup and go back to-"

"Butterbean!"

"Whatever. Take your wolf and go back to the wagon."

"I'm not leaving you alone with him."

"You don't have to get in the wagon," said Tim. "Just back off and give us some room to breathe." He looked at Captain Righteous. "And talk."

Katherine didn't move.

"Katherine," Tim pleaded. "I'm going to try to negotiate a safe passage home."

Katherine turned around to look at him.

"Real home," Tim said.

"If your home is located in the deepest pits of the abyss," bellowed the captain, "then rest assured. You'll return there soon enough!"

"Shut up!" Tim and Katherine said simultaneously.

Much to Dave's surprise, the captain shut up.

"Come on, Kat," said Tim. "If things go badly, you can always summon a whole pack of wolves to rip that fucker to pieces." He made no effort to hide the message from the captain.

Katherine backed up, beckoning Butterbean to follow her.

Tim stepped forward. "What's your endgame here, Captain?"

"I will bring this murderous band of thieves to justice."

"You're outnumbered eight to one," observed Tim. "And that's not counting a wolf and a..." he lowered his head, "a bird."

"Eight to one, is it?" The captain sneered. "Do you include the wizard under the heel of my boot, who I could-"

"Sorcerer," Julian struggled to say with his face pressed in the dirt.

"Fine," said the captain. "The sorcerer whose head I can sever with a single thrust? Do you include yourself? The unarmed halfling standing right in front of me, who I could disembowel from where I stand?"

"All right, fine," Tim conceded. "But still."

The captain carried on. "How about the little goblin, and the ancient old man? Do you expect them to fight alongside you?"

Tim didn't respond.

"Let's see how loyal your new friends are," said the captain. "Shorty! Greely!"

The goblin and the old man shifted in their seats uncomfortably.

Shorty cleared his throat. "Um, yes?"

"I grant you your freedom. Go now and you shall never be pursued."

Shorty and Greely looked at one another.

"Um... thanks," said Shorty. He and Greely hopped down from the side of the wagon. "Good luck, guys. I think I speak for the both of us when I say that we've enjoyed the time we've spent with you, and we wish you all the best in your future endeavors." He looked at Greely for confirmation. "

Greely nodded. "Indeed," he said, and then turned to the captain. "So long Captain! All the best to you as well!" He and Shorty walked away, not on the road, but rather into the grasslands off to the side of it.

"So," said Captain Righteous. "How do you like my odds now?"

Tim shrugged. "Still not so good. Yeah, you might take down a few of us, but you'll never take us all down."

"Do you see this armor I'm wearing?" asked the captain. The sneer was gone from his face, and the contempt had left his voice. The sunlight shone off the armor so brightly that Dave had to squint in order to look directly at it.

"Yeah," said Tim. "I've noticed it."

"This isn't your typical soldier's standard issue suit of armor, you know."

"No," agreed Tim. "I wouldn't think so."

"This armor was passed down to me by my late father," said the captain. "It's been in my family for seven generations. I have no sons."

"Why not?"

"Haven't had time. Haven't met the right girl. You know."

"I'm sure she's out there," said Tim. "You're a good enough looking guy. Gainfully employed. Have you met my sist-"

"The point," interrupted the captain, "is that I would rather die by the hands of my enemies than dishonor my family line by letting a murderer escape justice under my watch. This is the armor I choose to die in."

"Seriously," said Tim. "You're going to talk to me about honor right after you tell me about how you're going to cut my helpless friend's head off, and disembowel me while I'm unarmed."

"It is unfortunate that-"

"And what about the dishonor to your family line by letting a murderer escape? Cooper's the one you want. As many of us as you kill, Cooper will surely be one of the last to fall. You'll still be letting a murderer escape under your watch."

"But I will have died in my attempt to uphold the law, and there is honor in that."

"What if we give you the chance to go mano-a-mano with Cooper? His axe against your sword?"

"Sure," the sneer returned to the captain's face. "And the rest of you lot will just sit back and watch while I cut down your friend, right? Forgive me if I don't trust a group of criminals to not stab me in the back. No, I think I'm going to decline your offer. I think I'll be able to take out at least four or five of you before you kill me. If the big guy remains standing, he's dumb enough so that he'll be easily captured later without all of his little friends to help keep him out of trouble."

"Um... Tim," said Dave.

"Not now Dave!" Tim shouted back at him.

"I think you ought to see this," Dave insisted.

Tim whipped his head around. "What?" He ran around to the

front of the wagon to get a better view of what Dave was looking at.

Dave knew what was coming. He'd seen this cloud of dust once before. He'd felt these same tremors. Horses, and lots of them.

Tim ran back to face Captain Righteous. "You talked a big game," he said. "But you haven't done anything. If you were going to die in a blaze of honor and glory, why haven't you started killing us yet? Why have we been standing around talking?"

The captain smiled down at Tim. "You are the one who wanted to talk."

"You've just been stalling, haven't you?"demanded Tim. "Those are reinforcements coming, aren't they?"

"How do you like my odds now, little man?"

"For such an honorable man, you sure are a sneaky motherfucker."

"And for such a sneaky rogue, you sure are a dumb motherfucker," the captain retorted.

"Listen, shitbag!" Tim shouted, taking a step forward. He stopped suddenly, his crossed eyes fixed on the end of the captain's sword at his nose.

The thundering sound of horses in the distance drew nearer. Whoever was coming was doing so in a hurry.

"It matters not to me," said the captain, looking down the length of his sword blade at Tim, "whether you die here by my sword, or die tomorrow morning at the end of a rope. Who knows? You may even concoct some sort of brilliant escape plan during the night."

Tim took a step back.

Captain Righteous laughed. "I wouldn't count on it, though. The prisons in Cardinia are far more secure than the little dungeon in Algor. And they are much more accustomed to dealing with prisoners with all of your different skill sets."

"I want to talk to Mordred," Tim said coolly.

"Who is Mordred?"

"You know damn well who he is."

The captain furrowed his brow in confusion. "I honestly have no idea who you're talking about. If this is some sort of last-minute trick, I can assure you that you're far too late."

"I know you're in there, you fat shit bucket!" Tim shouted.

"I beg your pardon!" The captain was taken aback. "I

understand you're upset, but I don't have an ounce of fat on my-"

"Are you having fun in there?" Tim continued shouting. "While we're all struggling for our lives, you're sitting in my restaurant —"

"You've gone mad!"

"Drinking my beer, eating my Popsicles, and jerking off to my sister!"

"Ew, Tim!" said Katherine. "Please don't give him any ideas."

Captain Righteous cocked one eyebrow. "Popsicles?"

Tim didn't seem to hear any of it. He just kept on shouting. "You think you're so great and powerful, with your magic dice, and your shitty car, and that stupid fucking velvet curtain that you wear on your back, and..." Anything else he said after that was drowned by the din of hooves pounding the ground around them.

Chapter 21

Tim's whirlwind of verbal abuse was drowned out by the stampede of horses surrounding him from all sides. His shouting degenerated into a mindless string of obscenities that even he couldn't hear anymore. Captain Righteous removed his foot from Julian's back and lowered his sword. Tim took the opportunity to breathe.

"Ho!" shouted the commanding officer, raising his right arm and bringing his horse to a stop. The rest of the horses stopped as well, forming what looked to be an impenetrable circle around the wagon. This was no band of lowly, first-level, throwaway guards. These were fully fleshed-out, multi-level characters that Mordred had obviously put some time into preparing. No amount of Cooper's rage, Julian's sorcery, Katherine's summonations, Dave's healing, Chaz's music, or Tim's slipperiness was going to get them out of this one.

The commanding officer removed his helmet, revealing a full head of gray hair, and a luxuriously long mustache to match. "Captain Righteous Justificus Blademaster," he said, smiling down at the captain. "It's been too long."

Captain Righteous got down on one knee and touched his forehead to the hilt of his sword. "Major Portheus," he said solemnly. "It is a great honor to be able to serve you again."

"Stand up, man!" the Major commanded cheerfully. Captain Righteous jumped to his feet. "So what do you have here for me today? A rowdy looking bunch they look to be."

"That they are, sir."

The major scrutinized the group. "An unusual mix of comrades as well." He shrugged. "So what are the charges you have against these... er... prisoners?"

"First and foremost, the cold-blooded murder of one of my men, sir. There is also theft, breaking into the manor of Lord-"

"One at a time, Captain," said the major. "Let's start with the murder. My sources tell me you have some pretty damning evidence to support this allegation."

"In addition to the dozens of eyewitnesses I can provide, you'll find the head of the victim in the half-orc's bag."

The major raised his eyebrows, and there was a rumbling murmur from the rest of the soldiers.

"Henderson!" Major Portheus called out.

"Sir!"

"Kindly fetch the half-orc's bag, would you?"

"Right away, sir!"

The major looked at Cooper, who was shifting in his seat, unsure of what to do. "Easy there, big feller. Don't put yourself in any more trouble than you're already in. You'll get your chance to speak."

Cooper looked at Tim. Tim nodded. Cooper reluctantly released his bag to the soldier that had ridden up to retrieve it.

"Orc scum," Henderson muttered as he took the bag from Cooper.

"I covered your mother in orc's come last night."

Despite the gravity of the situation, Chaz and Dave snorted.

"Nice one, Coop," said Dave when he got himself under control.

"I don't get it," said Katherine. "Orc scum? What's so funny about... wait a second... orc's co... ew, you guys are fucking gross!"

A few chuckles echoed from within the helmets of some of the soldiers situated near Henderson.

"Why you filthy son of a whore!" shouted Henderson, drawing his sword.

"Henderson!" shouted Major Portheus. "Put your sword away. Open the bag and let's see what we've got." He backed up his horse and muttered under his breath to the soldier next to him. "Orc's come. It was pretty funny."

"Yes, sir!" the soldier responded. "Absolutely hilarious, sir!"

The major flinched, and then exchanged an awkward glance with Henderson, who looked devastated even with the visor of his helmet down.

"Go on," said the major, casting an annoyed glance at the soldier next to him. "What's in the bag?"

"Yegh!" said Henderson. "It's a head all right." He grabbed the head by the hair and held it up above his head for everyone to see. The air was suddenly filled with echoing gasps, swears, curses, and angry grumbles.

"Silence!" shouted Major Portheus. "Stand up and be judged, half-orc!"

Cooper stood up.

"State your name."

"Donald McKinley Cooper."

There was another brief period of murmuring from the crowd on horseback.

"That, um..." said the major, "doesn't sound very orcish."

"It's not," said Cooper.

The major shrugged. "All right then, Mr. Cooper. What have you got to say for yourself?"

"Yesterday," Cooper began. "I couldn't even afford a night's lodging."

Tim and his friends exchanged confused looks.

Captain Righeous wouldn't have known what Cooper was leading up to any better than the rest of them, but the look on his face suggested that he knew it was bullshit. "Major Portheus," he interrupted. "It's obvious that he's-"

"Quiet, Captain," said the major, politely but firmly. "I would hear what the accused has to say before I pass my judgment. Go on, Mr. Cooper."

Cooper continued his story. "I had only one silver piece to my name, and I spent it." He paused, raising his eyes to face the major.

"I'm not sure I understand," said Major Portheus. "Are you saying that you blame... society, or something... for your decision to commit murder?"

"Not at all," said Cooper earnestly. "I'm just saying that I think Henderson's mom owes me some change."

The entire contingent of soldiers roared in laughter. Dave wiped tears from his eyes and fell backwards off the side of the cart, and then continued laughing. Major Portheus punched the arm of the soldier next to him and laughed so hard that he started coughing violently and went red in the face. The only two people who weren't laughing were Captain Righteous, who stood in place stoically, waiting for the laughter to die down, and Henderson, who was shaking and nearly boiling in his armor. His knuckles were white around the hilt of his sword.

After a few minutes had passed, Major Portheus collected himself, wiped a tear from each eye, and suppressed the tiny fit of giggles still bubbling to the surface. "Whew," he said. "I haven't laughed that hard in years." He brushed his gray hair back from where it had fallen over his eye. "But the time for laughter is finished. It is my judgment that the accused, Mr. Donald McCartney-"

"McKinley," Cooper corrected him.

"McKinley Cooper, is to be executed here and now by Henderson's sword." He looked at Henderson, eyebrows raised.

Henderson dropped to one knee. "Thank you, sir! Right away, sir!"

"Round the rest of them up," The major said casually. "They can stand trial and be hanged tomorrow morning."

"What!" shrieked Katherine.

"Sorry, dear," said the major. "Can't afford to make exceptions. You fell in with a bad crowd. There are penalties for murder in this realm."

Two of the soldiers dismounted and brought Dave to his feet.

Cooper stood tall in the middle of the wagon, staring the soldiers one by one in the eye, as if daring each to be the first one to try and grab him.

Chaz stood back to back with Cooper, but there was no defiance in his face. He cradled his lute in his arms as if he were trying to hide behind it. As a last ditch effort, he plucked at the strings with trembling hands.

"Sleep, baby, sleep," he sang weakly at the helmeted faces moving slowly and cautiously toward him. "Your father tends the sheep." Cooper collapsed in a heap behind him. "Fuck."

"Thank you, bard," said Henderson. He pulled the lute out of Chaz's hands and threw it on the ground.

It took three soldiers to haul Cooper's sleeping body off of the cart. They placed him on the ground as gently as they could to avoid waking him up.

Tim, Katherine, Julian, and Dave were rounded up easily, with Butterbean being spared on the condition that Katherine order him to keep his distance from the soldiers.

"Make it quick, Henderson," said the major.

Henderson walked over to Cooper, and drew his sword.

"Tim," whispered Katherine. "Do something!"

Tim looked up at Katherine helplessly. What could he do? Katherine looked down at him with tears welling up in her eyes.

"Wait!" shouted Tim. "Cooper is innocent, and I can prove it!"

Major Portheus sighed. Henderson, who had already begun to raise his sword, looked to his commanding officer for instruction. The major waved him down.

"This had better be good, halfling."

Tim scrambled around in his mind for something to say. Not the right words, necessarily, as he didn't think those actually existed. Just any words would do now. He turned to Captain Righteous. "Do you remember the first time you saw me?"

"I remember," said the captain in a tone of voice that suggested that he was only going to put up with a very small amount of this nonsense.

"Do you remember what I had with me when you caught me?"

"You had some small weapons," said the captain impatiently. "A bow and a knife or something. What of it?"

"That's right," said Tim. He paused and looked around, making sure he had everyone's full attention. "But what didn't I have?"

"A week left to live?"

The major chuckled, as did his men. Even Henderson joined in this time.

"That's yet to be seen," said Tim. "But that's not the point I was trying to make."

"I do hope you intend to share that with us very shortly," said the major.

"Of course, sir," said Tim. "Your majorness, er... your majesty, er... ah! Your majority!"

The major sighed again, and folded his arms.

"Ravenus!" Tim shouted.

Ravenus, who had been hiding under the canvas, scooted out, stood up, and flew to perch on the edge of the wagon near Tim.

"There," said Tim, triumphantly. "You see?"

"I see a bird," said the major. "What about it?"

"Well," said Tim. "First of all, look how big it is!" He glanced over at his friends and his sister. They were all staring back at him with wide-eyed disbelief.

"What are you doing?" Katherine mouthed.

"This is nonsense!" said Captain Righteous. "He's stalling for time."

"Time for what?" asked the major.

"Yeah," said Tim. "What could I possibly hope to accomplish by buying a few more seconds?"

"He's a sneaky one, sir," the captain warned.

The major looked down at Tim. "If you have a point, make it now," he demanded. "Otherwise, stand aside and let me... wait... what's this?" His eyes went wide. He dismounted his horse and approached Tim. "You little shit!"

The soldiers looked at one another.

Captain Righteous stepped back, momentarily confused. He cleared his throat. "Um, sir?"

Tim heard something behind him that might have been a small explosion an instant before Major Portheus snapped his fingers. Startled, he whirled around to investigate the noise. The whole world had become silent and still.

Cooper's eyes were clenched shut, and his cheeks bellowed out like ship sails. In front of his face was a frozen mist of snot and spittle. Two balls of snot hung still in the air like a photograph of twin comets racing through an asteroid field.

Tim scanned the crowd. No one moved, not even so much as to breathe. Not a single blade of grass betrayed the slightest hint of a breeze.

"I suppose you think you're pretty clever," said Major Portheus.

Tim turned back around. Time, apparently, hadn't stopped for him or the major. It could only mean one thing. Tim swallowed.

"Not really," he said. "You kind of gave yourself away, stepping out of character like that."

"That's not what I'm talking about!" said the major, scowling.

"Then what are you talking about?" asked Tim, feigning innocence.

"I'm locked in the goddamn freezer!"

"Oh, right," said Tim. "Then I'd like to change my answer to 'Yes'. Yes, I do think I'm pretty clever."

"Fine," said Mordred. "Ha ha. You had your little joke. Now tell me how to get out of here."

"Wow," said Tim.

"What?"

"Who's living in a fantasy world now?" asked Tim, walking away to examine a butterfly.

The major followed him. "What do you mean?"

Tim got down on his hands and knees. He blew softly against the butterfly, but it didn't stir. He looked up into the major's face. "Do you really expect me to help you murder my friends? You seriously believe that I'm just going to let you out of the freezer and trust you to be a decent guy? This is what you call leverage."

The major's face grew livid. Impotence and hatred shone out of eyes that were unmistakably Mordred's. Tim tightened his lips to a position just short of a smile.

"Here's the deal," said Mordred. "You and I both know there's a poorly designed handle around here somewhere that I just can't see because it's dark. But I'm feeling around, and I'm eventually going to find it. If I find it before you tell me how to get out of here, I'm going to kill all of you, and it's not going to be quick and painless either."

Tim yawned. "I'll wait."

"Fine," said Mordred.

Tim crossed his arms and tapped a foot for a few seconds, and then felt his jaw slacken. The red rage flowed out of the major's face. His skin turned pale, almost gray. Dark circles formed under suddenly heavy eyelids. He looked tired and haggard, and was shivering in spite of the warm sunshine.

"I've been at it for hours," said the major through chattering teeth. "I can't find the latch."

"Seriously?" said Tim. "Hours? How can it have been hours?"

Mordred sighed. "Time passes differently here. I paused the game, so it's only been a second for you. I'm fucking freezing, man. Please let me out of here."

"Did you at least find the Popsicles?"

"Fuck you."

Tim laughed shallowly. "You know my biggest regret? I won't be around to see your obituary. 'Fat nerd dies alone in chicken freezer.'"

"You're really going to let me freeze to death?" asked Mordred. "That's really the sort of person you are?"

Tim frowned and gazed into the distance. Then he turned back to face Mordred sighed.

"No, Mordred," he said. "I'm not going to let you freeze to death."

"So there's a way out of here?" Hope sprang into Mordred's voice, though his teeth still chattered.

"Oh yeah," said Tim. "Piece of piss. No problem." He turned around and started walking back toward his friends.

"Where are you going?" asked Mordred.

"I'm gonna go watch all my friends get killed. You coming?"

"Do you think I'm fucking around?" the major shrieked after him. "I will murder every last fucking one of you!"

Tim stumbled to a stop and turned around. "I swear to God, Mordred. The first one of them that you lay a finger on is the deal breaker."

The major slumped towards him and dropped to his knees. "Come on," he pleaded. "You said you weren't going to let me freeze to death."

"And I won't," said Tim. "It's barely below freezing in there. You're much more likely to die of dehydration or asphyxiation."

"And you're just going to let that happen? Yeah, you're a real fucking hero."

"I saw on TV once that you can drink your own piss. I think it was on the Discovery Channel."

"Come on, man. I'm begging you."

Tim waved to his friends and shouted, "Sorry guys! Looks like we're all going to die!"

The major grabbed Tim by the shoulder and spun him around. "If I spare you and your friends, will you tell me how to get out of the freezer?"

"Absolutely," said Tim. He gave the major a cheeky grin.

Major Portheus and Tim returned to where they had been standing when time had stopped. Any slight deviation from their original postures went unnoticed when the major snapped his fingers, as everyone's attention was briefly diverted by Cooper's sneeze.

"Is everything... okay, sir?" asked Captain Righteous.

"Everything is fine, Captain. Don't worry about a thing." He cleared his throat, and commanded silence before addressing his men. "It is my order that these prisoners be released immediately and unmolested, and that all charges against them be dropped and forgotten."

A loud murmur rolled through the crowd. Once again, Tim's group of friends looked at him in astonishment. He winked back at them.

Henderson removed his helmet and threw it on the ground. "What is the meaning of this?" he demanded.

"Begging your pardon, sir," said Captain Righteous. "But I must agree with young Henderson. This is most irregular." A murmur of approval echoed out from the soldiers at the captain's words.

Major Portheus shifted on his feet and lowered his head. "I find there is... um... insufficient evidence to warrant further prosecutory action."

Henderson shoved his sword into the ground, and picked up the severed head. He raised it once again above his head. "How's this for sufficient evidence?" he shouted.

The major glared down at Tim. Tim shrugged.

The major sighed. "Let's ask him what he thinks," he said, pointing to the head in Henderson's hand.

The head came to life. "I'm... uh... in a better place now. I don't wish to press charges."

Henderson screamed and threw the head away as if it was suddenly on fire.

"Fuck this," came a voice from within one of the helmets. He was easily identifiable afterward, as he was the one on the horse galloping away. A few more followed after him.

"Deserters!" Captain Righteous shouted, moving as if to go after them.

Major Portheus put a calming hand on him. "Let them go. It's been a rough day. They'll come back around."

"Sir," said the captain with some hesitation in his voice. "I know it is not my place to question your judgment, but I-"

"You are correct," said the major sternly. "It is not your place." Captain Righteous shut his mouth.

"However," said the major. "If you will join me for a very very strong drink, I will explain everything. I could use a man like you under my direct command."

"Of course, sir. As you wish."

"Come on, men" the major called out. "Let's head back to town. Drinks are on me tonight."

The command was met with a series of shrugs and contented murmurs. One soldier, however, would not be subdued with the promise of free liquor.

"Major, sir!" shouted Henderson in a decidedly defiant tone of voice.

"Yes, Henderson. What is it?"

"This barbarian monster has besmirched the honor of my mother. I cannot let that go unavenged. I demand his ugly head!"

Major Portheus looked down at Tim. Tim shook his head.

"How about..." said the major slowly and thoughtfully. "How about I promote you to the rank of captain?"

Henderson's jaw and shoulders dropped. "What, really?"

"You did well today, son. I see a lot of potential in you."

"Okay," said Henderson, walking away from Cooper, who was still asleep on the ground. "That'll do."

"I hear there's an opening in Algor," said the major, looking over at Captain Righteous. "Let's get back to town," he said, stepping into his stirrup and mounting his horse. "If ever there was a man and a drink who needed to be together..."

Chapter 22

Tim slapped Cooper lightly on his huge gray cheek. "Cooper, wake up."

Without waking, Cooper yawned, grabbed Tim one-handed around the waist, and tossed him away as if he were a doll. He turned over, smacked his lips a couple of times, and resumed snoring.

"Dammit, Cooper! Wake up!" said Tim, rising to his feet and dusting himself off. He stomped back toward Cooper and gave him a swift kick in the ass.

"Hey, fuck off!" Cooper barked. "Can't a guy get any sleep? Show some fucking consider –" He sat up, eyes wide open. "Hey. Where did all the soldiers go?" He looked around. "Why aren't we all dead?"

"I think I may have just bought us a ticket home," said Tim.

Everyone gathered around Tim, speaking at once. "What?" "How?" "What happened back there?"

Tim picked up the severed head and placed it on the back end of the wagon, where it was low enough for him to reach. "Hey Mordred. You in there? How are you feeling?"

The head came wearily to life. "Cold," it said.

"Cold?" said Cooper. "It's in the middle of summer, and you're on the Gulf of fucking Mexico. How can you possibly be cold?"

"You sneaky son of a bitch," said Dave, laughing and punching Tim in the arm. "Popsicles, indeed!"

One by one, the light of understanding shone on everyone's faces. Everyone, that is, except for Chaz.

"What the hell are you guys talking about? What do Popsicles have to do with anything?"

Dave answered. "Tim lured Mordred into the freezer by mentioning that he had Popsicles in there." Chaz looked less than satisfied with this explanation, so Dave continued. "The freezer door only opens from the outside."

"He's locked in the chicken freezer?"

"Yep," said Tim. "The indoor latch is broken. Major safety hazard."

"Wait a second," said Mordred. "If the latch is broken... Didn't you say getting me out of here would be a piece of shit?"

"Piece of piss," corrected Tim.

"That means it's easy, right?"

"Incredibly easy."

"So what do I do?"

"Bring us home, and I'll open the door."

The head on the wagon closed its eyes. "I can't bring you back."

"Look," said Tim testily. "I appreciate your dedication to the game, but it's time to concede defeat."

"No," said Mordred. "I mean I really can't. Not without the dice."

"What dice?" asked Katherine. "What's he talking about?"

"The dice he used to send us here," said Tim. "Wait... You did roll a die, didn't you?"

"No, I didn't roll any fucking die. He threw a rock at me and I threw it back at him."

Tim rolled his eyes. "Did the rock have twenty sides?"

"How should I know? I didn't stop to count them."

"Excuse me!" the head on the wagon shouted, silencing everyone else. "The dice are on the table up front. I can't get to them from here, and I can't get you back home until I get those dice. Think of another way."

"Dude," said Cooper. "Sounds like you're fucked."

"Tim," the head pleaded. "I swear on my mother's soul, man. If you tell me where the latch is, I promise to bring you and your friends back here right away."

"It's not a question of whether or not I believe you," said Tim. "I don't, incidentally. But I'm being perfectly honest with you. There's no latch. It's broken. Maybe a customer will come in tomorrow morning, and you can bang on the door and hope they hear you."

Mordred sighed through chattering teeth. "I locked the front door."

"Well," said Tim. "Then it looks like Cooper's pretty much spot on. You're fucked."

"Come on, man!" the head shouted. "This isn't fucking funny anymore. I'm fucking freezing to death in here! I've learned my lesson. Just let... me... out!" The pauses in his voice suggested that he was pounding on the freezer door as he shouted those last three words. The head closed its eyes and started crying.

"Shit," said Julian. "That's a hell of a way to go."

"Good for him!" said Katherine. "The fucker deserves it."

"Nobody deserves that," said Julian.

Chaz took Tim by the elbow, and nodded his head off to the side. Tim willingly followed him. The rest of the group followed as well.

"Dude," said Chaz in a tone just above a whisper. "I don't want to come off as like... insensitive, or whatever. But if he dies in that freezer, what's going to happen to us?"

"We'll definitely lose our business license," said Tim. Nobody laughed. "Honestly, I don't know."

"I know," said Katherine.

"You know what?" asked Tim.

"I know what will happen when Mordred dies," she said. "We'll be stuck here for good."

"But if Mordred's not there to run the game, who runs it?" asked Chaz.

"She's right," said Dave. "I remember Mordred said something about that in the woods. If he's not around, the game goes on autopilot or something."

"That's right," said Cooper. "I remember. He said he's been the one controlling our encounters so far, which is why we've been fighting leopards and ants and shit. But when he's gone, there's no telling what we'll run into out in the wilderness."

Tim looked around. They were still in the grass near the road, and had a wide range of vision in every direction. But forests were visible off in the distance on both sides, and they suddenly looked a lot darker and more uninviting.

"Well then I guess we'd better get out of the wilderness," said Tim.

"Come on, guys," the head on the wagon called out, making everyone jump. "Don't let me die in a freezer! I'm so cold. So fucking cold."

"What should we do with him?" asked Dave.

Tim answered. "I don't think we should bring him to- what's this city called? The one we're headed to?"

"Cardinia," said Julian.

"Yeah. I don't think we should bring him there."

"But we need him," said Katherine. "What if he thinks of a way to bring us back? What if we think of a way to get him out of the freezer?"

"Fuck getting him out of the freezer," said Cooper. "If he gets out, he's not going to bring us back."

"How do you know?" asked Katherine.

"Would you?"

"Of course I-"

"I meant if you were him," said Cooper. "He knows that the second we come back we're going to beat the shit out of him. Anyway, he's a sad little fuck who gets off on having power over other people. As soon as he got out, he'd just laugh at us and send a bunch of shit out to fight us."

"But if it's our only chance to get back home," Katherine argued.

"Mordred can talk to us from anywhere and by whatever means he likes," said Tim. "Be it a horse, a mosquito, or some random asshole on the street. We've just been given a clean slate with the law of this land, and I don't think it's wise to go marching into one of its largest cities with a severed human head in our bag."

"So you just want to leave it here?"

"We'll bury it. Cooper, can you dig a hole?"

"Yeah," said Cooper, his voice uncharacteristically somber. "No problem." After a few strokes of his axe into the thick, green grass, he lifted out a chunk of earth that they could have buried an entire body under.

Tim walked over to the head. "Mordred?"

Moist eyes looked dolefully at him.

"I'm truly sorry you're going to die in my freezer. I genuinely thought you would be able to bring us back, and that this was the only way to force your hand. You didn't leave me any choice."

He waited for a response, but the head just stared back at him coldly, its teeth chattering.

"We're going to bury this head, so it's probably time to find a new conduit if you think of any ideas."

The eyes in the head grew heavy. They lost the coldness in their stare, and succumbed to exhaustion. "I've tried... everything," it said, the words broken by a yawn.

"Dammit, Mordred," said Tim. "Did you go away again? How long were you gone?"

"Hours," it said. The eyes in the head struggled to stay open. "It's probably sometime in the morning now. It's all over. I'm sorry I put you guys through this."

"Come on, Mordred," said Tim, slapping the head on the cheeks. "Wake up. You know, the chicken in there is pre-cooked. I mean, it's frozen, and probably tastes pretty shitty, but it's okay to eat."

The head wheezed a hollow laugh. "I know. I've eaten a box of it already. Not bad."

Katherine started sobbing. She dropped to her knees and buried her face in Butterbean's fur.

"If you run into any of the others," the head said wearily, "let them know I'm sorry too."

"What others?" demanded Tim. "Who are the fucking others?"

"He's sent people here before," said Dave. "We can talk about this later. Let's just get this done."

"I'm going to go to sleep now," said Mordred, yawning. "And I don't think I'm ever going to wake up again. Good luck, guys." The eyelids slowly closed, and the head's breathing became soft and steady.

A whirlwind of reality hit Tim all at once. He grabbed the head by the ears and shook it. "Wake the fuck up, man!" he shouted. "We need you to get us the fuck out of here! We don't fucking belong here!"

Cooper's giant hand gripped Tim's arm, gently but firmly, until he stopped shaking the head. Once again, it was just a cold and lifeless hunk of flesh and bone. "Let him go, man. You did the best you could." With his other hand, he removed the head from Tim's grasp and tossed it unceremoniously into the hole.

"Should we say something?" asked Julian, cradling Ravenus in his arms. All eyes immediately went to Dave.

"What?" asked Dave, taking a step back.

"You're a cleric," said Julian.

"Guys, I'm just fucking Dave. I haven't been to fucking seminary. I haven't taken any fucking vows. I- fuck. No, I don't want to say anything."

"Chaz?" said Julian. "A song maybe?"

"All I've got on me right now is a Whitesnake song that will help us all fight better. I don't know if it's appropriate for... this."

"Fine," said Julian. "Let's just cover him up. Coop?"

Cooper covered the hole and patted the earth on top of it.

Tim looked up at Cooper with tears in his eyes. His sister's crying had caught hold of him. "What are we going to do?"

Cooper stood up. He spoke confidently and authoritatively. "We're going to grab our shit, go into that town, find the nearest tavern, get shitfaced drunk, and then see how things look in the morning."

Tim smiled through his tears and nodded. He looked around. One by one, the rest of the group nodded as well. Katherine wiped the tears from her eyes.

The setting sun cast a pink light across the evening sky, dotted with purple, wispy clouds as the friends walked together in silence toward the city of Cardinia.

The End.

Don't stop now! The adventure continues with…

<u>Critical Failures II: Fail Harder</u>

<u>Critical Failures III: A Storm of S-Words</u>

Also, take a look at the growing selection of Tim, Julian, Dave, and Cooper's continuing mini-adventures in the world of Caverns and Creatures.

ABOUT THE AUTHOR

Robert Bevan is an American author and university English teacher living in South Korea. He is a husband and father of two. When he isn't busy writing, teaching, fathering, or husbanding (a small window of time on Friday nights), he still plays third edition Dungeons and Dragons.

Look for me on Facebook:

www.facebook.com/robertbevanbooks

Or visit the Caverns and Creatures website at...

www.caverns-and-creatures.com

Made in the USA
San Bernardino, CA
17 March 2017